KU-335-336

Making A Killing

Iain McDowall

PIATKUS

❧ Visit the Piatkus website! ❧

Piatkus publishes a wide range of exciting fiction and non-fiction,
including books on health, mind, body & spirit, sex, self-help, cookery,
biography and the paranormal. If you want to:

- read descriptions of our popular titles
- buy our books over the internet
- take advantage of our special offers
- enter our monthly competition
- learn more about your favourite Piatkus authors

visit our website at:

www.piatkus.co.uk

Copyright © 2001 by Iain McDowall

First published in Great Britain in 2001 by
Judy Piatkus (Publishers) Ltd of
5 Windmill Street, London W1T 2JA
email: info@piatkus.co.uk

This edition published 2002

The moral right of the author has been asserted

A catalogue record for this book is available from the British Library

ISBN 0 7499 3303 8

Set in Times by
Action Publishing Technology Ltd, Gloucester

Printed and bound in Great Britain by
Bookmarque Ltd, Croydon, Surrey

Iain McDowall was born in Kilmarnock, Scotland. He worked as a philosophy lecturer and as a computing specialist before turning to crime (writing). Currently, he divides his time between Crowby and his home in Cheltenham. *Making a Killing* is the second in a series of novels featuring Chief Inspector Jacobson and DS Kerr. For further details visit www.crowby.co.uk

To the memory of Roselynd Wray, 1959–1991

August

Chapter One

The summer heat shimmered on the pavements, glimmered on the red-hot roofs of red-hot cars, sweated through the pores of people on the street below. On the fifth floor, Chief Inspector Jacobson felt too tired to work, too hot to think. A memory flash came to him of the sublimely cool interior inside the Banque Populaire in Avignon, the tellers coolly efficient in white shirts, loosened at the collar. He reflected that global warming would have come and gone – that the planet would be staring down the barrel of the next ice age – before decent air-conditioning was likely to reach the Divisional building.

He mopped his brow ineffectually with his hand, his heart sinking before the mountain of untouched paperwork on his desk. His holiday had been over less than a week but already it was starting to feel like some vivid dream which held you enthralled and enraptured only to fade at the first moment of waking. He checked his watch. One thirty. There was still half an hour to go before Chief Superintendent Chivers' operational briefing. Time to deal with some of the burgeoning pile of overtime claim forms for instance – or time for a quick one in the Brewer's Rest. It was hardly what you could call a contest: Jacobson swivelled in his chair and stretched his arms before he stood up. He picked up his pager from his desk, switched it on and tucked it into his shirt pocket.

He went out of his office and along the corridor to the back stairs, his exit route of choice in moments like these. Unlike the main stairs or – worse still – the lifts, you minimised your chances of running into someone you didn't want to see, save for the final sprint past the reception area on the ground floor. The route was known to the cognoscenti as the Denby Dash in memory of Detective Sergeant Denby, an early colleague of Jacobson's, long since deceased and even longer retired. Denby's ability to sneak in and out of the Divi unseen by superiors and inferiors alike had been very nearly as legendary as his famously extended lunch hours in the Brewer's Rest.

Jacobson imagined he felt the benign smile of Denby's ghost over his shoulder as he carried his drink away from the bar and out into the beer garden. A half pint of English draught lager was a far cry from a glass of local red in the shadow of the Palais des Papes but it beat the hell out of overtime calculations. He sat down at a table protected from the sun by the faded green of an elderly Perrier umbrella. He eased off his jacket and began to feel almost human again. He'd been lucky to get a table to himself. The heatwave had temporarily boosted the BR's takings to the level of the fashionable cafe-bars and phoney Irish joints which threatened its survival. Not that Jacobson would be especially sorry to see it go. Like others in the know, he used it only because – as Denby had long ago discovered – it was near enough for convenience to the Divi without being so close that you were actually visible from there while entering or leaving.

The woman he was trying not to look at had dark-red hair in pre-Raph ringlets. Her left hand fidgeted with the end of her short summer dress while her right clamped her mobile tight to the side of her head. Jacobson hoped for her sake that the health risks he'd read about in the paper were just scare stories, space-fillers. He made her thirty, maybe younger, before he managed to look away. He lifted his glass and swallowed a good third of its contents in one

4

gulp. At least, he thought, it was properly chilled. He seemed to spend an undue proportion of his time these days trying not to look at women, trying to reconcile the laddish impulses in his brain to the constraints of its middle-aged casing. He took another swallow, wishing the half were a pint or – better still – two pints. But even in his restless, post-holiday mood, he wasn't about to turn up at the Super's briefing with anything other than a clear head.

He checked again that his pager was properly switched on and risked another look. Her phone had disappeared – presumably into the giant-sized leather bag which lay at her feet – and now she was tapping frantically into an expensive-looking laptop. Underneath the white plastic table, her uncrossed, sun-tanned legs momentarily challenged Jacobson's Platonistic belief that true perfection was unattainable in the human realm. He made a show of reading the headlines in a drink-sodden copy of the *Guardian* which a previous customer had left abandoned on the table. When he looked up again she'd gone and he realised that it would soon be time to make a move himself.

Chivers, the force's most senior detective, was finally retiring, his leaving-do only seven nights away. Jacobson made it to the briefing room just minutes before the great man got up to speak. Greg Salter, Chivers' replacement, sat to his left, his arms folded high on his chest. Jacobson slid into the empty chair next along. The chief rose briskly to his feet.

'Our watchwords in the new century must be those of the old. *Law and Order*—' Chivers paused, then repeated his mantra. '*Law and Order*. If that's not why you joined, if that's not why you're still here, then *go now*. If you can't put your duty before your personal feelings then *go now*.'

A second pause, a second repetition: Chivers' eyes scanning every face in the room.

'The proper authorities have decreed that Robert Johnson is to be paroled under licence. His wish to return to this community is a *lawful* wish. There will be no vigilante

5

justice in Crowby. Robert Johnson will be under a voluntary curfew. Robert Johnson will be subject to the fullest supervision of the Probation Service.'

Chivers paused a third time. Jacobson looked around for a groan, maybe even a catcall, but somehow an uneasy silence persisted through buttoned lips, bitten tongues. He glanced at Greg Salter, who seemed to be working a nodding dog routine, his head bobbing vigorously in support of the party line. Chivers made a run for it while the going was good.

'Our uniformed colleagues already have their contingency arrangements in the event of any incidents of public disorder. As Frank Jacobson will now describe to you, our role, the proper *Crime Management* role, is discreet preemptive surveillance. Not only Johnson himself but also those members of the public who are regrettably unaware of Our Lord's retributive prerogatives.'

Jacobson ran through the surveillance arrangements in detail. Johnson would be tailed round the clock for at least the next month and there would be regular checks on those who'd made the most noise against him, victims' families mostly. Before he sat back down, he put his own spin on the official policy which Chivers had taken pains to spell out.

'It's bad news that the bastard's going to be back in Crowby. Bad news, plain and simple. No one feels that more than I do. But the way to deal with it is to stay professional, to do our jobs properly. As long as Johnson's on our patch, it's up to us to ensure that he doesn't so much as drop litter or cross the street against the traffic.'

Salter caught up with Jacobson by the lifts after the meeting.

'Nice speech, Frank, if I may say so. You did more to calm the troops than the old boy did in my view.'

Say what you like, take any view you like, Jacobson thought. Never met me before and already he's using my Christian name. It was the first time he'd encountered

Salter face to face. He'd arrived at the Divi while Jacobson had been in France, had apparently spent the last two weeks *shadowing* Chivers, if Jacobson had got the management buzzword right.

'Thanks, *Greg*,' he said, managing somehow to keep his face deadpan. Eight passengers crammed into a lift constructed for six. Jacobson was no giant yet Salter's balding head just about came to his shoulders.

'I'm inviting some of the movers and shakers over for drinks and a meal come Sunday night. You'd be more than welcome, Frank. My wife is quite a sought-after cook, if I say so myself.'

Say so anyway you care to.

'That would be good if I can make it, eh, Greg. I'll need to check my diary.'

'Do that, Frank, do that.'

A civilian clerk with an armful of documents struggled out of the lift at the third floor. Jacobson seized an opportunity and exited after him, having decided he'd rather walk the rest of the way down. He'd heard on the grapevine that Salter was a smoothie but he hadn't realised that the soon-to-be Super was quite definitely in training for Slimy Schmoozer of the Year. Since he was headed out on official business this time he treated himself to the broad sweep of the main stairs, a welcome pretence of cool air hitting his face.

It took him fifteen minutes to walk to the railway station. You could probably do it in ten minutes tops but he wasn't going to hurry in heat like this. Besides, walking at any pace was still quicker than driving through the post-lunchtime traffic. When he got to the station he found the usual mass of dissimilar elements in close proximity. Beggars, businessmen, back-packing tourists – the lost and the found. The two lonely tables reserved for smoking pariahs in the Costa coffee franchise were wedged in an unattractive corner. Jacobson lit up proudly what was only his second B and H of the day so far, less proudly realising that he was still in overtime form denial. There was no compelling operational need for the meeting he'd arranged here – only his own desire to be out of his office, away from his desk. By reputation, the two Brummies were skilled stake-out merchants and could probably be safely left to get on with it. Not that he had any other real option: the success of this part of the surveillance depended on the use of outside officers and – trickier – of Jacobson and his team steering well clear. The Mill Street bail hostel, where Johnson would be put up, crawled with locally based career low-life who could take the membership of Crowby CID as their specialist subject on *Mastermind* if the programme ever came back. Mill Street itself likewise: petty thievery, drugs, prostitution – the kind of area where a bail hostel was tolerated, even welcomed, by the locals.

Jacobson had ordered a latte with an extra shot. Despite the paper cup it tasted good. There was no doubt that the peripherals of rail travel had improved since the days of British Rail when your choice was foul tea or instant coffee or piss-off. The problem was the trains themselves. The one with Jacobson's outsiders onboard was already twenty-five minutes overdue.

Robert Johnson. King of the Delta Blues Guitar. It had been Kerr inevitably, Jacobson's Detective Sergeant, who'd made the musical link. The man whose playing was so angelic they said he'd made a pact with the Devil. But not this one. This one was Robert Johnson aka the Crowby Crawler. The newspapers at the time had acted as if he WAS the Devil. Eight violent rapes in eight months. The youngest victim had been seventeen, the oldest seventy-three. Each one had been committed on the thirteenth day, each one had tabloid-friendly elements of 'bizarre ritual': right from the beginning, Johnson had made sure an insanity plea would be his fall-back position if caught. As far as Jacobson was concerned, what had really been bizarre was that this plea had been believed by six experienced psychiatrists and ultimately by a unanimous jury guided by a judge who'd looked like seventy going on a hundred and five.

Jacobson finished his cigarette, drained the latte: still no-show from the Brummies.

So in the end Johnson had been put away for – what was it? – eight years, nine at the outside. A special hospital job: assessment, counselling, rehabilitation. From the release notes it looked like some super-duper special programme in Johnson's case. Skim reading, he'd taken in enough keywords to get the flavour. Experimental. Behaviour Modification. Impressive Results in Scandinavia and Holland. The notes also testified to Johnson's genuine repentance, his deep personal sense of regret. All very convincing no doubt. Except for one, central detail ... Johnson's ceaseless insistence on returning to Crowby. A town where he had no prior roots. A town where his victims endured their wrecked lives.

Emerging back on to the concourse, Jacobson was astonished to see the woman from the Brewer's Rest, the woman with the legs, hurrying towards him, smiling. He drew up, gobsmacked, waiting. Quickly he pretended to check his pager for messages – as if that had been his purpose all along – when she swept straight past him. From the huddle of doomed commuters in front of the departures board, vainly trying for an early escape home to the barbecue or the golf course, he tracked her destination, saw her meet two men, one young, one old, both in leather jackets despite the heat, both camera and camcorder laden.

Jenny Mortimer nursed her hangover all the way from the master bedroom to the breakfast bar at the far end of the large mahogany-fitted kitchen. She switched the massive ghetto-blaster moodily between Classic FM, Radio Four and her cd of Billie Holiday without finding something to distract her. She was too sober now to think about anything but Kevin's exasperating, stupid deadline. *Tell him Jenny, tell him before I get back. If you won't tell him, I will.*

She took the precious photograph from her dressing-gown

pocket, her only still from the movie which played relent-
lessly in her head. She looked again at his tanned body, lean
and lightly muscular, his tight cut-off jeans, the sunlight
catching his eyes and his smile. She'd always thought that
only men were really turned on just by looking but now,
tracing the line of his face with her finger, she wondered if
that were really the case.

She poured herself a cup of instant coffee, realising she
couldn't face the hassle entailed by the expresso machine.
She tried Radio Four again only to hear the unwelcome pips
before the three o'clock news. Today was the day she'd
dreaded – the day when she could no longer put off a decision – and it was already a lot more than half-gone. She
lifted the coffee cup to her lips but it was still too hot to
drink. The phone rang but she didn't pick it up, let the
answerphone act as her barrier to the hostile world. Gus
Mortimer's voice sounded gruff, confident and as cold as
the Arctic. He wasn't asking his wife about their invitation
to the Trayners' summer party, he was telling her.

'They're expecting us around eight, Jen.'

What he meant – what he always meant – was be there,
do it, play by my rules. She gripped the coffee mug tightly,
felt the day's first full shudder of fear. For the tenth time
since waking, she told herself to get a grip. All she had to
do was not panic. All she had to do was think it through.
She finished her coffee and then she forced herself to make
and eat two slices of wholegrain toast with marmalade. She
washed up, showered, got dressed. She was easing the ice-
blue Jag out of the garage on to the smoothly raked red
gravel of the curving driveway when the fear gripped her a
second time.

She cut the engine and sat there for a few moments,
fighting it. Anyway, there was no point just driving off
with no destination in mind, driving just for the sake of it.
Not with her head pounding her eyes behind her Ray-Bans.
She shoved her head back into the soft leather of the head-
rest, tried to do the deep breathing they'd shown her at

Skyros the summer before last. The worst thing was knowing that Kevin had consciously and deliberately forced her into this hellish corner, into a confrontation that she really didn't want, really didn't need. It wasn't enough that she loved him, that every cell, organ and membrane of her body was his and his alone. Kevin wasn't Gus but Kevin, she realised, was still a man; men always needed their ownership to be public. She shook her head, bit her lip. Finally, she turned the ignition again, lurched the car recklessly forward, her foot heavy on the pedal.

Ten minutes later, as high as it was possible to get above Crowby, Jenny followed the narrowing path to the summit of Crow Hill. Below and to her left was the woodland clearing where she'd parked. Above and around her: scraggy rain-parched grass, outcrops of hard rock, unreal powder puff clouds in the perfect summer sky. It was the nearest thing to a local beauty spot. By day you could see right over the town as far as the motorway. By night, the lights of Crowby twinkled like a film set, making it seem larger than it was and somehow more important. She'd come here as a girl on family picnics and, much later, with Gus in his after-dark car – when she'd first known him – when he was still with his first wife.

An Indian or Bangladeshi family nodded politely to her on their way back down the hill. The woman's sari was a dazzling, sumptuous orange, her little boy's eyes big and smiling, like shining black saucers. She turned and watched the three figures disappearing, carefree, down the path. She toyed with her mobile, considered phoning Gus at his office right there and then. Just state the facts without drama. Gus, I've been sleeping with the guy who does the gardening and now I'm going to live with him. God! He'd hit the roof. He'd probably hit her when he could get hold of her, might even hurt her badly. But then at least it would be over; everything would be out in the open and Gus could file for the divorce which both of them knew was long overdue.

11

It wasn't that she expected Kevin to last. Ten years younger than her, he'd wake up one day and realise her breasts were less than perfectly firm, her stomach not as flat as it used to be. Or she'd wake up the next day, her physical need of him finally sated, her mind at last numb and bored by his juvenile enthusiasms for crop circles, conspiracy theories, alien abductions. That would be a bad time obviously. The immediate time – today, tomorrow – would be even worse. But at least there would be the beginning of an end in sight. Six months from now – a year – and she could be somewhere else, leading another life. She could even get some kind of a job, earn her own living again. This last thought came to her shockingly, almost thrillingly. As if she were a prisoner newly awakened to an unlocked cell door and the jailers all fled. She looked down across Crowby, the traffic crawling like shiny beetles through congested streets. It would hardly be fair that Gus, with his string of office bimbos and sales conference pickups, would legally be the wronged party, would hang on after all to the lion's share of 'his money'. But it had been a long time in any case since she'd believed that life could be fair.

She reached in her shoulder bag for the last of her Marlboro Lights, realised that her hands were shaking. Two lank youths swaggered by, passing a joint between themselves only barely surreptitiously. The one with the least spots gave her a lecherous wink. She fingered her mobile again but then put it back in the bag. OK. Today if it must be. But later and in person, not now by phone. She would have had to tell him anyway, would have had to force the issue sometime. She lit the cigarette, her fingers a little steadier. All Kevin had really accomplished had been to compel her to act sooner rather than later.

When Gus Mortimer put down the phone after calling home, he walked through to his outer office for no good reason other than to watch the girl called Faith swivel away from her word-processing and await his instructions.

Angie, his regular secretary, was on her annual screwing-fest in Ibiza and now he almost wished he'd let her have the extra week off she'd asked for. The strange thing was that her temporary replacement didn't actually match up to Gus's normal recruitment criteria. Obviously they had to be able to use a computer and answer the phone. But above this minimal baseline, Gus gave priority to other qualities. Angie for instance was classic office furniture. Blonde, leggy, size-able bust and a manner that suggested you were in with a chance. This girl on the other hand gave the impression that her Doc Martens were permanently targeted on any set of bollocks within striking distance of her long, thin legs. He still couldn't really say why he hadn't just booted her right back to the agency the very first minute he'd clapped eyes on her. She wasn't exactly bad-looking but she certainly wasn't a typical Gus sex-object either. She was tall and pale, her long, straight hair dyed jet black. What they used to call a Goth a few years back, maybe still did for all he knew.

She was good enough at her work, better than Angie if the truth be told. But that was hardly relevant. Competence wasn't material if you didn't want someone around, just didn't like their face or their bad breath or – which was the issue here – their attitude. He *ran* the company after all: what was the bloody point otherwise?

'I need a quick breakdown of last month's figures, love. Just run them off on Excel or something, could you?'

Gus looked into her hazel eyes as if probing a mystery. You couldn't even get a proper angle on her figure under the black sack she wore as a dress. All he was sure of, apart from she was slim, was that her chest, unfettered, was probably bigger than she allowed it to appear.

The girl looked away from him and back to the screen.

'No problem, Mr Mortimer.'

Ordinarily, Gus liked formality in the office. Even when he shagged them he didn't want them taking liberties on company time. But somehow this girl wielded her unvarying politeness like a sharp stick. He watched her for a further moment, her thin fingers resting on the keyboard, the finger-nails painted a deep, dark purple. You could do some damage with those love: the kind of thing he would have said without thinking to Angie. With this girl he said nothing at all. Instead, he astonished himself by closing the door and leaving her to it without a single, patronising word.

Jacobson had been ready to give up on Aston and Dennett, the two Birmingham DCs, when their train finally crawled in a full fifty-five minutes late. He blew most of his hospitality budget on a round of drinks at the Yates' Wine Lodge which had recently opened up in the building opposite the station that had once belonged to the *Evening Argus*. He left them there half an hour later waiting for a mini-cab to Mill Street; both looking convincingly dodgy, both getting wary glances from the bar staff. Jacobson wouldn't have blamed the driver for turning down the fare. He walked back to the Divi, picked up his car and drove – late himself – to his next destination.

He parked unobtrusively at the bottom of Riverside Avenue and got out. Tall plane trees lined the pavement at regular intervals, keeping the glare of the sun at bay. When he reached the unmarked Astra, he opened the passenger door and sat in.

'All quiet, lass?'

Detective Constable Emma Smith nodded.

'Barnfield and his wife got back about twenty minutes ago. Supermarket trip. From what I could see it looks like the only thing they're planning at the moment is a barbie.'

Jacobson looked across and down the street. The house was solid, detached and, like its neighbours, a century and a half old. On foot you were no more than four minutes away from River Walk and the river itself. Another couple at most to get you across the nearest bridge and into the Memorial Park: feed the swans, exercise the dog or call into the Riverside Hotel for a swift one.

'Not your typical rent-a-mob area,' Jacobson thought out loud.

Yet the Barnfields were undoubtedly the potential troublemakers to be taken the most seriously. On the first day of the trial, John Barnfield had urinated on the supposedly tight security by waving Linda Barnfield's sharpest Kitchen Devil, a veritable cleaver, within two feet of Robert Johnson's throat. Thereafter, with the husband banned from the court and its environs, the wife had become the unofficial leader of the braying hordes who'd shrieked, jeered and spat at every one of the Crawler's coat-shielded entrances and exits from the building. 'A Mother's Fury' had been how they'd billed it, the day she'd made the front cover of the *Sun*.

'What do you really think they'll do, guv?'

Jacobson shook his head, glad that DC Smith didn't smoke, glad of an additional reason to postpone his next lighting-up.

'I just don't know, Emma, I just don't know.'

Anyone could feel sympathy for the Barnfields' position. Their only daughter had been eighteen when Johnson had broken in and found her alone in the house with a boyfriend while they were on holiday in Florida. Overpowering the youth, he'd held her there for sixteen hours, the most sustained and degrading of all his attacks. Bulimia, wrist-slashings and heroin had all followed predictably in its wake. Jacobson never wanted to know how he'd feel or act in their situation. If the case had become an obsession with him, as his ex-wife claimed it had, then the nightmare that a girl like Sally, his own daughter, could be next had certainly played its part.

'It's okay, guv, I don't mind on a day like this with the windows wound all the way down.'

Jacobson had unconsciously been tapping the cigarette lighter on the dashboard.

'You're more than kind,' he said. 'But I'll hold out a while yet.'

From the pavement outside the house next to the Barnfields', an elderly resident was trimming his hedge. Every now and then, he stopped to rest, gazing contentedly up and down the street. Each time he looked straight past the Astra without a second glance. If he noticed them at all, he'd probably assume they were a couple. Provided there were only two of them, it was what officers in a surveillance car were usually taken for, regardless – as in this case – of any age difference or other incompatibility. It helped – but was no longer essential – if they were male and female. The whole world, Jacobson thought, loves a lover. The Barnfields had kept up the pressure by more conventional middle-class methods too. Constant letterwriting to press, politicians and the Home Office was the least of it: Mrs Barnfield was a regular on local radio phone-ins, had even made a couple of appearances on regional television. As a victim's family, they'd had to be legally informed of the release date, would undoubtedly have passed the information on to their media contacts. It would be a minor miracle if Johnson's whereabouts remained unknown to them for long. Jacobson watched the old boy's shears glistening in the sunlight, wondered whether – next door along – they might be quietly sharpening up the cutlery again.

Aston and Dennett had barely set up in their shabby room above the Atlantis laundrette when, at the pre-arranged time of four o'clock, Colin 'Santa' Marshall, the Head of Crowby's Probation Service, parked his ageing Volvo estate at a dangerous angle on the double yellow lines outside the bail hostel. One tearaway racing too quickly to beat the traffic lights up ahead, Aston thought, and he's looking for a new bumper minimum. The hostel was directly across the street from the laundrette. Robert Johnson emerged on to the pavement carrying his worldly goods in a grey Adidas holdall. Johnson was thirty-six but from this distance he looked younger in his baggy jeans, hooded sweatshirt and number one haircut. You had to be up close to see the jail pallor on his face, the thick creasing lines on his forehead. Marshall, fat and with an unkempt grey-white beard, locked his car and followed Johnson into the hostel. Aston tapped out the Operation Control number on his mobile.

'Nasty looking piece of kit, mate,' said Dennett.

Aston held the phone to his ear, waiting for someone to answer. The lack of an instant response left him unimpressed.

'Which one? Chummie or Karl fucking Marx?'

Jenny stepped out of the bath feeling almost relaxed. She'd had the idea for ten minutes now. She'd looked at it from every angle, examined it, still couldn't see a flaw. She would tell him at the Trayners' party. There! Simple! She'd tell him quietly if possible but loudly in public if need be. If she took a few overnight things with her then she could leave alone by taxi, book in somewhere for the night, meet Kevin when he got back tomorrow. She towel-dried her hair, an almost-smile across her face in the mirror. The Trayners' invitation meant so much to Gus. That kind of thing always did. He'd either have to take it in silence, behave himself, or become a public spectacle. Even if he did lose his rag, she would surely come to less harm there in public than back here on her own. She pulled the long T-shirt she wore as a summer bathrobe over her head and walked out of the bathroom. At the top of the stairwell she stood, listening. Gus's carwheels made a distant scrunging of gravel. He was home. He was here. He must have left early for once but there would still be a good twenty minutes before she'd have to face him. Hot and indefinably irritable, he'd make straight for the pool. He'd strip, plunge straight in, his clumsy, angry crawl like an elephant on speed. When he finally sought her out, he'd find her semi-naked in the bedroom, trying on dresses: just where – the gospel according to Gus – his wife should be.

Chapter Two

Aston and Dennett settled down on a couple of junk-shop chairs with two cans of Stella apiece. While they would be on-site round the clock for the duration, they would be virtually off-duty eight pm till eight am. These were the hours of Johnson's voluntary curfew during which – this was the theory of it anyway – his electronic ankle tag was supposed to do their work for them. All Johnson had to do was move out of range of the bail hostel's hall telephone and an alarm signal would be triggered in a computer terminal at the tagging company. Within seconds of that – so it was claimed – a hotline phone would ring at the Divisional HQ. In point of fact Johnson had barely stirred so far anyway. About six o'clock, he'd sauntered down to the twenty-four-hour Londis store and returned a few minutes later with a carrier bag of over-priced groceries. By now, Aston thought, he'd be settled into his room, doing whatever it was sociopathic maniacs did on a quiet night in.

He pulled open the ringtop, swigged. At least the local side had been decent enough in that respect: pizzas in the freezer, a few beers in the fridge. Dennett switched on the television, flicked dismissively through the channels.

'Fuck,' he said. 'Sat TV would've been a nice gesture.'

Aston's mouth edged as close as it ever did to a smile.

'Just think about the overtime, mate. Not to mention the disbursement. Anyway – this is the original *Get Carter* this is. One of the great moments in British cinema.'

Dennett grimaced.

'All that seventies shit. Give me Tarantino any day.'

Aston had worked with Dennett for two years now, trusted him implicitly in any operational crisis, wouldn't hear a word against him in that department. Which in his view made it all the more surprising that – despite hundreds of hours on surveillance – the guy still knew nothing worth knowing about films: sod all, zero, nada.

'Watch this next bit anyway,' he suggested.

The TV set which had been laid on courtesy of Crowby CID looked like it had been hand built by John Logie Baird himself but the picture was surprisingly clear. Dennett looked on doubtfully as Michael Caine warmed up to deliver Aston's favourite line to the actor whose name he could never remember, the one who'd been Alf Roberts in Coronation Street.

'You're a big man, but you're in bad shape,' Aston said, pre-empting Caine and enjoying the look of puzzlement on Dennett's face. 'With me it's a full time job.'

Detective Sergeant Ian Kerr left his wife, Cathy, pointedly weeding the strawberry patch in the neatly tended back garden of their semi-detached Bovis home. Gardening had become one of her recent passions. One that Kerr didn't share, or claimed he didn't have time to share. Their twins, Samuel and Susanne, were soundly asleep in the second bedroom which Kerr had used as a kind of den before their startling arrival three summers earlier. It was after they'd put them to bed, after Cathy had suggested a glass of wine or maybe a walk over to the Lonely Ploughboy if they could get the baby-sitter in for an hour at short notice, that Kerr's mobile had so conveniently rung.

He stopped his car for a moment at the exit junction from the estate. Turn right and you were headed out of the suburbs towards the centre of Crowby. It was the direction in which his police business usually took him. Kerr turned

19

the car decisively left, the direction that took you out of Crowby altogether, put you on the back road for Wynarth. Sometimes, when he was feeling devious or paranoid enough, he drove partway towards Crowby as a precautionary measure and then doubled back. Tonight though he decided just to risk it. You could only, he thought, put up with so much of covering your back, with so much of the dreary mechanics of deceit.

He shoved Steely Dan on to the tape deck, *Two Against Nature*, turned it up louder than he'd ever think of at home. They were still cutting good stuff, he thought, even if it did take them twenty years between albums. The road got bendier and the trees seemed to get leafier as he drove on. The Chief Constable himself lived out here somewhere. Not that you could actually see his house from the road. Only the seriously wealthy or the seriously connected could contemplate the asking prices of the secluded properties, situated well back from public view, which lined the route from Crowby to the outskirts of Wynarth. Kerr eased off the accelerator. It was no more than a ten-minute drive at this time of the evening anyway: 'Almost Gothic' had barely turned into 'Jack of Speed' before he was circling the picture-postcard market square and finding himself a parking space near the war memorial.

Kerr walked across the square in the warmth of an English summer evening. Humphrey's Wine Bar and the Wynarth Arms were both as busy outside as in; crowds of mainly youngish drinkers spilling out on to the pavements, chatting, laughing, giving each other the eye. The Bank House, built in 1882, was the newest building in the centre of Wynarth. It had actually lasted out as a bank until the mid-1990s, but now one half was occupied by an estate agent and the other half had been taken over by the Viceroy Tandoori. The stonework had recently been sandblasted back to its original state of gleaming whiteness. Kerr ducked into the alley at its left and emerged a minute later on to Thomas Holt Street.

Rachel's flat was just along from the Looking East Gallery and one floor above a self-styled antique shop which flourished, like three others further along the street, like maybe a dozen others in Wynarth altogether, on the indefinite line between genuine antiquity and fashionable junk. Kerr glanced in the window as he fished for his key. Victorian lace, Chinese carved bears, Hornby train sets, Guinness toucan table lamps, busted bakelite radio sets. The domestic detritus of one century was being recycled as the incidental decoration for another. He opened the door and stepped in. Rachel was standing at the top of the narrow flight of stairs waving a chilled bottle of Mexican beer.

'I thought you might be thirsty,' she said by way of a greeting.

They made love more or less straightaway, more or less without preamble. Later, drying himself fastidiously after using her shower, he told her that they really needed to talk. Talk properly. She looked at him from across the room where she was stepping back into her white Gap jeans.

'All this ... it can't go on,' she said mock-dramatically. Her eyes were blue smoke, instantly weakening his resolve.

Kerr wrapped the towel round his neck, reached for his boxers and trousers.

'Well how can it?' he asked her, balancing precariously on one leg, pulling on his clothes. She picked up his shirt from the chair at the foot of the bed and threw it at him.

'If I can go on with it, Ian, you can. I'm the one who spends six nights out of seven alone while you're playing happy families.'

He fastened his belt, made no attempt to catch the shirt which landed rumpled at his feet.

'It's not like that Rayche. I've told you—'

She walked over to him, used the towel to pull him close.

'You tell me whatever you think I want to hear,' she said, kissing him. Then: 'Look, lighten up. Let's at least enjoy tonight. How much longer can you stay?'

*

Robert Johnson stared into Mill Street from the third floor of the bail hostel. The room was actually smaller than the one he'd had, pre-release, at the secure hospital. The difference was this one locked from the inside. The head screw – or Centre Manager as he preferred euphemistically to be known – would have a pass key obviously but the other roomies wouldn't, not legitimately anyway. Not that he was taking any chances. He'd already pushed the chest of drawers across the door, intended leaving it there till morning. It wouldn't keep out a determined punishment squad, but at least it would give him a bit of warning. He lit up another Marlboro for the sheer luxury of it. Inside he hadn't smoked, had concentrated on keeping himself fighting fit. But there was nothing in his plans to prevent a day or two's laxity at this early, interim stage. A tart appeared on the corner as he looked out. Short skirt, fuck-me heels, gold handbag. He felt the smoke deep in his lungs, watched her parade nervily to the edge of the pavement then back to the whitewashed wall of the Bricklayer's Arms. Still trying to flog their addled fannies, he thought, when *would* they ever learn? A souped-up, bashed-in Golf Cabriolet screeched to a halt near the Londis shop. A tall, gangly youth loped inside leaving three others in the car, shaved heads nodding like cattle to Fatboy Slim. Thump, thump, thumpity-thump. He fetched himself a can of Special Brew from the plastic bag he'd dumped on the bed. Another luxury to be allowed only because he knew he didn't need it, knew that a warrior must always trust himself. When he turned again to the window, the youth was back at the Golf with a six-pack, the driver already turning into the stream of traffic with the door trailing wide. Johnson watched the passenger scrambling in, the driver accelerating hopelessly away. Always, he thought, it begins with observation. Just like Musashi said: 'large people must be familiar with the spirit of small people.'

Chief Inspector Frank Jacobson ensconced himself on his

balcony with a thick book and a tumbler full of ice and Glenfiddich. There was only just enough space for his solitary sun lounger and his ailing cheese plant. But that was just as much space as he needed. Jacobson's flat – his *apartment*, as the estate agent had insisted on calling it – had a rear view, which meant it looked over the park rather than the street. With the dust on his divorce settled and the family house sold, Jacobson had at last acquired the bachelor pad of his dreams. Thirty years too late, he thought ruefully. He'd put his offer in the day he'd first seen it, had bought it with as many fittings intact as the departing owner had been prepared to leave. Jacobson had no time and even less inclination for DIY and he'd liked the flat exactly how it was: subdued lighting, black leather, minimalist.

There were irritations obviously. The couple upstairs for one, whose screwing could be even noisier than the slanging matches which usually preceded it. Wellington Drive wasn't River Walk either and Wellington Park wasn't the Memorial Park. In the middle of an average night, you ran the risk of being roused from sleep by the noise of drunken cursing or smashing glass as Crowby University students took an unsteady short cut home to their tower block hall of residence on the opposite side. But it was still more than pleasant to look out over the trees early morning, watching the squirrels watching the dog-walkers and the dogs; more than pleasant right now to feel the air finally starting to cool. All in all, it was the first time since his break-up with Janice that Jacobson had felt at home, had felt that he *had* a home.

He read half a paragraph then picked up the glass. He jiggled the ice cubes around with his finger before taking a sip: as if the clinking sound was the primary pleasure on offer, the drinking only secondary. *Pagans and Christians* by Robin Lane Fox. He'd read the book in full a couple of years ago, still liked to browse it from time to time. Especially at this precise moment with Nîmes and Arles clear in his memory. Jacobson's real fascination was with

23

the Sumerians and the Babylonians rather than with relative newcomers like the Romans. But modern-day Iran and Iraq remained tricky holiday destinations for a British policeman in contrast to the South of France. He traced the cult of Mithras in the index, knowing it had been especially popular in the army. He liked to think of some Mithraic centurion far from home but sustained by his faith. Jacobson envied any kind of believer their certainties. Mithras had slain the divine bull and made all the good things of the material world possible; he had also – conveniently for another religion – celebrated his birthday on the twenty-fifth of December.

The B and H packet sat on the little table next to his lighter. His ex-wife, Janice, had bought it for him a lifetime ago – before they'd been married – before he'd even slept with her for the first time. *To FJ with Love*. Not that he had actually slept with her, had fumbled instead on the settee in the front room while her parents were at the British Legion club; while her little brother had been despatched to the pictures with half a crown in his pocket. Two and sixpence: a currency as impossibly remote, as buried in history, as the Roman denarii.

He read a few more pages and finished his drink. He got up from the lounger and stood over by the rail, lit up his goodnight cigarette. His route had taken him erratically through Languedoc, across Provence and finally into the Pyrenees. He'd spent the last proper night of his holiday, the night before the long drive back to Cherbourg, in Perpignan. He'd dined in the Can Marti, watching the Sardane dancers in the square, had ended up getting plastered with two raucous German couples from Dusseldorf. It had been gone four when he'd crawled off to his hotel room. Crowby, he thought: less than a week back and already all he wanted was an early night and – Robert Johnson permitting – an uneventful weekend.

Chapter Three

Out of Crowby and on through Wynarth, Gus sat in the back of his merc with Jenny. Old Bob Hicks from the company's storeroom acted as chauffeur; his white shirt short-sleeved and neatly pressed, his tie well-knotted. When Hicks at last turned the car off the public road, Gus took a stiffener from a silver hip-flask and more or less smiled at Jenny. Geoffrey Trayner was big-time: which meant that Gus, his invitation card still childishly in his pocket, was also big-time. Deer – some kind of special breed of scientific interest – grazed on one side of Trayner's very own, strictly private road. Gus couldn't see any sign of the racehorses but didn't doubt that they were around somewhere.

The road dipped to the left and Boden Hall itself came into view, old and solidly elegant. It pleased Gus that in size it was only marginally bigger than his own gaff. But Gus's place was new and by his own admission a standard Andy and Fergie job. A suburban bungalow grown bloated and disproportionate like a giant insect in a 50s B-movie: he was surprised that no one had ever mistaken it for the out-of-town Sainsbury's. Size, Gus thought, wasn't the point. The point was that the Hall was – what was the word? – redolent. Yes, redolent.

'This is what I call style, Jen.'

He patted Jenny's knee, not seeming to notice whether she answered or was listening.

The merc was in a queue for parking now, behind a brand new beamer and a dark-brown Morgan. Gus decided to let Hicks deal with it. Jenny followed him out and they set off across the front lawn, green and thick like a carpet. Ahead of them, immaculate white linen covered the surfaces of small, intimate tables set out in formal rows. Each one was resplendent with candelabra, the candles already alight not so much for the approaching dusk but as a deterrent against midge and mosquito. The diners were seated four to a table according to a complex formula of personality, background and wealth. A waiter on a generous fawning bonus showed them to their seats. Gus and Jenny had been partnered to Charlie Walsh and his wife, Pamela. Gus reckoned the sums added up when it came to cash between himself and Walsh but he was a little put out that Walsh's gross dog of a wife had apparently been judged a suitable counterpart to Jen. Even so, Gus felt like a dweller on the threshold of the inner sanctum. After all, the barbecue or a buffet in the marquee had been deemed a sufficient choice for the needs of the lesser guests. Every time he lifted his glass to his lips it seemed that one of the hovering waiters would instantly fill it up to the brim again.

Walsh told them he was just back from closing a deal in Tokyo where he'd travelled alone, Pamela having been consigned to decorating and sunbathing duties at their holiday house outside Remoulins. Gus risked a wink at him. The guy was evidently smarter than he looked although not smart enough just to have slung the old trout out permanently. Gus watched her fat fingers swallowing up the stem of her champagne glass as she drank. She had probably been a looker twenty years ago but now her paunchy jowl made a mockery of the brown eyes and the shinily auburn hair. Her biggest problem in France, she told them, had been the constant streams of day-trippers on their way to the Pont du Gard.

'The manners of some of the coach parties ... really. More the kind of people you expect to find in the Spanish resorts than in the Midi.'

The idea of some beered-up English hooligans spoiling the view for the schoolteachers and social workers appealed enormously to Gus but he said nothing. Instead, he treated all three of them to his whitest smile and lifted up his own glass.

'To success,' he said, reverting to the topic of Japan and making a mental note not to mention his own recently acquired villa at Playa d'Aro.

Course followed course and the conversation ebbed and flowed. Walsh told an only mildly tedious anecdote about Japanese executives and their propensity to drink themselves unashamedly sick in public. Jenny glanced at Gus but could tell he wasn't hearing a word. In all probability, his mind would be focused on Geoffrey Trayner alone, wondering when and if Trayner would press the flesh in his direction. Above the clamour of chattering voices, she listened to the music drifting on the still air. Live jazz from the other side of the knot garden; a Fleetwood Mac cover band, their amps turned tastefully low, near the barbecue. After the coffee and liqueurs, the four of them headed into the marquee where the third alternative, a chamber orchestra, was limbering up for a spot of after-dinner baroque.

On the way, Jenny helped herself to another glass of champagne from a passing waiter. Another two glasses maximum, she thought, and then it would be now or never: booze-confident enough to state her case, sober enough to look out for herself. Once, she thought, she'd needed all this the way that Gus still did. No one here was poor, no one here settled for any material thing that wasn't the very best. Diane Coulter, the dentist who did Jenny's own teeth, smiled at her as they made their entrance. 'We never know when there's a recession on,' Jenny heard her telling her companion. As if dentistry wasn't a branch of medicine but a part of the Stock Exchange, which to Diane it probably was. It had taken Kevin to show her that the choices weren't limited to the obvious triad of filthy rich, mortgage slavery or sink estate hopelessness. That there were other, viable ways; cracks in the wall where slivers of light glinted.

Knee deep in potted palms, the orchestra got into its stride. Gus's hand felt hot and sweaty, proprietarily flat in the small of her exposed back.

'What are they playing, Jen?' he asked her.

'Vivaldi, one of the cello concertos,' she lied, mainly for the pleasure of watching Pamela nodding in agreement like she knew Vivaldi from *Grease*. Or Albinoni in this case. With his other hand, Gus took a pack of cigars out of the pocket of his DJ, offered one to Walsh. That's my girl, he would be thinking now. He'd tired of fucking her two years after their wedding but she knew he still liked it that creeps like old Charlie-Boy couldn't keep their eyes from straying over her body when they thought he wasn't looking. She bent down to straighten the heel of her shoe, half-hoping the sight of her cleavage would throw Walsh's cholesterol-red face into a terminal spasm. That she knew culture too, could play the snobboes at their own game, was a delicious icing on the cake for Gus. Too bad, she told herself. I wasn't the one who let it all go stale.

Since Trayner was nowhere in sight, Gus evidently wanted to be quit of the marquee and quit of the Walshes. Jenny suggested a walk down by the lake, thinking it would be a quiet spot. But he refused to consider it, looked at her as if she was crazy.

'I'm here to network, Jen, not to look at bloody swans in the moonlight,' he told her.

They made their excuses and she followed him instead into the Hall itself where the charity auction had already started in the library. He wanted to go straight in – flash some cash around – but she tugged at his sleeve, managed to halt him. He stood there staring at her, already aggravated, his dwarfed head directly under the frame of the John Martin canvas, big and apocalyptic. Something in her eyes told him to listen.

The slap seemed to echo up the marble stairs, reverberate

all the way to the chandeliers. Then he was dragging her by the hair, as if he would tear her scalp off, parting his way through the sea of partygoers like Moses, slamming her on to the back seat. Bob Hicks surprised her, getting out of the car, refusing to drive, telling him he was a disgrace. Two young men even tried to intervene. But one was hopelessly drunk and the other bespectacled, his build too slight for the job. Gus headbutted both of them, kicked the drunk one gratuitously where he lay.

She heard the doors click shut, felt the car lurch forward and away. She pulled at his head, her nails trying for his flesh. But he braked, turned round, punched her straight in the face. His fist seemed to come at her in slow-mo, clenched knuckles extending towards her frame by frame. She only thought it, never had the chance to utter it. *You'll have to kill me to stop me. You'll have to kill me to stop me.*

Chapter Four

Jacobson had detailed a constable to drive the postman and his van safely back to his depot, had wanted to make sure he thanked him personally before they drove off. He'd known police who'd done much worse as the first caller at the scene of a serious arrestable offence. The postman hadn't just noted the time of discovery accurately – eight forty am – he'd even had the nous to use the bottom of his tobacco tin as a makeshift mirror, checking under her nose and mouth for signs of breathing but not finding any. Apart from that, he'd touched nothing, moved nothing. The fact that he was shaking like a leaf now did nothing to lessen Jacobson's gratitude. He'd kept his head in the few seconds that counted.

'Usually I just drop them in the letterbox at the gate post. Only today there was a registered item, see.'

Jacobson saw perfectly: the simple twist of fate that put you in one place and not another, made you a key witness instead of an unaware passer-by. He nodded through the van window as the constable started the engine, found the reverse.

'Mind you take it easy when you get home. Tell the wife you're to have a whisky on police orders.'

The van retreated down the driveway. As if reluctantly, Jacobson turned back towards the blue and white line of police tape which threaded off the area in front of the house.

Young Robinson was waiting for him, tall and stooping from too many nights spent poring over his textbooks. It was Jacobson's second consolation of the morning after the postman's presence of mind. Professor Merchant, Crowby's senior pathologist, it transpired, was still in Tuscany, would be gone for at least another fortnight. Good news for the nurses, Jacobson thought, too bad for the Italian housemaids. If Merchant's understudy lacked his experience and flair, he also lacked his egomania and self-obsession. As far as Jacobson knew, Robinson had no side to him at all: What You Saw Was What You Got.

The naked body lay motionless on the red gravel. Jacobson had already looked into the bulging, stone-dead eyes but now Robinson gave him the official tour. The blue ears, lips and fingernails were what he called cyanosis, a sure sign of strangulation. So were the purple bruises on either side of the neck, each as big as a navvy's thumb. So was the trail of blood which had dribbled from the mouth, the ghastly froth crusting under the nose.

'. . . asphyxia, obviously enough, as the direct cause of death, Inspector. Unless of course the heart gave out before the lungs. In which case call it vagal inhibition.'

Jacobson, kneeling over the corpse, became aware of DC Mick Hume standing close by.

'There's only two names listed on the voters' roll, guv. A Mr and Mrs Mortimer. Exactly what the postman said. He's forty-six, she's thirty-six. Also the jag out back?'

Jacobson hated the way the American style of turning a statement into a question had become an English common-place.

'What about it, old son?' he interrupted deliberately.

'Registered to Jennifer Mortimer, this address, same DOB. Born in Crowby, it looks like.'

'Right: better try and trace some relatives. But concentrate first on the husband. If this is Mrs Mortimer lying here, I want to know where the hell hubbie is.'

Robinson looked across from the other side of the body.

'The age fits, Inspector—' he said, hesitating.

A couple of years ago, Jacobson thought, he would probably still have blushed.

'For a childless woman who kept herself in shape anyway.'

Jacobson nodded. Alive, Jennifer Mortimer, if that's who she was, must have been a sought-after package. Even now the contours of desirability persisted – if you didn't look at the face – if you could ignore the welter of bruises on her arms and legs.

Mick Hume left them but was instantly replaced. Looking like an extra from *Star Wars*, a soco in protective clothing was impatient to make the video record. Robinson got to his feet and moved out the way. Jacobson followed him up at a substantially slower speed.

'Time?'

It was a question which would scarcely have been worth putting to Merchant before the post-mortem. Even then the answer would be supercilious and drenched in sarcasm. Robinson dealt with it matter-of-factly.

'Two hours maximum as far as rectal temperature is a guide. The absence of rigor points that way too. I'll be able to give you a better estimate this afternoon but it's—'

Jacobson saved his breath for him.

'I know, it's only ever an estimate.'

There was nothing more that Robinson could do until they'd moved the body to the morgue. He headed off towards his car and Jacobson turned towards the house.

According to the postman, both the porch door and the main door had been wide open. He'd called inside but hadn't got an answer, hadn't fancied looking. Jacobson didn't blame him for that either. He stepped into an entranceway which was larger than many front rooms. Socos were dusting, filming, testing in every direction. Jacobson retraced in reverse the signs of a violent struggle that led all the way back through the hall, up the wide stairway and ended at its beginning in a small back bedroom on

32

the first floor. Upturned chairs, broken flower vases, pictures knocked off the walls, two smashed telephones: Mrs Mortimer looked to have clung to every last second of life even as it was being squeezed and choked out of her. The senior soco barred his way to the bedroom itself. For once, Jacobson didn't argue. Once the socos had gone, he would be free to peer into every nook and cranny of the house. From the little he'd seen so far, it wasn't a task to be relished.

Back outside, Jacobson watched as the MIU, the Major Incident Unit, was unloaded and moved into place. Despite its grand title, the MIU was basically two linked porta-cabins. Once set up it would provide the crucial first hours of the inquiry with computer terminals, a fax machine, somewhere to protect and classify potential evidence. Above all else, it would also have a bog, a microwave and a drinks dispenser. Mick Hume had moved off the driveway out of its way and was standing under the shade of the English oak which faced the entrance to the house. It was old, an awful lot older than the house itself, its trunk knotted and gnarled. Hume was muttering into his mobile, still on the trail of the absent husband. Jacobson lit up what was already his third B and H of the morning just as DS Kerr drove his blue Peugeot up to the line of police tape.

Kerr parked the car well out of the trajectory of the MIU and got out. Not for the first time, he wondered what he'd do if he wasn't police. Even for a man who was avoiding his home life, there was a limit to the amount of overtime your mind and body could stand. He'd felt almost obliged to book the weekend off, had been staring over his break-fast cup of tea at the prospect of two long days with his wife and family when Jacobson had called him on his home number. Cathy had answered the phone, had passed it over to him in stony silence. She'd been wiping milk and cereal off the front of Sam's best Thomas the Tank Engine T-shirt when he'd made his escape.

The soco with the camcorder had just finished videoing

the corpse. The orderlies from the morgue were on their way over and soon it would be sealed into a body bag and en route to the mortuary. Jacobson looked on as Kerr performed the grim ritual of studying the victim in situ. There was no practical need for him to do so – Jacobson had just summarised the essentials for him, Robinson's report when it was completed would be expert and comprehensive. But it was an essential preliminary – psychologically necessary, symbolic – which no true detective would ever shirk. The last thing he noticed as he stood back up and moved away was a tiny tattoo of a butterfly high on the right arm, just below the shoulder.

With the socos still busy inside, Kerr and Jacobson took a walk around the circumference of the house. There were half a dozen or so similar properties in the area. Secluded, set well apart from each other and surrounded by farmland. You were close to Crowby but no longer of it. The gardens were expansive yet sparse in detail. Green rolling lawns in every direction, punctuated only occasionally by simplistic floral borders: poster-paint colours mostly – primary reds and yellows. A couple of garden centres' worth of leyland cypress had been stuffed along the perimeter walls. It scored high for privacy but not for much else. The leylandii had grown big enough for the job but it was still new, somehow weirdly insubstantial. You wouldn't want to give it odds against a strong wind, Kerr thought: only the old oak round the front would be left standing if the big, bad wolf came calling.

'You reckon the hubbie then, Frank?'

Jacobson stubbed out his fag on the grass with a typical smoker's disregard for nature before he answered.

'As the first port of call certainly. It's early days yet but there's no obvious sign of a burglary or a break-in. Though it's such a bloody mess in there it's hard to be sure of anything at the minute.'

The Mortimers' big, deluxe swimming pool was covered over by a canopy of glass, steel and white plastic. Behind it the landscape changed abruptly. The lawn had been dug up and there were piles of timber, bricks, stones. Someone had stacked bags of organic fertiliser inside a mini-skip next to a concrete mixer. Jacobson kicked a watering can out of his way and stood on a paving stone which marked the start of a winding but far from complete footpath.

'Let's hope it *is* the hubbie, old son. A nice, clean, good old-fashioned domestic.'

Seemingly unconscious of the fact, he lit up another cigarette to follow the one he'd just extinguished.

'Anything else is going to be a bloody nuisance. August is a shit time for a full-scale murder inquiry even without the Robert Johnson farrago to worry about. As it is, I've just had to pull Emma Smith and DC Williams off the surveillance team. God knows who upstairs will try to replace them with.'

They turned back in the direction of the house. Kerr suggested DC Barber as another useful officer to draft in.

'I've already thought of Barber, old son. He's back from Barbados all right but the bugger's jet-lagged. No use to us till tomorrow, tops. Barbados! I can remember when coppers went to Bognor and liked it.'

Past the conservatory and nearing the front again, they saw the mortuary vehicle arriving. From the outside it looked – discreetly – like any other ambulance. The driver did a U-turn, coming perilously close to Kerr's Peugeot at one point, then started to reverse into position. He'd nearly completed the manoeuvre – but not nearly enough – when a white Ford transit screeched up the driveway and blocked him in.

A youngish male figure jumped out of the van, was running, screaming. He was through the police tape and less than a foot away from Jenny Mortimer's body before two burly plods – one of them Sergeant Ince – wrestled him to the ground.

'Jenny! Jenny! What's going on? Why's she just lying there?'

Ince held him in a secure arm lock.

'Try to calm down, son. Take it easy.'

'Let me see her. Let me *see* her. Get *off* me. If that bastard—'

With the help of two others, they half lifted him, half dragged him into the first portacabin, shoved him into a red plastic chair in front of an ancient, formica-topped table.

'What's going on?' he asked again. But in a whisper this time, his body no longer struggling, his mind already grasping – already starting to know – the worst part of the answer. Jacobson and Kerr came in, pulled a chair each up to the table. From somewhere of his own devising, Ince produced a quarter bottle of brandy and poured a measure into a Klix paper cup. He handed it to the unknown arrival.

'I'm Chief Inspector Jacobson. This is Detective Sergeant Kerr,' Jacobson said.

The newcomer swallowed the brandy in one hurried gulp. Kerr made him mid-twenties, an outdoor type. He was in hiking boots, green combat trousers, a sweaty, purple singlet. More than his angular face, his most distinctive feature was his hair: light brown in long, stubby dreadlocks.

'She's dead, isn't she?'

The needless question hung in the air: Jacobson nodded.

'She's dead, yes. I take it you know who she is?'

Silence: a look across the table that said one of them at least must be mad.

'I really need you to tell me if you do. It's important for our procedures,' Jacobson persisted.

'It's Jenny. Jenny Mortimer.'

The panic found him again.

'I need to see her. I've got to—'

He would have flung the chair back, made a try for the exit, but Ince held him in check. Jacobson promised he'd see her again as soon as things could be sorted out. He didn't specify what things, didn't indicate a timescale. Mick Hume stuck his bluff head round the door.

'There's nothing on the PNC, guv. According to Swansea though, this is Mr Kevin George Holland, DOB 4-9-75, Crowby address – assuming the vehicle belongs to him.'

'It's mine all right,' Kevin Holland said.

He looked contemptuously straight at Hume.

'I've always given Babylon its due,' he added. 'Extend the courtesy to the outer. That's how the Sufis put it.'

Render unto Caesar, Jacobson thought. He'd heard the wheels whirring in Hume's standard-issue police brain himself, caught the familiar whiff of canteen prejudice. White rastas in combats weren't supposed to have clean records, weren't expected to own legitimate vehicles. He offered him a cigarette, put the pack down on the table when he said no.

'Just tell us what you know, Mr Holland. Please. We've got to get things moving here.'

Kevin Holland toyed with the empty paper cup. His anger at DC Hume seemed to have given him a road back to some level of composure. He told them he was a self-employed landscape gardener, that he'd taken the Mortimers on as clients back at the turn of the year, that he'd been trying to give their land a soul. He'd been away at a festival all week, had only just got back. Jacobson didn't have time to waste skirting the issues. He played his hunch as quickly as he could.

'What did you mean outside Kevin? When you said "if that bastard"?'

Kevin Holland stared at him, tried to weigh him up. Before he could speak again, Mick Hume was back in the doorway.

'Mr Mortimer, guv?'

Jacobson endured a whole string of Americanisms this time.

'He's Gus Mortimer as it turns out. Managing Director out at Planet? Planet Avionics? The wife's sister worked there for a couple of years as I recall.'

Kevin Holland looked from Jacobson to Hume then back again.

'There's your answer, Chief Inspector,' he said.

Sergeant Ince poured more brandy into the paper cup. Holland ignored it for a moment then swallowed it down in one again.

'Look, it's like this. Jenny and me.'

His voice started up then stopped again. He took a cigarette out of Jacobson's B and H packet, produced an orange plastic lighter from deep inside one of his trouser pockets.

'She was going to leave him,' he tried again, lighting the cigarette but not bothering to smoke it.

Chapter Five

The Science and Business Park was completely on the other side of town. They took Kerr's car, Kerr driving. He gambled on the motorway traffic and the bypass against the route via the town centre, made the journey inside a respectable twenty minutes.

The SBP, as it was known locally, housed a dozen or so hi-tech companies in a circular formation of buildings around a central linking road. It didn't look too bad a spot on a hot summer's morning with the ducks paddling dozily on the regulation mini-lake, the gentle cascading hiss of the regulation water features, the picnic tables set out under the trees. But for most of the year it was a windswept, lifeless hell-hole. In the firms that offered flexitime, Kerr thought, you'd take the minimum lunchbreak, eat inside at your desk or workbench, get the fuck home as soon as you could. He asked a security guard outside the Fujitsu building for directions. Not that there was any real need: you just kept going along the link road and eventually you passed everything there was to pass.

Planet Avionics was a long, low-rise building at the far end of the site. There were less than half a dozen cars in the numbered spaces outside. Kerr pulled in as near to the entrance as he could and cut the engine. Jacobson opened the passenger door and heaved himself out.

'Right, Ian. If hubbie's not at home, let's see if he's at work.'

The glass-fronted main entrance was locked. A sleepy-looking watchman eyed them from behind the reception desk, might never have moved if Jacobson hadn't waved his ID vigorously in the direction of the nearest security cameras. Something electronic buzzed and the doors slid open.

'Is Mr Mortimer on the premises? We need to see him if he is.'

The watchman lifted a telephone receiver but Jacobson shook his head.

'It's a personal matter, urgent. Just take us right to him.'

They followed him up a flight of stairs and then along a cool, air-conditioned corridor. Every now and then large-scale prints broke up the monotony of the pale-lime walls. Aircraft history was evidently the theme: Flying Fortresses, Sopwith Camels, Spitfires.

'Not exactly bustling,' Kerr commented.

'Never is on a weekend, mate.' The watchman's voice was professionally gloomy. 'Only some maintenance guys on the production floor and the Big Man in his office.'

At the top of the corridor, they turned right.

'You'd have been on duty when Mr Mortimer arrived then?' Kerr asked.

'I'm on twelve to twelve, mate. Midnight till twelve noon.'

The watchman paused at the third door along where an elegant steel plate read *Managing Director*.

'The Big Ma— eh, Mr Mortimer came in at eight o'clock on the dot. Often does, Saturdays.'

He was about to knock on the door when it opened from the other side. Before Jacobson had even brought out his ID, Gus Mortimer was smiling like the proverbial crocodile, wanting to know how he could help them, what he could do for them. Jacobson's – and Kerr's – world divided sharply between those who knew you instantly as police and those who didn't. Kerr placed Mortimer definitely in the first category. Sub-Division B: smarm in preference to hostility.

40

'I think this needs to be in private, Mr Mortimer,' Jacobson said evenly.

The watchman made himself scarce. Mortimer looked casually relaxed for the heat in a white Lacoste T-shirt, dark-blue shorts and light-brown leather deck shoes. He made a ludicrously expansive gesture with his left hand, indicating that they were welcome to enter his humble premises, that what was his was surely theirs.

Mortimer's lair, a smaller inner office and a larger outer one, occupied a corner position with windows along two walls. In one direction you looked over the link road towards the artificial lake; in the other you could keep an eye on the loading and unloading bays at the back of the building. Mortimer had evidently been working in his outer office: in the middle of the room a chair had been pulled back in front of a computer terminal. A complex spreadsheet – pound signs, numbers, delivery dates – danced, dazzling, in front of your eyes if you looked at the screen.

'I was just checking the sales, Chief Inspector. You know how it is.'

Actually I haven't a clue how it is, Jacobson thought.

'There's no easy way to say this, Mr Mortimer,' he said – and then said it: 'The body of a woman has been found murdered this morning. We've very good reasons to think it might be your wife.'

Mortimer had been about to show them into a couple of comfy, visitors' chairs near one of the windows, had almost certainly been about to mention drinks. *Tea, coffee, something stronger perhaps, Inspector?* The usual, insincere offer. But now his expression turned from lizardly smile to near blankness. He stared at them, his large flat hand patting the top of the computer screen defensively. Finally he spoke.

'Jenny? Is this some kind of jo—'

'I'm not joking Mr Mortimer.'

Jacobson told him that the postman had reported suspicious circumstances at their home address. But he didn't say when, didn't say that the woman who was a hundred and ten per cent certain to be Mortimer's wife had been found naked and strangled in front of his over-sized porch. Jacobson, like every policeman, knew that the human responses to sudden death were stock and limited. You cried or you fainted or you got angry or you went numb. So far Mortimer's reaction to the news was a masterclass in numb.

'When did you last see your wife yourself?'

Mortimer's brain-stem answering service replied. The synapses where his consciousness actually resided seemed to have disengaged themselves from any external communication.

'I – I didn't actually see her this morning. I left to drive over here about seven thirty. She ah – she slept in one of the spare rooms last night.'

He sagged more than sat down into the chair, the fingers of his right hand resting idly on a green mouse mat as if its surface was somehow comforting.

Jacobson caught Kerr's glance, nodded in return. What to do next was so obvious they didn't need to confer outloud. They'd get Mortimer over to the morgue, make the formal identification. Then they'd haul his arse down the Divi for some serious question and answer. Today on Who's Murdered Their Wife, Jacobson thought, let's give a big welcome to Mr Gus Mortimer of Crowby.

Kerr used his mobile, asked Sergeant Ince to get a patrol car and a couple of plods out to them A-S-A-P. Jacobson spoke quietly to Mortimer.

'You'll understand we'll need you to fill in the details later, build up a picture. But right now what's important is to identify the body.'

Mortimer was staring at him or staring through him.

'I'm sorry,' Jacobson added, lying.

Jacobson and Mortimer travelled over to Crowby General with the plods, Kerr followed on alone. The mortuary and the pathology department were in the new wing of the hospi-

42

tal, up on the fourth floor. By general jocular agreement of those who worked there, it was the coolest place to be in the middle of a heatwave. There were three new arrivals in the refrigerated anteroom designated for the purpose. A car crash victim, an alcoholic suspected suicide and the putative Mrs Jennifer Mortimer, listed as Caucasian, 5 feet 4 inches, 112 pounds, blue eyes, natural blonde hair. Gus Mortimer was still deep in numbland, gave only the slightest nod of his head when the attendant drew back the sheet.

'I'm afraid we need a verbal confirmation, Mr Mortimer,' Jacobson prompted.

Mortimer let out a quiet noise that might have been a sigh.

'Yes. It's Jenny. It's my wife,' he said.

Kerr played Mr Sympathy, led him out of the room.

'You'll see her again later, spend some time with her when they've – eh – tidied her up a bit.'

Jacobson had rehearsed a whole set of glib rational-isations and half-truths on the journey over as to why Mortimer couldn't go home yet, wouldn't want to trouble relatives yet, ought to make his statement at the police station. In the event, none of them were needed. Mortimer didn't even query where they were going while Kerr guided him into the lift, out through the reception area, back to the patrol car. Jacobson travelled with Kerr this time, left Mortimer to the plods.

'We'll play this absolutely by the book, Ian,' he said, mopping his brow with an old-fashioned white linen hand-kerchief as they pulled out of the hospital car park. 'We'll get the police surgeon to check him out for shock, make sure he's compos mentis for questioning and then we'll take his statement. The minute it's looking useful, we'll caution him, suggest he calls in his solicitor too.'

Kerr let the patrol car get well ahead, watched it disappear in front of a red container wagon.

'Open and shut then, you're still thinking?'

'Attractive woman, older fat cat hubby, bit of rough

43

boyfriend? It's on Channel Five at nine o'clock most nights, Ian, old son. The weather forecast on the other side's more unpredictable in a normal summer.'

Jacobson wound the passenger window all the way down in preparation for his fifth cigarette of the morning.

'It could be very nearly a text book case. He loses it over the boyfriend, does the business, goes straight into denial.'

'Following his normal routine like nothing's happened you mean?'

Jacobson fished out his cigarette packet then apparently changed his mind, put it away again.

'Exactly. No attempt to hide the body, no attempt to get away.'

Kerr took the inside lane as they pulled nearer to the Flowers Street junction. They were three minutes on foot from the Divisional building but at least another ten minutes by car in the Saturday morning traffic.

'So all that "what can I do for you, Inspector" bollocks was part of the Norman Normal act too?'

Jacobson nodded but before he could reply his mobile rang. Mick Hume: they had an address for the victim's parents at last, Emma Smith and DC Williams had showed up at the crime scene, Kevin Holland was still sitting with Sergeant Ince, still wanting to know when he could see her. Jacobson scribbled the address details in his notebook.

'Cheers, Mick. Let young Emma and Williams have a word with him. For yourself, start thinking about the nearby properties. We need to know who's living out that way, whatever's known locally about the Mortimers.'

He winked at Kerr as he spoke to Hume. It was hardly the kind of neighbourhood where you called round to borrow a cup of sugar but he badly needed a detailed statement from Kevin Holland, was more likely to get it with Hume as far out the way as possible.

DC Aston brewed up wearily while DC Dennett took the next stint at the window.

44

'Gross,' he exclaimed. 'The bugger's playing with himself.'

Aston poured the tea into two, ugly chipped mugs and looked for the sugar.

'I hope for your sake you're joking.'

Dennett focused the lens expertly until he had a clear line of vision all the way into the room. He was rewarded with the sight of Robert Johnson covering his face with shaving foam then wetting his razor in a sink that would have been happier as a goldfish bowl.

'Hurry up with that tea, mate,' he said to Aston. 'Looks like chummie's sprucing himself up to go somewhere.'

Aston stirred an industrial quantity of sugar into each mug.

'At last,' he said. 'I could do with going walkabout.'

Despite Aston's and Dennett's doubts, the Crowby side had insisted on a low-key approach. No bugs, no cameras, just straightforward observation of the hostel while Johnson was indoors and old-fashioned tailing if he looked likely to leave the vicinity. Dennett stayed in position, crouched behind the Zeiss ClassiC telescope and the tripod.

'Me too, mate,' he replied without taking his eye away.

Aston poured the milk in from a clumsily opened carton.

'Let's hope it's not just another trip to Londis. Bastard probably only wants to find out if Nutter Perv Weekly's come in yet.'

Kevin Holland, still hunched in the red plastic chair, had progressed – if that was the right word – from Ince's brandy on to a cup of Klix instant coffee. DC Emma Smith saw right away how he was precisely the kind of ragamuffin an unhappy wife might eagerly take to her bed. Even in the circumstances, his eyes held an easy, friendly knowingness when he looked at her. Even in the circumstances, she had to suppress an instinct to finger his dreadlocks, to explore their rugged texture. She suggested they walk in the garden to clear his head. He shrugged non-committally, asked for the twentieth time when he could see her.

'Kevin—' she said, then asked if it was all right to call him by his first name.

He gave another equivocal shrug.

'Kevin,' she said his name again, 'I'll level with you if no one else will. They've taken Jenny to the morgue. This afternoon there'll be an autopsy, other formalities. It's going to be this evening before they let you look at her. You need to get used to that idea.'

They followed the same route that Jacobson and Kerr had taken earlier. Holland and Emma Smith in front, DC Williams trailing behind, opting for a deliberate back seat. They stopped behind the swimming pool building.

'Your handiwork then, Kevin?' she asked.

Holland righted the watering can that Jacobson had knocked over, moved it to one side.

'The Garden of Heart's Delight,' he said. 'Or might've been, eventually. I don't expect he would've let the work carry on once Jenny'd moved in with me.'

Emma glanced over her shoulder at Williams. His face said that he didn't think it was very likely either.

'And that was the plan? To move in with you?'

'That was the plan, detective lady,' Holland said. 'She was supposed to leave a text message on my mobile yesterday telling me where and when to meet her. That's why I came over, when I hadn't heard anything. I knew he could be handy with his fists but I—'

She heard him struggle to keep the shaking emotion out of his voice.

'I never – I never thought anything like this.'

'So her husband had been violent to Jenny before?'

'That's what she told me. If there was a problem with his business shit he'd take it out on her. The rest of the time, he'd ignore her, leave her on her own in this great, ugly place.'

Holland turned round, looked back to the house.

'All that money and still up for more. Stupid, shallow bastard.'

Emma Smith looked back with him.

'Kevin, when did you last see Jenny?'

'Last Friday, a week ago yesterday. A group of us were heading over to the Larmer Tree Festival in Wiltshire. I asked her to come with me, just *go* I said. But she said she wanted a few days on her own, promised she'd tell him what was what, make the break when I got back.'

DC Williams joined the conversation at last: 'You don't think Mortimer might already have known what his wife was planning anyway?'

'No, I don't. The only thing that interests Gus Mortimer is Gus Mortimer – that and his bank balance. I don't think he'd have had a clue until she told him.'

'And you think she did?'

Holland nodded slowly, emphatically.

'Yes I do. And then the bastard killed her.'

His voice was choked up but his words were distinct.

'It's not like you and me, mate.'

He was talking to Williams now. Emma Smith, side-lined, decided his eyes were grey-blue, not blue-grey.

'Not normal jealousy, nothing like. Just didn't want someone running off with *his* property. Especially not without paying.'

Jacobson checked into his office. There were maybe twenty minutes to spare while the police surgeon gave Mortimer the once over; time, Jacobson thought, for his mind to process events, to formulate his plan of campaign. Idly, he picked up the neatly typed yellow form which he'd left on the top of his swollen in-tray. He'd been about to read it more than two hours ago when the postman's 999 call had disrupted the Divi's daily routine.

The Incident Sheet was produced twice in every twenty-four-hour period, contained summary details of all incidents logged or reported to Crowby police stations in the previous twelve hours. On an ordinary, non-murder case morning, it was Jacobson's bible, the basis from which

47

existing inquiries were progressed, new inquiries actioned. He scanned down the usual dreary scroll of burglaries, Friday night pub brawls, indecent exposures, car thefts. It took his eyes less than thirty seconds to be drawn to the conjunction of the surname Mortimer with the police code number for the report of a violent assault.

The incident had been phoned in at midnight, there had been a police response at twelve forty. Not bad, he thought, for the rural hinterlands. The Wynarth sub-station had been closed a couple of years ago and nowadays patrolling the lonely B roads between there and the county border had become a Divisional responsibility. Which would have been fine if any additional resources had been made available for the job. Jacobson located his telephone on the sprawl of his desk, knocked half a dozen unread copies of the *Police Gazette* on to the floor in the process. World peace and universal brotherhood were probably good ideas too and just about as imminently likely. The best the Divi could do – and didn't always manage – was to have one single patrol car per shift, one single constable only, on the rural beat. Two phone calls later – one to the desk sergeant, one to last night's shift supervisor grumpily disturbed in bed – and Jacobson knew not only which officer had responded to the reported incident but also that the said officer might still be currently in the building. PC Ogden: apparently, he'd stayed on after his shift to write up his reports and catch up with his paperwork. An example to us all, Jacobson had commented unkindly.

He found him in the canteen, didn't even try to resist the opportunity to grab a plate of egg and chips at the same time. The last occasion he'd spoken to him, other than in passing, was when Ogden had been hospitalised during the Roger Harvey case. About four years ago maybe. He'd been a raw recruit then, barely recognisable as the confident, smart-looking officer he'd evidently grown into.

Ogden ran through the highlights while Jacobson tucked into what was either his second breakfast of the morning or an early lunch. It seemed there'd been some kind of big summer do out at Boden Hall. One of the guests had treated his wife to a slapping. Then he'd proceeded to put the head on the couple of bystanders who'd had a go at stopping him:

'It was all over a good hour before I got there, sir. I think there'd been a bit of discussion as to whether to report it at all. The two young guys who'd got butted weren't having anything to do with pressing charges, anyway. Too embarrassed I reckon.'

Jacobson pronged a thick, greasy chip with his fork.

'But you got their names and addresses at any rate?'

'Of course, sir. It was actually Geoffrey Trayner who called it in. Though he hadn't actually seen anything himself, had been – eh – auctioneering in the library when the altercation took place.'

Jacobson passed him his notebook.

'Pencil the details in there, old son. I take it your witnesses are absolutely certain *who* the happy couple were?'

'It seemed so, yes. I've got a half a dozen names all told. They all said Gus Mortimer and his wife.'

'You were thinking of making a case of it then?'

'If I could've done. Bit tricky when the two assaultees don't want to play ball. But I'd definitely planned to pass the details on to the Domestic Incident Unit. Only – too late now.'

Ogden's confident air waned in an instant, the obvious thought finally hitting him.

'You don't suppose I should have—'

Jacobson wiped a dribble of egg yolk from the side of his mouth.

'What? Chapped up a respected citizen in the middle of the night to see if he was strangling his wife? No, old son, I don't think so. You did as much as the job demands. They don't pay us enough to be clairvoyants as well.'

Ogden neatly copied the name and address details from

his own notebook into Jacobson's while the latter cleared his plate. Jacobson's mobile rang: Robinson from the pathology lab.

'We're setting up for the autopsy, Inspector, I've been able to take a closer look. I've found clear evidence of sexual intercourse sometime in the last twelve hours. I thought you'd want to know.'

Jacobson sensed a pause, maybe a mental blush.

'Rape then?'

'Possibly. But there's so much bruising to the body in general it might never be possible to say for sure. Rough sex certainly. Anal penetration as well as vaginal. The main thing is the presence of semen though – we should be looking at a full DNA profile, no problem at all.'

Jacobson thanked him and then thanked Ogden too. He made his way out of the canteen with a speed which belied his full stomach. Back in his office, he phoned Kerr and the custody sergeant in turn. Kerr had accompanied Mortimer to the medical suite, was still waiting there for the police surgeon to complete the assessment which had been sold to Mortimer as just a simple chat with the doctor. Jacobson's idea had been to do the interview there also, keep the whole thing as casual as possible initially. But the input from PC Ogden and then from Robinson had changed his gameplan. Now he'd be cautioning Mortimer *before* he quizzed him, getting everything on tape too. He noticed that a fresh load of paperwork had found its way into his in-tray while he'd been in the canteen. Well it could all wait now. Everybody, even the bureaucrats upstairs, had to agree that murder investigations took the highest priority. At the top of the pile there was a small card, white with gold embossed edges.

'*Greg and Christine Salter request the pleasure of your company at their housewarming event . . .*'

Another slice of tedium which no longer compelled his attention: he could hardly be expected to call round for drinkie-poos while he had a murder case to clear up.

Jacobson binned the card with a flourish as he made his way out.

Until the point where Kerr ushered him into the interview room and Jacobson read him the formal caution as required by the Police and Criminal Evidence Act, Gus Mortimer could have exerted the absolute right of any citizen to walk straight out of the Divisional building via the revolving doors at the main entrance. But now it was too late: now he could be kept there without charge for twenty-four hours while Jacobson's team carried out their inquiries, held if necessary for a further twelve on the approval of Detective Chief Superintendent Chivers.

'I take it I can call my solicitor?' he asked.

His voice was very nearly animated. As if – at last – his brain was starting to de-numb itself. Jacobson pulled his chair in closer, leant his elbows on the table, rested his chin for a moment on his left palm before he replied.

'In the case of a serious arrestable offence such as murder, I can ask my superior officer to delay access to a solicitor for up to thirty-six hours if I think the situation merits it.'

'And do you?'

Jacobson ignored the question.

'Let's get this straight then, Mr Mortimer. You left for work at seven thirty this morning. You didn't notice anything unusual and you didn't see your wife because she was sleeping in another bedroom.'

'As I've already told you. Now about my solicitor—'

Kerr had been checking the sound level on the tape recorder. Now he joined them at the table, sat down in the chair next to Jacobson.

'So when exactly *did* you last see your wife, Gus?'

'Now look here—'

Kerr was already looking: the managing director of Planet Avionics had hated the disrespectful use of his first name every bit as much as he'd hoped.

51

'Bedtime last night. About midnight probably. We'd been out at a party,' Mortimer said finally.

'That would have been the summer party at Boden Hall, Gus?'

'I want to speak to my solicitor. I'm entitled.'

'Just a few straightforward questions first, Mr Mortimer. Any solicitor would advise you to answer them,' Jacobson said, almost reasonably. 'Unless you want to brand yourself as hostile and uncooperative. That can amount to an offence in itself in a serious case like murder—'

'All right. All right. You've made your point. Yes, we were out at Boden Hall. Got back about midnight like I said.'

'And then you and your wife went off to separate bedrooms?'

'She's a restless sleeper after a few drinks. That's why if you must know.'

Kerr feigned a laugh.

'Restless after a punch in the face, perhaps. Restless after she'd been dragged off to your car by her hair.'

Mortimer made no reply.

'You deny assaulting your wife in front of several witnesses last night, Mr Mortimer?' Jacobson asked him.

'I want to speak to my solicitor.'

'Do you have any witnesses who can account for your whereabouts between eleven thirty last night when you left Boden Hall and eight o'clock this morning when you arrived at your place of work?'

'I want to speak to my solicitor.'

Kerr got up, moved behind Mortimer, leaned into his ear.

'When did you last have sex with your wife, Gus? This morning was it? Trying to make it up: only maybe she was calling out for someone else to do it properly?'

Mortimer unfolded the arms he'd been clutching to himself, leaned two clenched fists on the table. But said nothing. Kerr spoke mockingly, almost in a whisper.

'Oh Kevin, Kevin.'

Mortimer's bottom lip might have quivered slightly. He kept his gaze straight ahead, his eyes fixed solely on Jacobson. Kerr moved away.

'Was last night the first time you knew about your wife and Kevin Holland, Mr Mortimer?'

Jacobson waited a few seconds then pressed the button under the table.

'For the benefit of the record, Mr Mortimer made no reply to my question. This is Chief Inspector Jacobson terminating interview at eleven fifty-six am,' he said, standing up.

The door opened and two custody officers entered.

'That's as much as we need to know for now, Mr Mortimer. As the investigating officer, I'm placing you in police custody while I make further inquiries. The custody sergeant will make arrangements presently for you to contact your solicitor as you've requested.'

Gus Mortimer's mouth opened as if he was going to speak after all but no words came out. Instead – before the nearest plod could stop him – he banged his head down on the table. Three times. Hard.

Chapter Six

Jacobson paid himself back for his earlier egg and chips indulgence by skipping his lunchbreak altogether. Unusually, he commandeered a patrol car for the drive over to Boden Hall, used the journey time to review the progress of the case.

Smith and Williams were working through the list of witnesses to the assault which young Ogden had put together, taking half each. But Jacobson had decided that he wanted to talk to Geoffrey Trayner personally. The case against Gus Mortimer was purely circumstantial so far and the Boden Hall incident was crucial to establishing a pattern of violence against his wife. Frankly, they needed as many statements about it as they could get. Trayner hadn't been a first-hand witness but it seemed he *knew* the Mortimers. He was worth speaking to for that reason alone. Especially since – as expected – Mick Hume's tour of the properties which neighboured the Mortimers' place had been pretty much a wild-goose chase. Apart from the odd Christmas drink, there didn't seem to be a huge amount of social mixing going on from one over-lengthy driveway to the next. They all knew who their neighbours were, probably had a shrewd idea of *who* was worth *what*: but well-heeled English homes remained fortresses of solitude to judge by Hume's meagre results. Jacobson had told him to keep at it for the afternoon anyway. You never know, old son, you never know.

The sun was high and fierce overhead as the driver turned the car into Geoffrey Trayner's private road. Surprisingly it was PC Ogden behind the wheel. He'd wangled a bit of overtime when somebody else had called in sick. He must be the keenest man on the force, Jacobson had thought: or the most in debt. Jacobson had already wound both the rear windows down. Now he let his left hand dangle out in the air stream so that some part of his body could remember what cool felt like. At least Smith and Williams had managed to get a full statement from Kevin Holland – one which gave Mortimer a classic motive for the killing. Not that Jacobson was taking it at face value. Before he left the Divi, he'd assigned Kerr to check out Holland's story about his *own* whereabouts. Even though he felt in his bones that Mortimer was guilty as hell, he wasn't about to fall into the lazy copper's trap of putting his eggs entirely into one basket, focusing on the one obvious suspect to the exclusion of the wider picture.

The patrol car neared the Hall itself. Jacobson saw activity in every direction. A gang of workmen were dismantling the marquee, a litter team was clearing up the fag ends, the stray wine glasses, the discarded bottles of Bollie. He'd never been out here on police business before but he had a dim memory that he'd visited Boden Hall once a long time ago: with Janice and Sally when Sally had still been a toddler. Some kind of fête or Open Day, some kind of happy memory.

Geoffrey Trayner was in the thick of the ongoing toil but strictly in a supervisory capacity. If I have been here before, he thought, it would certainly have been pre-Trayner. When the last of the Bodens had finally dissipated away the last set of fivers from the family coffers, Boden Hall had lain unoccupied for a good dozen years at least. Trayner had caused a splash locally when he'd moved in, not least because he'd acquired the pile for a song on the basis of his pledge to restore it to its former glory. Trayner had made his money back in the nineteen eighties in a way that Jacobson only dimly understood. Speculation, hostile takeovers, company buy-outs. There was a word for it – carpetbagging maybe – that he couldn't precisely recall. He remembered Kerr talking about him sometime, come to think of it. The main point had seemed to be that Trayner had made money from *other* money, without the messy need to actually produce any goods or services himself.

Ogden had made good time for a driver who'd been up all night. Jacobson thanked him, asked him to wait. Trayner was already headed towards him as he got out of the car. As far as Jacobson knew, money wasn't the main thing for Trayner any more. Now that – presumably – he had more than enough of it, power, influence and public status had become his overriding bags. He'd joined the New Labour bandwagon sometime in the nineties, had been the region's MEP since the last Euro elections.

Jacobson showed him his ID, introduced himself. Trayner gave him a vigorous handshake, his thumb darting momentarily from one significant knuckle of Jacobson's hand to another equally significant knuckle. Jacobson took his hand away quickly, quite definitely not reciprocating.

'I must say, Chief Inspector, I didn't expect someone of your rank on a matter like this. I thought your constable had sorted it out last night. Delighted though I am to meet you.'

Trayner was younger than Jacobson, older than Kerr. He looked exactly in the flesh how he looked in the papers or on television. Jacobson had caught him on *Question Time*, the last time the programme had been in the area. Not that the spectacle of a bunch of pontificating prats pandering to the ill-informed prejudices of Middle England was Jacobson's idea of a fun evening at home. He'd just been too tired, too slumped, after a particularly enervating day's work to switch the damned thing off. He'd probably, he thought now, slept through most of the programme. He made him forty-five at a guess. A man of medium height and thin receding hair but with a healthy glow to his skin and the kind of good muscle tone most painlessly achieved by frequent hours in an expensive gym.

'So you didn't see what happened yourself, Mr Trayner?'

'Please: Geoffrey. No I didn't, I'm afraid. Neither did my wife. I think your constable spoke to the guests who did see it though.'

Trayner invited him indoors but, despite the heat, Jacobson declined the offer. Instead, he gestured to a nearby bench, invitingly shaded by a tall lime tree. He just wanted to cut the crap, didn't have time to play at *An Inspector Calls*, wasn't about to go on first name terms either. Jacobson sat down first, then Trayner alongside.

'If you could just tell me what you know about Mr and Mrs Mortimer, Mr Trayner. It could have a bearing on a more serious inquiry.'

Trayner shook his head before he answered.

'They're not personal friends, Chief Inspector. That's the first thing to say. Neither are three quarters of the people who were here last night. It's just become something of a tradition in the last few years. A get together for the local movers and shakers. Oil the wheels of business as they say.'

You should meet my new friend Greg Salter, Jacobson thought.

'But you did – do – know the Mortimers?'

'I probably know all the top company men in Crowby, Chief Inspector. One way or another. The Rotary, the – ah – the Lodge, the Chamber of Commerce. And Planet Avionics is a big concern, a significant employer for the local workforce.'

'So you know the Mortimers then?' Jacobson repeated, not caring if he sounded as tetchy as he felt.

'I've met them on a few, formal social occasions yes. Gus Mortimer, because of his directorship, is also on the CEG. That's the Crowby in Europe Group. Local employers who're pro Europe, pro my work at Strasbourg.'

Jacobson dug into his pocket, found his lighter. B and H

tally of the day: six and, thanks to Trayner, rising. He let the party political drone on for a few seconds more while he lit up. Then he told him an edited version of what the postman had found, watched the smarm drain from a second smug face.

'I – I see. Could I – ah, could I trouble you for one of those?'

He handed him the packet, then the lighter. Trayner lit a cigarette awkwardly. He took two or three quick puffs but didn't seem to inhale. Maybe politicians never did, Jacobson thought.

'I – I still don't think I can help you very much. Planet Avionics is a go-ahead company, Gus Mortimer is a competent MD from everything I've heard. Before last night, I didn't know anything negative about his personal life—'

Trayner took another quick, non-puff.

'In fact I didn't really know anything at all about his personal life. His wife was younger of course, pretty.'

Jacobson watched the workmen struggle with the last section of the marquee. Rather them than me.

'No rumours, gossip?'

'Nothing that reached me, Chief Inspector.'

A blonde woman emerged from the path behind the tree, a French poodle panting at her heels. Trayner introduced her as Elaine, his wife. What was it he'd just said? *His wife was younger of course, pretty*: if Trayner's own wife wasn't Jenny Mortimer's twin, she was her younger cousin. Jacobson entirely failed for a moment to take his eyes off the blue gemstone studded into her tanned belly button.

Elaine Trayner was as helpful or as unhelpful as her husband. She'd never seen the Mortimers other than at a few functions, hadn't spoken to them beyond a few pleasantries. 'Who'd have thought a thing like that?' was the best extent of her contribution to Jacobson's investigation. Jacobson thanked her anyway then cut his losses. It had been worth a try, he told himself. The Trayners might have been the Mortimers' best mates. The wives were certainly well matched as regards looks. Maybe the problem was that Mortimer wasn't in the same money league as Trayner. Wealth, he reminded himself, was a strictly relative concept.

He clambered back into the patrol car, only just on schedule for his next destination: Mrs Jennifer Mortimer's parents. It hadn't taken long for the local media to get wind that something juicy was up. Possibly as a Chinese whisper from one of Mick Hume's housecalls, possibly more directly. Crowby CID had switched to pagers and mobiles operating with strong encryption. But the plods still relied on old-fashioned radios which were easily and routinely scanned by petty crooks, bored pensioners and news-hungry reporters. Jacobson had caught the twelve thirty bulletin from Crowby FM on the ride over to Boden Hall: '*Murder squad detectives are believed to be on the scene of a serious incident at a property outside Crowby. No more details are available at present.*' They would have to make an official press statement soon, no question: someone had to speak to the parents before that happened, before the hacks battened on their doorstep.

Ogden knew his fair share of short-cuts, found a route through the town centre that Jacobson hadn't known was possible. Inside fifteen minutes, they were pulling up outside the location. The Beech Park estate was on the north side of Crowby. It was regarded by both police and residents as 'decent'. Ex-council houses in good repair, hard-working families with newish cars, jobs, tidy gardens: with what politicos like Trayner called A Stake In Society. He had it in mind that Kerr's father lived around here somewhere. Being the last living Stalinist though, Kerr Senior was known to take a less Panglossian view of his surroundings. To Jacobson's relief, there was another patrol car already parked in the street outside. Someone else had broken the news; all he'd have to do would be to mop up the intelligence. He thanked Ogden for his time, told him he'd get a lift back in the other car. He opened a green-painted gate and walked up the garden path to the front door. The female plod who'd drawn the short straw of the day showed him in when he rang the bell.

Jenny Mortimer's parents looked to be in their seventies. Later Jacobson learned that she'd been born relatively late for a couple of that generation, had also been their only child. The mother was trying her best to drink the tea that the young policewoman had made for her. Every now and again she put the cup shakily back down on the saucer, wiped more tears away from her cheeks. Next to her, neglected on the sofa, lay a copy of the *TV Times* opened at today's programmes. The father was a pacer. A small, wiry man with silver hair, close cropped. Over and over again, he repeated the same two or three steps up and down in the centre of the room, his hands shoved into his trouser pockets, his face sinking forward into his neck. There was a bowling trophy on the mantelpiece and half a dozen framed photographs. Post-war newly-weds: the husband awkward in his de-mob suit. The little girl on Santa's knee. The smiling graduate with the mortar board and the prop ribboned scroll. In the centre a black and white close-up showed an engine driver, oily-handed at the gleaming wheel of a steam train. Jacobson was good at resemblances, recognised the father in what must have been his prime. Years ago: before Beeching, before old age, before his daughter had been beaten and strangled to death.

He told them who he was, that nothing he could say could make things better.

'All I can promise you is that we'll get who did it.'

The old man stopped pacing, stood with his back shadowed to the fireplace. It was bright sunshine outside but somebody had drawn the curtains tight shut, an old custom that Jacobson hadn't witnessed for a long time.

'You mean you haven't lifted him yet?'

Jacobson struggled for a moment to remember Mrs Mortimer's maiden name. Then:

'Exactly who are we talking about, Mr Swain?'

60

'Him of course.'

Swain gestured to one of the photographs behind him: Jenny and Gus spraying champagne, showered in confetti.

'Never even had a proper wedding,' Mrs Swain managed to get out between sobs. 'Married on some cruise ship somewhere. Off on their own.'

'Manila,' Swain volunteered, 'I knew he was a wrong 'un. Said it all along.'

The policewoman made another round of tea and a cup of instant coffee for Jacobson. There were less than maybe five miles between Beech Park and the Mortimers' house but the story Jacobson got was that her parents had seen Jenny less than half a dozen times in the five years the Mortimers had been married. Mrs Swain rubbed her eyes again.

'It was bad enough when she was with the one before. Eric. But we'd see her at Christmas and her birthday any road. Or on an odd weekend – if she'd nothing better to do. At least she pretended to be a real daughter then. They weren't properly married or nothing. But he was good to her, Eric was. A mother can always tell that.'

Jacobson sipped at the too-milky coffee. The social psychology of the family had been a course unit on his Open University degree, how there were always as many family histories as there were family members. In Mum and Dad's version, Jenny had been a quiet girl, studious. She'd done well at school, gone to university, come back to Crowby as a teacher. Eric Brown had worked at the same school. If they hadn't seen her as much as they would've liked, at least she'd seemed settled for a few years. Then she'd suddenly taken up with Gus Mortimer.

Swain paced again as he talked.

'We hardly saw her at all after that. Foreign trips was part of it. New York, Hong Kong. All over the shop. I wouldn't have minded that. Good for her, I'd have said. But she didn't want to know her mother and me even when she was right here in Crowby. We used to give them a helping hand. Eric and her, like. A bit of DIY and what have you. Just taking an interest. But after Mortimer – well, she more or less turfed us out the only time we went over there. We were only passing by. Told Elsie what a rotten mother she'd been. How we'd brought her up all wrong. How she didn't want us breathing down her neck. We won't be back if that's what you think, I told her.'

The wife buried her face in her hands. Jacobson finished off the coffee to get the taste over with.

'What makes you think her husband would've harmed your daughter, Mr Swain?'

'It's always the husband, isn't it? You see them on the telly asking for witnesses. Next thing you know, they're being arrested, charged with it. Besides, he *hit* her.'

Swain picked up his daughter's wedding photo, waved it as if it was material evidence.

'Elsie ran into her in town. Six months ago it was. Couldn't get away fast enough, could she, love? A big black eye covered over with make-up. Where'd she get that then, eh?'

Elsie Swain nodded.

'She told me to mind my own blankety-blank business. I wouldn't care to repeat the word she used. I've never spoken to her from that day to this. My husband neither.'

She gave another quiet sob, her voice weirdly child-like.

'Now – now I never will.'

'You can't have known Mr Mortimer very well then?' Jacobson asked after a moment.

Mrs Swain tried another sip of tea.

'He came round here in his big car just the once. Just after they got married,' her husband answered, 'All smiles to your face. All surface. I know him about as well as I know you, son. But I trust him a damn sight less.'

On another occasion, Jacobson would have smiled at the epithet. There was always someone older than you, he thought: until you were dead. He asked them for Eric Brown's details, assured them it was a matter of pure

62

routine, a question of filling in the background to the case. The policewoman persuaded the Swains to let her phone up their GP, have him call on them later. Then they were gone, out of there. The outside air and the hot afternoon sun on Jacobson's brow had never felt more welcoming.

Kerr parked up a couple of houses away from the address. The Longtown area. Bedsits, students, three vegetarian restaurants, coffee shops that you didn't see how they could possibly make enough profit to keep open: the closest that Crowby came to bohemia.

He tried Cathy on their home number, then on her mobile. Answerphone both times – most likely she'd taken Sam and Suzy to the park, just hadn't bothered to switch the mobile on. He left her a message anyway: he'd definitely be home for tea, they might even have put the case to bed by then, tell the kids he loved them. He checked again for incoming messages but there were none. He tapped out Rachel's number but then seemed to think better of it, cancelled the call before it connected.

Kevin Holland's white van was outside his front door next to a Volkswagen beetle and a converted ambulance which somebody had thought it would be a good idea to paint dayglo orange and red. Holland had checked out clean on the PNC but he shared a rented terraced house with half a dozen other tenants, mostly aged between eighteen and thirty. Two of them had minor drug-related convictions, another one had got probation for affray after the Stop the City action in London the year before. A plump young woman who said she was Wendy opened the door, told him she knew exactly *what* he was as he flashed his ID.

Kevin Holland himself was sitting on a white sofa in the front room, expertly constructing a joint over a round, elaborately crafted table. Some kind of Eastern design. Kerr thought it went well with the magic carpet of a Persian rug on the floor.

'Going to do me for this then?' Holland asked.

'Not my department,' Kerr answered. He noticed the Moloko cd, the one that used to be Rachel's favourite, playing quietly on the hi-fi. 'Even if it was, I wouldn't bother right now. Not in the circumstances.'

Wendy had followed him in, made herself a seat on a large cushion next to an even larger rubber plant. Her expression became maybe one per cent less hostile than it had been a moment before.

Kerr invited himself on to the other end of the sofa.

'I just need to know your precise whereabouts for the last twenty-four hours, Kevin. It's the standard routine that's all.'

Wendy interjected before Holland had time to open his mouth.

'Jesus! Kevin's already given you lot a statement. What more do you want? Blood?'

Holland left the unlit joint on the table, waved his left hand in her direction.

'It's OK, Wendy. The man's got a job to do. It's what he has to learn in this life, what he's got to work through.'

She gave an acquiescent shrug, drew her short legs up into an uncomfortable-looking approximation of the half lotus position. Kerr checked his notes: Wendy Pelham, DOB 10–3–77, the one who'd been caught waving a Metropolitan police helmet on a stick outside Moorgate tube station.

'Whenever you're ready,' he said to Holland, trying to keep the irritation out of his voice. The guy's girlfriend had just been murdered, he reminded himself; the least Kerr could do was to leave him with his pretentions intact.

'Like I said when I gave my statement – we were at the Larmer Tree site from last Saturday to yesterday. Wendy was there, so was Chris. He lives here as well. A couple of others who don't. We've run a food stall over there for the last two or three fests. Just a sideline really. But it brings in a bit of cash – pays for us being there anyway.'

'Where's Chris now?'

64

'At work I expect. He's got a second-hand place. Cds, rare vinyl, that kind of thing.'

'I'll need the address, Kevin. When did you actually get back here?'

Holland leant back on the sofa, clasped hands on the back of his neck, brushing back his dreadlocks.

'Between ten and eleven. We'd packed up around eight and it's about a two-hour drive.'

Wendy Pelham nodded her head. Her mousy hair was cut short and straight. If you could call it a style at all it was a pudding-basin. Kerr's dad had used to threaten him with one when he'd been eleven or twelve, when he'd failed once again to rendezvous voluntarily with the barber.

'It was quarter to eleven to be precise,' she said. 'I can vouch for Kevin one hundred per cent. So can the others.'

Just one big, happy, smiley family, Kerr thought.

'The others. I'll need *their* names and addresses too.'

He turned a page in his notebook, clicked the plastic top of his pen. Holland gave him the details of something called CD Heaven, gave him two more names with a shared address.

'That's fine, Kevin,' he said. 'It's just so we can corroborate your statement. I take it you didn't go out again?'

'Smoked some draw, had a cup of tea, hit the sack before midnight.'

'And you didn't see or hear from Mrs Mortimer?'

'No. No, I didn't.'

Holland's left leg suddenly shot forward, kicked the table over. He flung himself to his knees, his fists battering futilely into its upturned surface.

'I didn't, I didn't, I fucking *didn't*.'

Wendy tried to put an arm around his shoulders but he shrugged her off, banged his fists down half a dozen more times. Kerr noticed Moloko again: *Give up yourself unto the moment*.

Holland stood up finally, righted the table back on to its legs. On both hands, his knuckles were scraped, a couple of them looked to be bleeding. When he spoke again, his voice was barely a choked whisper.

'I knew there was something wrong when she didn't leave the message. I should have listened to this – not this.'

Kerr watched him stab his forefinger to his breastbone and then tap the side of his head.

'I should've gone out there last night, not waited till this morning.'

Kerr told him not to blame himself, that only the murderer was to blame.

Wendy pulled herself up to her full height: five feet and maybe a couple of inches.

'I think *you'd* better go.'

Kerr had been in the job too long now to believe what the textbooks still taught, that you had to dominate every situation, win every confrontation.

'I'm going,' he said.

He told Holland that someone would phone him, let him know when he could see the body.

'Don't worry,' he added for Wendy Pelham's benefit, 'I can see myself out.'

CD Heaven was less than two streets away. He decided to leave his car where he'd parked it and walk. The shop turned out to be in a basement underneath a second-hand furniture store. There were at least six customers poring over the racks. Not bad, Kerr thought, for a hot Saturday afternoon in August. He allowed himself a quick look at the new arrivals box. Graham Parker, *Squeezing Out Sparks*, tempted him – a medium-sized hole in his collection filled for a mere six quid – but he passed it up, had more important business to deal with.

The guy behind the counter was nearer fifty than forty, what was left of his ginger hair tied back in a pony-tail. Kerr had thought nothing in particular about the name when Holland had mentioned it but now he had a flash of instant recognition: Chris Parr – Career Activist – Crowby's first and last Green councillor. He'd lost his seat at the last local election. But his memory lingered on, had become the stuff of canteen legend, although Kerr had never encountered him personally before. Parr had been a noisy presence on the Police Consultative Committee for a couple of years, had allegedly brought the Chief Constable to the verge of apoplexy more than once. Whatever the cause – anti-roads, housing asylum seekers, Say No to Land Fill – Parr was for it, against whatever handling the police took of related demos and direct actions.

Kerr waved his ID. Parr was tall and thin apart from the beer gut which challenged the capacity of his faded red T-shirt. There was a political slogan written in Spanish on the front. Whatever it meant was beyond Kerr's holiday phrasebook knowledge. But it was probably a safe bet that it didn't say God bless the World Bank, British Nuclear Fuels, Monsanto and Ronald McDonald.

'Mr Parr? Is there somewhere we can talk privately?'

Parr reacted without a trace of surprise. If Wendy Pelham hadn't phoned him in the last five minutes, Kerr thought, *that* would've been surprising. Parr gestured to a youth in an Eminem T-shirt who'd been clearing out-of-date gig announcements and amps for sale ads off the noticeboard to the left of the entrance. The youth took over the counter and Parr led him through to the backshop.

'Yes, mate,' he said unprompted, 'I was with Kevin and Wendy and co all week. We got back to Crowby last night. Not sure exactly when: round about eleven say. Fancy a cuppa?'

Kerr nodded a second too late to hide his mild amazement at the offer. You got so used to hostility in the job, you had to be careful you weren't wrongfooted by simple courtesy. Parr found a kettle and a couple of very nearly clean mugs.

'Wendy phoned me half an hour ago. I thought I'd give it till three then shut up early. We've been closed over the last week anyway. Not that there's much I can do. But you need your friends don't you?'

Kerr ignored the cliché, answered with a question of his own.

'Knocking on a bit for the rock and roll lifestyle, aren't we?'

Parr's grin would have been boyish once, even charming. When he'd still had all his front teeth for instance.

'Don't you read the quality papers, Sergeant? Forty-plus teenagers. We're all the rage. Guys packing in the rat race, trying to find something more meaningful. Only in my case, I never joined the fucker in the first place.'

'So you're dossed in a bedsit, recycling old records for a living. I thought you lot wanted to change the world.'

Parr handed Kerr a mug of tea and a haphazardly opened carton of milk.

'They're only bedsits to the landlord. It's a communal space for the people living there. And the world *has* changed, mate. Tories 'fessing up to toking. Suburban housewives raiding animal laboratories, kids re-inventing the barter economy, refusing to be wage slaves. The last days of the Evil Empire for sure.'

Kerr poured in the milk, decided to sideline the state-of-the-nation debate for the time being.

'Getting back to Mr Holland. Were you aware of his relationship with Jenny Mortimer?'

'We all were, mate. She came round to see him twice, three times a week. Usually on weekdays, usually in the afternoons. Everybody liked her. A sweet lady. Making changes, getting her head sorted, y'know?'

Somebody had certainly sorted it now: but Kerr kept the thought to himself.

'I don't expect her visits appealed to her husband very much.'

Parr slurped his tea. Somehow Kerr already knew he would be a slurper.

'As far as I know, Mr Fat Cat hadn't a clue what Mrs Cat was up to. Nobody at the house would've breathed a word in his direction. And we don't get many invites to the cocktail party circuit round our way. 'Sides, he seemed to spend most of his time at his office or away on business trips from what Jenny used to say.'

'Did you know Kevin Holland had demanded she tell him herself, threatened that he'd tell him if she didn't?'

Parr scratched the back of his head, the part which still had hair.

'That I didn't know, mate. I know he wanted her to move in with him. But I thought that meant her just doing a moonlight on the QT. Especially with him prone to thumping her. The husband I mean.'

'Where did you get that item of information from?'

'Straight from the horse's mouth, mate. She told me one afternoon. Kevin was held up, doing a job somewhere the other side of Wynarth. We were just talking in the kitchen. Like you do.'

Parr made as much of a whistling sound as his missing teeth permitted.

'Jesus. No wonder Kevin's blaming himself now.'

Robert Johnson, observed by DC Dennett, had boarded a number forty-three from the bus stop outside the Neighbourhood Advice Centre. DC Aston had got on at the next stop, had taken a seat right at the back, buried his head in the sports pages of the *Daily Star*. Johnson had stayed on the bus all the way to the Flowers Street bus station. He'd taken the moving staircase which led him from the back of the station up into the shopping centre. He'd poked around in the Indoor Market, looked through a couple of paperbacks at one of the second-hand book stalls. He'd examined – but hadn't purchased – a nasty-looking hammer at Desai's DIY before making his way next door to the Market Tavern.

At the bar he'd ordered a pint of Grolsch and the Captain's Special, was chomping his way through the latter right now. AKA battered cod, chips and peas, Aston thought, nursing his half pint of badly kept Marston's

Pedigree in an opposite corner. For the third time, he told the malodorous drunk at the next table to fuck off. The Market, Aston had quickly surmised, was the kind of town centre pub ready to serve anybody with the cash in their hand for immediate payment: this all-embracing policy meant in practice that most of its clientele were street people, thieves, dole wallahs. The market traders themselves and the God-fearing, mortgage-paying, *Daily Mail* reading general public gave it the very widest of body swerves.

'It's a fucking guid ray-dio,' the drunk started to tell him for the fourth time. Just what he needed: a run-in with a Scotch alkie. Aston hated Jocks. The BNP could have his subscription as soon as they liked, provided they stopped targeting blacks, turned their bigoted attentions northwards instead. Either they were useless wastes of space like this one or they were clever bastards like Gordon Brown, taking over the country at the top. They were also, as in Aston's own case, keen on running off with other men's wives.

'If you don't sit down and shut up, you're going to have Radio One coming out of your arse, mate,' he told him.

'Away tae fuck,' the drunk replied but left it at that. He swayed on his feet, very nearly falling, as he shambled back to his own table. Aston paged his whereabouts to Dennett then pretended to study the racing section until it looked like Johnson was ready to move on. He followed him out into Flowers Way and out finally into the High Street where some kind of rockabilly revival band was being studiously ignored by the passers-by. The overweight tea chest bass player had a dangerous-looking sweat on in the heat. Don't croak on my blue suede shoes, Aston thought. He gave them three cursory minutes of his time, enough to let Johnson get just far enough ahead, dropped a pound coin into the hat for their unknowing contribution to law and order.

At the top end, the High Street broadened out into a wide pedestrianised square. The Town Hall took up the far side.

A white 1930s building with art deco flourishes prefaced by a line of oak trees. Somehow they'd both survived the planning vandals back in the nineteen sixties. Bugger all else had as far as Aston could see. The Public Library was a sixties monstrosity as was the Divisional building across the way. Which left your eyes a choice between the multistorey car park and the back side of the shopping centre. He bought a copy of the local paper from the news stand next to the Häagen Dazs concession. A Brummie born and bred, he was starting to feel quite at home.

Johnson stopped in the middle of the square, pretended to watch the pigeons. He hadn't spotted the tail yet but it was common sense there'd be one around somewhere. They didn't wire you up to a computer all night and then leave you to your own devices during the hours of broad daylight. The local coppers would hate it that he was back here. On their turf. Invading their space. Tough shit, he thought: he should have bought the hammer really, just for the wind-up value. A married-looking slag hurried past. Thirty-five or something ancient. But good legs. You'd give her one if you were feeling in a generous mood. She lowered her eyes when he gaped at her. That's it, bitch, he thought. Look away, pretend you're not desperate for it. Why walk around with your tits hanging out then? Slag. Slapper. He noticed she was carrying a basket of books on her left arm. Terrif. He'd been headed to the library anyway: with any luck she'd think he was following her.

Chapter Seven

The autopsy had been scheduled for three o'clock. Its strict Sunday name was the post-mortem, but Americanisms were taking over in medicine as in everything else. As the senior investigating officer, Jacobson – like the chief soco and the Coroner's Officer – was officially obliged to take a ringside view. He'd got there just in time, had been relieved to find that the last remaining seat was on the back row and near the door: dissection wasn't something you got used to – it was something you learned to endure. There'd been some kind of fuck-up with the video camera. Jacobson stared at his shoes while the operator checked it out, got it sorted.

Before he did anything else, Robinson x-rayed Jenny Mortimer's neck. Professor Merchant, whatever his other faults, had taught his pupil well. A tiny bone, the hyoid, located just above the Adam's Apple, nearly always gets broken by a strangler. It was an old courtroom trick for the defence to claim that the little bone could have been damaged *during* the autopsy and not before but Robinson, Jacobson realised, had cleverly excluded the possibility. Now he began his naked-eye examination, talking his findings out loud for the benefit of the record as much as for his immediate audience. Jacobson watched and listened with only half his brain. The other half had just realised something which very nearly shocked it: he had finally lost count of the precise number of times he'd had to sit through this miserable game of soldiers. Despite the hysterical bollocks that surfaced from time to time in the tabloids, the murder rate in Britain had barely fluctuated in the last hundred years. But that still meant, for a biggish-sized town like Crowby, you could expect half a dozen unlawful deaths in a bad year. Or a good year: Jacobson wasn't exactly a fan of murder but he'd come to appreciate the clear sense of moral purpose which came with catching a killer. A lot of crime was just need. Provided they hadn't used violence or caused unnecessary damage, Jacobson sometimes felt sorrier for the perpetrators than for the well-insured, self-righteous victims. Mainly you banged up the unfortunates, the incompetent and the misbegotten. Their only way into a nice house was to burgle it, their only way to a credit rating was to nick a credit card. But killing was different. No one had a right to take life except God. And God, in Jacobson's considered opinion, either didn't exist or was in need of a bloody good kicking.

Robinson had commented in detail on the exuded material from the nose and mouth, had lingered over every cut and bruise, had debated inconclusively – again – as to whether the genital abrasures pointed to rape or to rough, consensual sex. Now he was scraping under the fingernails for any debris. It was the stock forensic check you saw on every TV crime drama, in every *Morse* and *Wexford*, yet never once in Jacobson's career had it yielded a clue of the slightest importance. The queasiness in his stomach told him that the external examination was very nearly over. Once the samples of hair had been taken, the body would be washed down and then they'd be in for it: the Y-shaped incision from the shoulders down to the pubes, the organs snatched out and examined, the brain popped out of its casing like a Halloween walnut, the hundred and one tests by which the dead can still – sometimes – speak.

Robinson took a short break. He removed one pair of surgical gloves, washed his hands, took a drink of water from the cooler, washed his hands again, put on a fresh pair. Jacobson fidgeted, a restless schoolboy trapped in Assembly. Come on, old son. Let's get on with it. He wanted to get the team together for its first formal briefing before five. He wanted to track down Eric Brown before then. He needed to catch up on the Crawler operation as well. These were the things he wanted to do, needed to do. Instead, he was compelled to witness Robinson's grim parody of surgical procedure. No matter how well he'd trained, how skilled he might become over a lifetime, his patients would always be dead on the table. Why do it then, Jacobson wondered, why not bring babies into the world instead or cure cancer? He looked away as Robinson made the first incision. They were unanswerable questions. Worse: they applied just as much to himself.

Kevin Holland's third alibi source after Wendy Pelham and Chris Parr was a couple Holland had referred to as Josh and Lynne. Josh was an art teacher and Lynne was several months pregnant, he'd said. Their address was a narrow terraced house on a street midway between Parr's record shop and Holland, Pelham and Parr's shared gaff. Kerr tried a bell which didn't seem to be working and then knocked briskly on the door. A dark-haired, bikini-clad woman in her mid-twenties opened it with a paint brush in her hand. She was tall and slim. If you were feeling unkind you might have said she was anorexic. But whatever else she was, she definitely wasn't pregnant.

She led Kerr through the hall, past the back room which was fifty per cent on the way towards pink and blue kiddification and out to the back yard where a smaller but distinctly fuller figured woman was basking in a sun lounger.

'I'm Josh. This is Lynne,' the tall one said. Lynne looked up from her book and read the question on Kerr's face.

'Artificial insem, donor sperm,' she said, reaching out for Josh's offered hand and giggling. Kerr felt fourteen again, trying to figure out sex and knowing that his sister understood more than he'd even imagined. His mind played him the likely thoughts of Chairman Jacobson. *The wonders of modern effing science, old son.* But he kept the transmission to himself, asked them instead when they'd last seen Kevin Holland. After they'd confirmed Holland's story about the time frame of their return from the music festival, he told them about Jenny Mortimer. Watching their faces, it was certain that nobody *chez* Holland had phoned ahead this time. Which probably meant, he thought, that Chris Parr hadn't been lying when he'd said that he'd heard the news *before* Kerr had called on Holland and Pelham.

'Had you ever met Mrs Mortimer yourselves?' he asked.

Lynne shook her head. Josh said they hadn't but they'd heard Kevin talking about her often enough.

'He's crazy about her, smitten. He used to be a bit of a wanderer. But I don't think he even *sees* other women these days. Sees with his eyes, I mean.'

Lynne stood up, said she'd had enough of the sun for now. Kerr watched her waddle indoors. Not for the first time he wondered about the biological imperatives of parenting. How much they'd pulled on his own wife for example. How little they pulled on him. They hadn't needed someone else's sperm but there'd been years of tests and screwing by the calendar before Cathy had suddenly, unexpectedly, conceived after a drunken night of recrimination and lustful reconciliation.

He told Josh he was finished with his questioning and she followed him through to the front door. He wished her luck with the sleepless nights and set off back towards his car, the sun baking his face. He decided he'd probably wear his baseball cap tomorrow even if it did piss off Jacobson. That's if the inquiry *needed* a tomorrow of course. Most murders were straightforward, solved in hours not weeks. Which was exactly how this one was shaping up. It was looking worse for Gus Mortimer by the minute. Even Josh and Lynne had heard the rumours about wife beating. As for Kevin Holland: unlike Mortimer, he would probably never be invited to a Rotary dinner – but his alibi was tighter than a duck's arse.

Eric Brown wasn't Known To The Police and the address Jenny Mortimer's parents had given Jacobson was long out of date. Not just that Brown didn't live there anymore, nobody lived there anymore: a set of streets that had stood in the way of the inner ring road and the expansion of the Waitrose complex. Jacobson had worked all this out by phone and pager as the patrol car had wheeled him away from the mortuary and back to the Divisional building. Now he was back in his own car and headed over to the Riverside area and a possible connection to Brown.

The Swains had mentioned that their daughter had met Brown through the school where they'd both worked, the Simon de Montfort Comprehensive. Jacobson suspected that tagging the name of a psychopathic despot on to a style of schooling that had originally aspired towards mutuality and equality probably hadn't helped its chances of success overmuch. But he didn't have time to ponder the issue fully right now. From his office at the Divi, he'd managed to raise one of the school secretaries by phone. It seemed that Eric Brown had resigned from the school a couple of years ago. She thought he'd given up teaching altogether. The best she could suggest was that he contact Mr Grant. Mr Grant had retired but he'd used to be Head of the English Department, where Mr Brown had worked. The secretary reckoned they'd been friends as well as colleagues. Mr Grant would know Mr Brown's whereabouts if anyone did.

Kenneth Grant lived practically around the corner from the Barnfields, though it was a less grand street and the houses were smaller. Jacobson drew his car up outside. He'd be able to do a quick check on the surveillance while he was here, kill two birds with one stone. He cut the engine and stayed put for a moment. The heat was stifling, even hotter today than yesterday. It certainly wasn't weather to rush about in. There was no need to anyway, he reminded himself. All they were doing was going through the motions, building up the background. He was ninety per cent certain they already had the murderer safely in police custody. He didn't know which particular nasty slime pit inside DS Kerr's brain had produced the 'Oh Kevin' line he'd used to such effect during Mortimer's interrogation. But it was sounding more and more like Kerr had hit upon the deep, dark truth of the matter.

Gus Mortimer was an alpha male, slugging his way to the top. His wife was his *property* – just like his house, his cars, his swimming pool. When she stepped out of line – or even if he just felt like it – he'd slap her one. Only this time she'd stepped out too far and he'd slapped too hard. He got out of the car and locked it. Even in an area like this you couldn't be too careful. He'd bet his pension that the semen inside Jenny Mortimer would match her husband's DNA bands. It wouldn't *prove* that he'd killed her but it would strongly back up the emerging scenario: Mortimer had dragged his wife home, enraged that she would dare to leave him. He'd beaten her, forced sex on her, finally throttled her and discarded – chucked away – her lifeless body on his red gravel driveway. The only wonder was that he hadn't bothered to drive over the corpse on his way out afterwards.

Kenneth Grant was sitting on an ageing wooden bench in his front garden, shaded from the sun by a healthy looking laburnum tree. He had a pot of tea and a set of tea cups in front of him and a copy of *The Times Literary Supplement* resting on his knee. Jacobson joined him on the bench, got straight to the point.

'Eric. Ah yes, Eric,' Grant said. 'Another good man lost to the profession. I've probably got his address in here somewhere.'

The former Head of English picked up a small palmtop which had been lying next to him on the bench, started tapping into the keyboard.

'You want to get yourself one of these, Inspector. Very handy in your line of work, I'd have thought.'

Jacobson could just about manage some basic word processing and a few elementary searches on the Police National Computer so he nodded as non-committally as he could. He usually rationalised to himself that computers were a young person's thing, that he couldn't be expected to keep up at his age. But Grant was seventy if he was a day. Everybody, it seemed, had joined the technological revolution except for DCI Frank Jacobson.

Grant passed him the palmtop. Eric Brown's address and telephone number pulsated on the screen in bold 12 point Courier.

'There you go, Inspector. Eric's not in any trouble, I hope?'

Jacobson scribbled the details into his notebook, told him an edited version of the facts; Jenny Mortimer was unlawfully dead, he needed to speak to everyone who knew her.

'It's just routine. We need to build up a picture. You say Mr Brown's not a teacher any more?'

'No – no, he isn't.'

Grant's voice had been relaxed and self-confident only moments before. Now his words sounded soft and hesitant. It was clear that the news of Jenny Mortimer's death *was* news, had knocked some of the wind out of his sails. His wife, as Jacobson assumed, appeared from around the side of the house. A small, bird-like woman in a floral dress and carrying a pair of secateurs. As soon as she'd established who Jacobson was, what was going on, she disappeared inside the house and came back with a bottle of Glenmorangie. She poured a generous measure into one of the unused cups, handed it to her husband.

'Inspector?' she asked, still holding the bottle.

Jacobson could think of little better in life than a decent dram or two in the shade of a well-tended English garden at the height of a long summer. Especially if there was a chance of ice too. But he managed to say no. He waited until Grant had taken a good snorter then asked him for the full card on Eric Brown and Jenny Mortimer née Swain.

'I barely knew the young woman, Inspector. Rather fetching though. She – she taught Modern Languages, I believe. Eric on the other hand was my right-hand man while he was with us. Some people are teachers by nature – most people aren't – Eric most definitely was. He could get essays on *Macbeth* out of kids who thought they were only interested in sniffing glue and watching *Driller Killer*.'

'But he left the school, gave up teaching?'

Kenneth Grant drained his tea cup of malt to the bottom. Then:

'A typical tale of benighted times, Inspector. You take on bright young people, give them one of the world's most difficult jobs and then constantly demoralise them. SATS, media hostility, OFSTED witch hunts, lousy pay. The weak go under, the strong get the hell out. Eric went into sales, doubled his salary inside six months.'

Jacobson took out his cigarette packet tentatively. Far from seeming to mind, Mrs Grant helped herself to one and squeezed on to the bench next to her husband, obliging Jacobson to slide awkwardly along to make room.

'Eric and Jenny came over to dinner a couple of times while they were together,' she said. 'But we never really felt that we'd got to know her. Ken's favourite conversations are about Dickens and Thackeray, Mr Jacobson. I rather had the impression that Eric's young lady preferred livelier ways to spend an evening.'

Jacobson lit her cigarette, then his own.

'Any idea how long they were together?'

Mrs Grant shrugged, looked to her husband.

'Three or four years,' Grant answered. 'It was all very yellow press when she left him – and us, I have to say. She threw a ruler at some young madam in the middle of period seven – that's about quarter to three back on planet Earth, I believe – and walked straight out of the school. Never to be seen again. Apparently she drove home, packed and moved out. Career and boyfriend both given the instant heave-ho.'

'And Eric Brown?'

Grant waved his tea cup at his wife. She gave Jacobson her cigarette to hold while she poured out another measure. Her eyes were the sharp blue colour that saw everything, missed nothing.

'Eric went on auto pilot for a while,' Grant said. 'Then gave in his notice at the summer term.'

'But you stayed in touch?'

'Oh yes. From time to time he gets over here, treats me to a pint or two in the Riverside lounge. He's done well for himself financially. But I think he hankers after the occasional dusty conversation about books. We saw him about a fortnight ago, didn't we Mary?'

Mrs Grant nodded.

'Yes. Just before he went away.'

'Away?' Jacobson asked.

Grant took a sip of whisky rather than a gulp this time.

'Yes, Inspector, away. Didn't I mention it? He's gone off somewhere Iberian on holiday. Spain or Portugal – I'm afraid I can't remember which. I don't think he's due back till next week.'

No, you bloody didn't mention it, Jacobson thought irascibly.

'I assume you never met Jenny's husband, Gus Mortimer, at any time?'

'You assume correctly, Inspector,' Grant said. 'I doubt if I'd know him from Adam.'

Jacobson thanked them for their time, tried to fight down his wholly unreasonable irritation. People *went* on holiday in August. In France, the entire country practically shut down. He was only just back himself. Besides: Brown had been out of Jenny Mortimer's life for the last five years. His testimony was unlikely to prove vital. Back at his car, he checked his pager but nothing important had come in. He wound both windows down and drove off, cigarette in mouth, into Riverside Crescent where he took the second exit left: Riverside Avenue.

From the street outside, there appeared to be nothing stirring at the Barnfields' house. No one in the front garden, no cars in the drive. Jacobson walked the length of one side of the street and then back down on the other side. Then he did the same in reverse. When he got back to where he'd left his car, he took out his mobile, dialled the appropriate number – and fumed.

There were a good dozen cars parked up and down the street. But none of them contained any passengers. And none of them was a police surveillance vehicle.

Chapter Eight

The reference section was on the second floor of the Crowby Central Public Library. Wearing cheap trainers, even cheaper jog pants and a fake Nike running vest, the unremarkable looking man who'd once been notorious in the press as the Crowby Crawler found a quiet desk well away from any other readers and sat down. Robert Johnson had the sacred text in his hands at last. He opened the book slowly, turned the pages with a reverence born of martyrdom.

When they'd realised inside what it had meant to him, they'd burnt his copy. When he'd got a second copy, they'd pissed on it and made him chew and swallow a few pages *before* they'd burnt it. After that, he hadn't bothered trying to get hold of another. He knew large chunks from memory anyway. Nights when he couldn't sleep, he'd recited them under his breath in his cell. Now here he was, the actual words in front of him again.

Miyamoto Musashi, known to the Japanese as Kensei, the 'Sword Saint', had first slain an opponent by single-hand combat in 1597 at the age of thirteen. Possibly during his career he'd killed as many as sixty men in this way. Often he'd opposed and won against a real sword armed only with a wooden stick. He'd taught that one man who'd truly mastered his art could overcome ten, that a thousand true masters could defeat ten thousand rabble. He'd spent the last two years of his life in seclusion in a cave where he wrote *Go Rin No Sho, The Book of Five Rings*, the ultimate distillation of what it was to be a Samurai: the warrior who defeats his opponents only because he has first declared war on himself. The modern translation had been a bestseller back in the nineteen eighties when an urban myth had spread that it was the secret bible of successful Japanese corporations. Johnson had his doubts about that one. Musashi had been anything but a salary man, anything but a cog in a wheel. It was true that he'd fought on behalf of noble patrons but it had been the fighting, the *way* itself, that had interested him. When honours, fortune and comfort could have been his, he'd spurned them, had followed his own stubborn, solitary path.

Johnson turned the pages to the third section, 'The Fire Book'. Musashi had never tasted defeat but his words were so true, so ultimate, that even the defeated could learn from them. You went inside your defeat, examined it, transformed it. If you went deep enough inside the mountain, Musashi said, you emerged at the gate. Johnson knew he had lost to the police, lost to the warders and hard nuts inside. He had no room for self-delusion. The first task – the first condition – of the warrior was never to lie to himself. When they'd moved him to the special hospital after the trial, he'd gone on losing. To the idiot shrinks and therapists this time. He'd had no better option than to follow *their* way, to give them what they'd wanted to hear about his childhood, his adolescence, about the so-called 'attacks', about his so-called 'remorse'. Without all that shit he'd still be banged up, still be inside. If you studied Musashi's words hard enough, diligently enough, eventually, Johnson thought, they talked directly to you. Even when your enemies caught you, *The Book of Five Rings* taught, your choices didn't completely vanish. You could be the pheasant held dumbly in the cage; or you could be the hawk waiting on its moment of counter-attack.

A library assistant passed close to his table, shoving a

trolley load of books for reshelving. He looked her up and down. Not a bad little bod. Best on offer anyway: early twenties, blonde. Not much in the tit line but sometimes he liked that. The librarian at the counter was definite granny material, probably hadn't been much to write home about when she'd been younger either. He'd done an even older battleaxe that one time, it was true. But that had been work, aimed at upping his terror ante, not something he'd actually enjoyed. As for the readers, he was probably the only one under sixty himself, apart from a dodgy looking geezer who'd come in with an *Evening Argus* under his arm. Johnson had watched him take a quick shifty at last month's *Empire* in the periodicals rack then bugger off like he was in the wrong place. He stared harder at her as she bent down to reshelf a gardening manual. When he didn't get a response, he turned his attention back to Musashi. Either she didn't notice or was pretending not to notice. A lot of them were like that. Closing their eyes, hoping the bogey man would go away.

Another thing about the book was how it could draw you to whatever you most needed to know – if you just let it, if you could just trust it. Take this next sentence: '*the "mountain-sea spirit" means that it is bad to repeat the same thing several times when fighting the enemy.*' It exactly described his situation now that he was back in Crowby. They'd have his profile, what they called his MO, nailed to the frigging wall in the cop shop. His only chance was to hit them with something new, something they didn't expect: '*if the enemy thinks of the mountains, attack like the sea. If he thinks of the sea, attack like the mountains.*' He read all the way to the end of the section then stopped, closed the book. Time to move on for now. He considered nicking it but rejected the idea. Point one: he hadn't come dressed for thieving. Point two: there was no reason why it couldn't become a regular pleasant little outing this. Consult the great man in peace and quiet. Plus keep an eye on blondie.

The Crowby Society of Artists' summer exhibition was

underway in the small gallery space to the left of the main doors in and out of the library. DC Aston was feigning an interest in a canvas which had been inspired by Cubism in the way that *Nutty Professor 2* had been inspired by *Battleship Potemkin*. He clocked Johnson's departure from the building and followed at a discreet distance. Johnson crossed the square to the left and went down the narrow street between the multi-storey car park and the side of the shopping centre which led directly back to the bus station. DC Dennett had been sunning himself in the square for the last half hour. Now he took over what looked like being the home stretch of the tail. Aston watched them disappear in turn around the corner. He enjoyed the sun himself for a minute or two then called up CrowbyCab. With luck he'd be back in Mill Street before Johnson's – and Dennett's – bus had even left the depot.

Jacobson had fumed down his mobile, fumed as he drove back to the Divi, was fuming now as he knocked – banged, really – on Detective Chief Superintendent Chivers' office door.

Once upon a time it would have been astonishing to find Chivvy on the premises in the middle of a Saturday afternoon while the sun was warm over the golf course and the beer was chilling nicely at the nineteenth hole. But the closer Chivers got to his retirement date the more time he seemed to spend mooching about the building, getting in the way. As if quitting the job had somehow reminded him of whatever it was that had drawn him to it in the first place. The advent of Greg Salter – and the 'shadowing' idea – had sent the process into overdrive.

Chivers had been a solid enough detective in his day. Twenty years or so ago, he'd solved a notorious series of murders – the worst in Crowby's history. But as far as Jacobson could see, the ten years he'd spent as head of the force's CID had turned him into a mere figurehead: a man who existed mainly in the medium of after-dinner speeches and PR, whose closest connection to the slog of real investigation was to hog the limelight whenever there was a witness appeal to be made on radio or TV or – better still – when he was able to announce an arrest.

Jacobson entered the room without waiting for a reply. Chivers was gazing out of his window, his hands in his pockets.

'Frank! We were just talking about you.'

Jacobson ignored the welcome. He noticed that Greg Salter was there too – ensconced in Chivers' seat – tapping into Chivers' computer terminal. He could have said 'nothing bad I hope' or grinned deferentially. But Jacobson had no plans to be any kind of a Super, hadn't dreamt of putting his name forward for the DCS vacancy, didn't give a toss what either non-combatant thought.

'Sergeant Ince tells me that you're supervising the surveillance operation personally now, sir.'

Chivers encouraged all his senior officers to call him by his first name. It was an informal rule that Jacobson pointedly ignored. There was a low, cushioned chair in front of Chivers' desk. He sank into it, took the weight off his feet.

'I've just been outside the home of John and Linda Barnfield. Unless my eyes have gone, there doesn't seem to be any surveillance happening in that neck of the woods.'

Salter looked away from the computer screen, stopped typing. Chivers turned away from the window, gazed into the room as if seeking – craving – a bigger audience than just these two.

'In conjunction with Greg to be precise, Frank. You've got your arms full suddenly and we've been looking for an opportunity to give Greg a hands-on feel for how we operate. Something that would angle him into the kind of systems we've got in place currently.'

Jacobson dabbed his brow with his handkerchief but the hanky was very nearly sodden itself. When he spoke again he was careful to keep his eyes solely on Chivers.

'Maybe Greg could *angle* me into why we've no pres-

86

ence outside the chief troublemakers' gaff then, sir.'

Salter leant back and swivelled in Detective Chief Superintendent Chivers' Parker Knoll, stretching his arms and resting them behind his neck.

'It's purely a matter of demographics and computer analysis,' he said. 'The resources for this operation were tight to begin with. Now that key officers have had to be transferred to your murder inquiry, there's been a need to prioritise.'

'Yes, but—' Jacobson tried to interrupt but Salter was a fast talker, practically a sprinter.

'What I've – what we've – done is to correlate the post codes of everybody on the list against local crime patterns. That way I've – we've – been able to rank them from highest to lowest in terms of risk. It's what the Americans call a felony anticipation index.'

Jacobson turned towards Salter and gawped, his attention involuntarily grabbed by this assault on the English language. But Salter wasn't even blushing.

'So what you're saying is that if one of these have-a-go merchants happens to live in a crime-infested area he's more in need of monitoring than John Barnfield?'

Chivers looked uneasy but Salter was oblivious to the incredulity which had spread all over Jacobson's face.

'Exactly, Frank, exactly. Statistical methods, patterns. Evidence-based policing is what we're all about now. Welcome to the twenty-first century.'

Welcome to a punch in the throat, Jacobson thought. He shook his head vigorously.

'Old-fashioned unthinking prejudice, I'd call it. John Barnfield very nearly cut Johnson's throat, Linda Barnfield's turned the case into a personal obsession.'

Chivers moved away from the window and stood behind Salter. Management on one side of the desk, plebs on the other.

'Nobody's saying we don't need to keep an eye on the Barnfields, Frank. It's just questionable in the light of

Greg's – our – analysis whether they merit the twenty-four/seven treatment.'

'But a few spotty kids out on the Bronx and the Son of the Bronx do? Even though they've most probably got no personal connection to the victims?'

Salter smiled like a second-hand car salesman who'd just swiped your credit card through his cash register.

'That's what the patterns suggest, Frank. Remember the paedophile riots in Portsmouth? Classic sink estate activity.'

Chivers looked straight to camera, still practising for *Crimewatch*.

'And you could hardly call the Riverside area a sink estate, Frank,' he said.

No you couldn't, Jacobson thought. But you couldn't substitute a bit of crude number crunching for serious police intelligence either. There were eight families in total whose lives had been ripped apart by Robert Johnson. They came from every walk of life. There was a threat or an outburst associated with nearly every one of them. Social class didn't come into it if your heart had hardened on revenge.

He got up from the chair slowly then stood facing them, his arms half raised, his palms spread open.

'Have it your way then, sir. I hope it's on record somewhere that I'm no longer executive in charge of Crawler fuck-ups.'

'I'm sure it's going to be very, eh, stimulating working with you, Frank,' Salter said.

He leant across the desk and proffered a handshake. But Jacobson had already turned his sweating bulk towards the door.

Outside in the corridor, the air felt like a single match would ignite it. DCS Chivers lived up on the eighth floor. Jacobson took the back stairs down to his own office on the fifth. Inside, his phone was ringing: DS Kerr on his way back from Longtown. He told him to meet him over in the

Brewer's Rest. He needed to catch up with Kerr before the team briefing, might as well sink a beer while he did so.

The custody sergeant, flanked by two constables, escorted Gus Mortimer into an interview room and left him there, shutting the door behind them. Mortimer didn't think the room was the same one they'd used this morning but he wasn't sure he'd be able to tell the difference anyway. They were probably all much the same: dingy, pokey, stinking of stale cigarette smoke. He sat down at the cheap table, squeezed his frame into a cheap, under-sized chair. Left to his own devices, he played with the rim of an ancient blue ashtray. He hadn't smoked for more than a decade. The smell of nicotine in the room made him feel unclean, nearly made him vomit.

He was thinking about her corpse again, couldn't stop himself really. The head and neck had been a welter of bruises when the orderly had drawn back the sheet. Creepy-looking little fucker, he'd thought. He'd heard they interfered with them sometimes. It was why they worked there. The shoulders had been a mess too except, funnily enough, the spot on the right where the butterfly was. That had still been perfect, unblemished.

The door rattled and then opened again. The sergeant moved to one side and Alan Slingsby, Crowby's top criminal brief, walked in. Mortimer had been dimly aware of Slingsby's existence, had dimly seen the name in the local paper when anything majorly criminal came to court. His company solicitor had told him he was the right choice – the only man for the job – when he'd finally got the chance to make his statutory phone call.

So this was him. He wasn't much to look at, Mortimer decided. An ordinary face bordering on expressionless. His handshake was soft, little more than an afterthought to the process of sitting down.

'When can you get me out of here?' Mortimer asked after the door had shut again and they were on their own.

Slingsby placed a black attaché case on the table, clicked it open. He took out his notes and scratched the back of his head, just under the scalpline of his neatly trimmed hair.

'You were formally cautioned at, let's see, eleven forty-five this morning. That means the police can keep you here without charging you until same time tomorrow. For another twelve hours after that if they think it's worth their while.

He ran his eye down the page as he spoke.

'My guess is that's exactly what they'll think. Unless they come up with something quickly that definitely eliminates you. They've taken a mouth swab for DNA?'

Mortimer nodded.

'That could be good or bad from our point of view. But it'll be Monday before any results are available. If then. I think you need to prepare yourself for the long haul, eh, Gus.'

Mortimer stared through him. *He* was the client, paying through the nose, yet already Slingsby was patronising him like he was some legal aid mugger or druggy.

'What do you mean long haul?'

Slingsby put down his notes, rested interlocked hands on the table. An accountant telling the shareholders the worst.

'I mean, Gus, that there's a very strong circumstantial case against you. Unless someone else stumbles into the frame, I'm afraid you're likely to be *it*.'

Slingsby coughed. Maybe he didn't like the bad air either.

'There's something I need to ask you before we go any further, Gus. Think carefully before you answer me. Did you kill your wife? I have to know. I can still represent you. But I can't plead your innocence if you tell me that you did it.'

She'd had the butterfly done the first time he'd persuaded her to cheat properly on her no-hope boyfriend, had snuck her away for a dirty weekend. Brighton: so much of a cliché she'd mistaken it for originality. They'd spent most of it in bed but somehow a stroll on the beach on the Saturday afternoon had turned into a pub crawl, had ended up with a visit to a tattoo parlour somewhere in the tacky depths of the Lanes.

'Gus? Mr Mortimer? Did you—'

Did I kill Jenny? Everything came down to that: Jenny being dead, Jenny being strangled until she was dead. He would've liked, he realised, to reach out and pound his fists into the lawyer's bland features until there was nothing recognisable left.

'No,' he said. 'No, I didn't kill my wife.'

Thinking: what the fuck do you expect me to say? You smug twat.

Chapter Nine

Superintendent Chivers kicked off the five o'clock briefing in person. But fortunately he didn't stay long. Fortunately he didn't have Greg Salter with him. Mainly he read through the press release which, he told them, would be sent out at six thirty. Mrs Jennifer Mortimer had been found dead at her home outside Crowby this morning. The finding of the post-mortem was that she had been strangled. Her husband, Gus Mortimer, was helping the police with their inquiries. An investigation into the full circumstances was being led by DCI Frank Jacobson. End of.

Jacobson lit up a B and H as soon as Chivers left the room. At least the old boy still understood timing, he thought. The last local news on Crowby FM went out at six pm on Saturdays. After that they just relayed the network bulletins. The BBC station likewise. As for the *Argus*, the next edition wouldn't hit the streets until Monday lunchtime. Maybe for once a serious case would be over and done with before the hacks got their teeth into it.

Kerr summarised his interviews with Kevin Holland and his associates then DC Mick Hume reported back. He'd visited seven properties in the area of the Mortimers' place all told. No one had seen or heard anything unusual either last night or through the night or this morning. Those who'd admitted to having actually met the Mortimers on some occasion or other denied knowing anything significant about them, whether good, bad or indifferent. He'd even called in at the farm on the other side of the narrow, country lane which bordered the back wall of the Mortimers' property. Nothing. Emma Smith spoke next. It sounded like Smith and DC Williams had been more successful. They now had a list of six witnesses who'd been prepared to statement Mortimer's attack on his wife at Boden Hall. Jacobson rescued an empty Coke can from the wastebin and stubbed the remains of his cigarette into it.

'Fine,' he said. 'It looks to me like we've got Mortimer by the proverbials. Motive, opportunity, method. We do have two or three potential problems though, courtesy of Robinson's preliminary report.'

Sergeant Ince, now officially co-opted as the inquiry's uniformed liaison officer, interjected to say that he'd just got the photocopies back from repro.

'Thanks, old son. Mandatory bedtime reading for us all. One: he still won't commit himself on whether the sex was rape or consensual. Two: surprise, surprise – he's putting the time of death into a nice wide frame. Not before six thirty, not after eight thirty.'

Jacobson picked up his copy, waved it as he spoke.

'The body didn't develop rigor until they were about to bung it in the mortuary van. Nine twenty-two to be precise. As we all know, it usually takes a couple of hours to set in. But only usually. Mrs Mortimer wasn't overweight to say the least. Unfortunately, that's a factor for speed. As is the hot weather.'

Emma Smith saw what he was getting at.

'So if Mortimer arrived at work at eight and left at seven thirty, it's not completely impossible that his wife was killed *after* he'd gone?'

Jacobson's fingers drummed the nearest surface.

'It's bloody unlikely if you ask me, Emma. But it could mean there's enough leeway for a barrister who knows what he's doing – or for a well-paid defence expert – to persuade a jury that there's *reasonable doubt*.'

Mick Hume groaned and ran through a list of popular expletives.

Kerr suggested that they check and re-check Mortimer's likely journey times. Hume, untypically, volunteered to do it first thing in the morning.

'You said *three* problems, guv?' Williams asked.

Jacobson flicked through his copy of the report.

'Page four. *A pattern of multiple round, reddish scars approximately one millimetre in diameter. Mainly on the chest, lower spine and thighs.* Nothing to do with the general beating or the strangling according to Robinson. He's still looking into it, says he's never encountered anything like it before. It's not necessarily a problem, could give us a more specific MO ultimately. But at the moment it's a mystery, an ambiguity. Just the sort of thing Alan bloody Slingsby loves.'

Mick Hume cursed again, wasn't the only one this time. Jacobson waited until the air was less blue then drew matters to a close. Along with Kerr he was going to have another crack at Mortimer. In the presence of Slingsby this time. Then they were going to check out the Mortimers' house. The forensic analysis in the laboratory was barely underway but the initial forensic sampling in situ had mostly been done; at last they should be able to get a good look inside. As for the rest of the team: in view of the stretched overtime budget – and in the absence of any other leads – they could file their reports and bugger off till tomorrow.

Jacobson grabbed a salad in the canteen after the briefing but couldn't resist a side plate of chips. Kerr bought two cheese rolls and a tired, melancholy-looking peach. Slingsby had been hassling for a further interview the past hour. Which to Jacobson's mind was a good reason to let him – and Mortimer – stew for another fifteen minutes or so. After he'd eaten the rolls, Kerr used his mobile, explained to his wife that the case had run on, that he wouldn't be home for tea after all. The look on his face said she wasn't delighted by the news.

'Trying to please two women at once, old son,' Jacobson said, shaking his head. 'One was beyond me at the finish up.'

Apart from Rachel and some of her friends, Jacobson was the only living soul who knew about Kerr's complicated personal life. Or so he hoped. He said nothing, bit into his piece of fruit.

'You're supposed to think with your head not with your prick,' Jacobson added after a moment, undeterred by the lack of response. Kerr gave up on the peach which turned out to be as juiceless as it looked. Jacobson could be a crude bastard, he thought. But he also happened to be right.

It was definitely the same interview room this time. Mortimer and Slingsby on one side of the table, Jacobson and Kerr on the other. Mortimer tried to work out which one he disliked the most. The younger one had been the nastiest this morning but the older one might be the most dangerous in the long term, was probably, he decided, the brains behind the operation.

Slingsby, gold pen in hand, was in his element.

'Now that I've studied the facts in the case and spoken with my client, I can see no reason for his continued detention in police custody.'

Jacobson grinned.

'The fact that he has no alibi at the time of his wife's murder might be one you'd want to consider, Mr Slingsby. The fact that by his own admission he left the property at seven thirty and the post-mortem suggests she was killed between six thirty and eight thirty; I suppose that could be another.'

'Mr Mortimer categorically denies any involvement. Everything you've got is purely circumstantial. If it isn't then charge him.'

Jacobson carried on grinning.

'Please. Ian. Explain the law to Mr Slingsby.'

'DS Kerr, Crowby CID,' Kerr said, for the benefit of the tape recorder. 'Our inquiries are continuing into the events that took place at Mr Mortimer's property. We believe he can assist us with those inquiries. And we are obliging him to remain with us for the time being. Unless of course he has something to say now which casts a different light on the situation.'

Mortimer looked at Kerr and Jacobson in turn.

'I didn't do it. I didn't kill my wife.'

'But you did assault her last night at Boden Hall?' Jacobson asked.

Slingsby touched Mortimer's arm lightly with his right hand. Then he dug into his case, produced a single sheet of typescript.

'Mr Mortimer has made a full statement which you may lodge in your records if you wish, Inspector. It is a full and generous statement which wholly fulfils his obligations as a citizen.'

Jacobson held out his hand to take the sheet but Slingsby was still having his day in the interview room, proceeded to read aloud.

'My wife and I had an altercation last evening while attending a social event at Boden Hall. Regrettably this became physical on both sides. I was distressed to learn from her that she had been unfaithful to our marriage. After we drove home, I went to sleep in our bedroom as usual and she chose to sleep in one of our guest rooms. This was around midnight. Around four am, as I recall, my wife returned to the bedroom and got into bed beside me. She told me she had made a dreadful mistake and asked for my forgiveness. We attempted a reconciliation which resulted in sexual intercourse. When I woke up about seven fifteen my wife wasn't in the bed. I assumed that she must have had second thoughts again and gone back to the spare room. I felt angry again but decided just to stay out the way for a few hours, give her time to think. I got up and dressed to go to my office at Planet Avionics. It's not unusual for me to do this on Saturdays. It gives me a chance to work without fear of interruption. I left in my car around seven thirty and arrived at eight. To the best of my knowledge, my wife was asleep on her own when I left the house. Signed and dated G. Mortimer.'

Slingsby stopped reading, passed the statement across the table to Jacobson.

'The pathologist examined your wife's corpse this afternoon, Gus,' Jacobson said. 'Only he feels you went a bit further than sexual intercourse. The word that appears more than once in his report is rape.'

Mortimer glanced at Slingsby.

'My client is under no obligation to comment on a report which his representatives have not yet had the opportunity of studying.'

Kerr leant forward in his chair.

'But he *can* tell us whether he raped his wife or not.'

Mortimer cleared his throat. Then:

'My wife has always – did always, like me to be forceful.'

Jacobson stood up, crossed the room to the tape recorder.

'This is DCI Jacobson terminating this time-wasting fiasco at six fifty-two. Gus Mortimer remains in police custody while my lawful inquiries continue.'

He pressed the stop button.

'There are times, Slingsby, old son, when even a copper who reads the *Guardian* yearns for the good old days.'

Kerr beeped for the custody officers. Slingsby was gathering his notes, closing up his case.

'What? When you used to just beat the so-called truth out of suspects?' he asked.

'I was thinking more of when defence lawyers used to take unfortunate tumbles down flights of stairs,' Jacobson replied evenly.

Kerr drove them out to the Mortimers' place. On the way,

Jacobson checked up on the Crawler surveillance. Messrs C. and S. could put themselves in charge if they liked, Jacobson still planned to keep in touch with the operation on the ground. The officers out at the Bronx and the Son of the Bronx reported all quiet. Infuriatingly, there were still no reports available on the Barnfields. Jacobson persuaded a DC who owed him more than one favour to call past Riverside Avenue on his way home when his shift ended. He called DC Aston last, was relieved to hear that Johnson was back at the hostel. Snug as a bug in a rug, the Brummie had said. Or as a sicko in the community, Jacobson had thought.

Two constables were keeping guard *chez* Mortimer as Kerr drove up to the line of police tape in front of the house. Jacobson's budget would have been happier with just the one. But the property was too large, the gardens too extensive, for that to be a realistic option. Kerr followed Jacobson indoors. The privileged nature of the job, *his* job, was never more apparent to him than when he poked around somebody's property, snooped around wherever he liked, took apart whatever he felt like taking apart. On one level, he thought, a good detective was nothing more than a nosey bastard with ID.

They looked in the bedrooms first of all. The socos had already confirmed the most likely sequence of events. Mrs Mortimer had been attacked as she slept, had tried to run out of the house, had never got further than the driveway outside. Only the master bedroom and one of the smaller guest bedrooms showed any signs of recent occupation. The forensic tests had a long way to go but already it was definite that Jenny Mortimer had spent some time recently in both rooms, both beds. The difficulty was that in this case the forensic evidence could be read more than one way. There would be traces of Jenny and Gus all over the house, in every room. If they 'found' Gus in the small bedroom where the first signs of struggle were evident, it would be consistent with his going in there in the middle of the night, dragging his wife out of bed, back to the other bedroom, raping her, then strangling her. But equally, as any decent defence team would argue, it was just as consistent with him having done no such thing: you'd *expect* his skin, his hair, in a room in his own house. There was nothing about human detritus that told you *when* it had been deposited. Or at least not in terms of the timescale that mattered here.

In the small room, Jenny's evening dress still lay folded across a chair in the corner which had somehow escaped the struggle with her attacker. Most of her clothes were back in the big bedroom she'd shared with her husband. Kerr and Jacobson checked the small room then the big one. They pulled out drawers, rummaged, looked under the bed, even checked the fixtures and fittings in the en suite. They weren't looking for anything in particular, they were just looking. There was a dvd player and television opposite the bed, half a dozen videos and laser discs stacked nearby. They were a bit more than soft porn but there didn't seem to be any minors or animals involved, nothing to worry Customs and Excise. Somewhere Kerr found a vibrator, somewhere else Jacobson found a pair of handcuffs.

'Pretty much your average suburban bedroom,' Kerr said.

Raunchy but not wildly so. No mirror on the ceiling for example, no DIY dungeon equipment. The socos had found a bit of cocaine on a mantelpiece in one of the lounges. Big deal not: they should do a shifty in Rachel's bedroom cabinet, he thought, if they wanted something pharmacologically more challenging to play with.

The main lounge downstairs was an airport hangar of a room. An endless expanse of expensive cream carpeting; original but non-threatening modern art punctuating the walls: visual Prozac. Through the double doors at the far end, there was a smaller, more intimate room which was almost cluttered, almost looked like somebody might actually have lived in it. Yesterday's *Evening Argus* and a copy of *Men are from Mars, Women are from Venus* had been left lying on an inviting-looking leather sofa. There was another dvd set-up opposite and a hi-fi system of second mortgage proportions. Kerr studied the cds which sat in racks possibly made of bronze, definitely not bought at Ikea. There was a load of classical stuff, arranged alphabetically. As far as his limited knowledge allowed him to judge, it was an informed collection. He looked at the titles top to bottom, left to right ... Wagner, Walton, Weil, Zelenka. By contrast, the pop selections which came next were a total and utter joke. Shania Twain, Chris de Burgh, even Phil Collins. It wasn't just lift music: it was crap, *shit*, lift music. Kerr's skin fairly crawled just thinking about 'Lady in Red' oozing out with crystal clarity through the state of the art, custom-built speakers.

Jacobson ran his hand along the mahogany bookshelves. Heavy-duty French and German classics in original language editions – Flaubert, Sartre, Thomas Mann, Nietzsche – competed for shelf space against Tom Clancy, Wilbur Smith, *The Dogs of War*. Jacobson had heard as much as he ever wanted to about post-modernism in his Open University days, about how you could read a comic book one minute, the *Iliad* the next. But for his money, the high culture was Mrs Mortimer's if it was anybody's. Which meant that the vintage Ferrari manuals and the signed Jeffrey Archer first edition had to be Gus's. Whatever else had brought husband and wife together, he thought, it had scarcely been a marriage of true minds.

Somebody had left a laptop lying, screen open, on the coffee table. Kerr switched it on but it turned out to be password protected, refused to boot up. It might be worth getting the civilian computer officer on to it. People left all sorts of stuff on computers. Jacobson was still studying the bookshelves. Kerr plonked himself on to the more than comfortable sofa.

'Slingsby was right though, wasn't he, Frank?'

It was a statement as much as a question.

'About it all being circumstantial, I mean,' he added.

Jacobson shoved *The Story of O* back into its position on the shelf, unsure of whether it advanced or contradicted his binary theory of whose books were whose.

'There's circumstantial and there's circumstantial, Ian. We don't have a video of Mortimer with his hands around his wife's throat, no. But the socos are saying definitely no break-in now. So who else? His story's changing in our favour too – even with Alan Slingsby on the payroll. With any luck, he'll want to get the whole thing off his conscience tomorrow.'

Kerr could only concede the point. In Mortimer's original version, he'd kissed his wife an innocent goodnight, hadn't seen her since. Now he was admitting to the punch-up at Geoffrey Trayner's stately gaff, admitting to some degree of violent sex afterwards.

Jacobson gestured his thumb towards a doorway they hadn't yet explored.

'Let's see what's cooking in the kitchen,' he said. 'Then I think we'll call it a day.'

Chapter Ten

Jacobson had left his own car in the car park at the Divisional building. Kerr drove him back there then headed out of town on the Wynarth Road. As he neared the turn-off for the Bovis estate, he played fleetingly with the fantasy of never going home again, of just leaving Cathy to it.

She was watching television when he walked into the front room, went on watching it, seemed to be pretending he wasn't there. He'd long since missed the twins' bedtime – again. He went upstairs and had a wash, changed his clothes. He came back downstairs to the kitchen, fed the cat, made himself a cup of tea, pretended to read the newspaper. He dialled the public number at Crowby Central from the handset of the cordless phone. Predictably – with Saturday evening in full swing – the line was engaged. He selected the ringback option, had to wait five minutes for the response. He let it ring five times and then cancelled the call, had a loud police conversation with nobody except himself.

Before he'd met Rachel, Kerr hadn't realised how much being police, especially being CID, was the perfect career move for playing away. Long, unpredictable hours were a constant. Whenever you needed it, there was always something unexpected, something last minute, that wanted sorting. As far as the job went, his only real fear was that sometime – unable to reach him – Cathy would check with

Jacobson. It was why he refused to ever switch his phone off when he was with Rachel. Jacobson wouldn't shop him, *hadn't* shopped him. But if it came to it, Kerr knew, he wouldn't lie to Cathy either.

He parked in the market square again, same as the night before. She wasn't expecting him but that was usually OK so long as he phoned ahead. There was conversation and music in the background when she lifted up the receiver.

'Rayche? Something came up, I'm just round the corner. I've probably got a couple of hours.'

'Shit, Ian,' she said. 'I wish you'd said sooner. Only I've a couple of friends here. We're going on to a party in a minute out at Tony's new place. Tony Scruton?'

'You mean I'm not invited?'

The line went quiet for a moment. When he heard her voice again, the background noise had disappeared. She must have moved into another room for privacy.

'You mean you'd like to come with me?'

'Sure,' he said, unsure. 'Why not?'

For one thing, the fewer people that knew about them, the safer he felt. Any time – anywhere – they went out together was a risk. For another, Tony Scruton was a painter, an old lover of Rachel's that she'd fashionably kept on as a friend. In the early days of their relationship, when he'd wanted to avoid either label, she'd persuaded Kerr that only a cave-man or a sexist pig would have an objection. By the time he'd met him himself, taken an instant dislike to him, it had been too late to backtrack. *Think with your head, not your prick*, Jacobson had said. But Jacobson didn't need to see her, didn't need to be with her.

He drove into Thomas Holt Street, waited in the car for Rachel and her girlfriends to emerge. The whole thing felt more and more like a time bomb. Sooner or later it was bound to explode right in his face. Crowby was a sizeable town. Rachel and Cathy moved in circles that could hardly be more distant from each other. Before the twins, Cathy had been in sales, her mates worked in building societies, estate agents, banks. Rachel had been to art college – thought of herself as an artist, even though she rarely sold anything – scraped by on temporary work as a gallery assistant or with her interior design and *feng shui* scams. But the way things worked – the way life was – surely meant that some time they'd run into somebody who *did* move in both of these little, partial worlds. Somebody with nothing to hide, who wouldn't be deterred by the idea of meddling with police, getting on the wrong side of a copper.

Only Rachel got into Kerr's car. To his relief, her friends, Kate and Judy, followed on in Kate's rusting Riva. He'd known her for four years now: ever since another murder inquiry, the Roger Harvey case. He watched her reach in her bag for the bottle of Evian water which seemed to accompany her everywhere. He loved the way she drank it in a big, bold gulp – then wiped her mouth with the flat of her hand afterwards, her fingers just skimming the top of her nose. He'd read in one of Cathy's magazines that the reason affairs dragged on for years was that you only had sex, only had fun, never got so familiar with someone that their habits began to drive you up the wall.

Scruton had moved out of Wynarth altogether, found himself an old farmworker's cottage at the wrong end of a narrow, bumpy dirt track. Kerr parked up, probably illegally, in somebody's field and they made their way to the front door. 'Block Rockin' Beats' pumped out into the night. Rachel took his hand, squeezed it, began dance-stepping along. Inside the cottage, Tony was hugging everybody, would probably have hugged *him* if he'd thought he could get away with it. All the same the expression on his face with his arms locked around Rachel looked less Findhorn to Kerr and more Dr Zhivago and Lara.

'It's great to see you – both. So glad you could make it.'

He opened his arms expansively as Rachel stood back and then gave Kerr the kind of firm, bone-shaking handshake he'd always detested.

'Wine, beer?'

Kerr pulled back the ring on a can of weak, under-chilled supermarket lager while Tony poured out a plastic cup of Chablis for Rachel.

'I'll show you round later if you like.'

Rachel took the cup.

'That would be brilliant, Tony. I'm dying to know what kind of stuff you're painting now.'

Scruton exited outdoors to where the dancing was, his white collarless shirt dazzling in contrast to the dull grey stripes of his Oxfam waistcoat. Rachel ran a finger down Kerr's arm, a mute plea for tolerance.

'The kitchen, it's so . . . brilliant,' she said.

Kerr could see that it was impressive. A full-range Aga, white-washed walls, an original timber or two.

'Very Linda McCartney, Rayche.'

The centrepiece was an old farmhouse table of solid oak, its surface currently laden with a buffet. He helped himself to a piece of quiche and a pork pie. The meat, he thought, was probably organic. He wondered if a holistic pig was happier than any other kind to have its throat slit open for the benefit of Tony's party guests. Rachel stood close to him. Running her hand down his spine as he ate. Making eating difficult. She'd wanted to come here, wanted to be *seen* with him. But now that she'd got here, it seemed she'd sooner they were alone. After a minute, he gave up, put the food down, kissed her.

He'd asked her more than once what she saw in him. He was thirteen years older. He only knew about art what she'd told him. Most of her friends thought police were fascist scum. Most of the time he couldn't be with her. When they paused to draw breath, a woman that neither of them knew came up to them with an eager smile.

'Carla,' she announced, 'I work at the Ikon in Birmingham. What do you do?'

Taxidermy, Kerr thought, meaning get stuffed. He wiped a crumb that Rachel must have missed from the corner of his mouth.

'Nothing special, Carla,' he said. 'Public Services, I doubt if you'd be interested.'

It was gone nine thirty by the time Kerr had driven him back to the Divi to pick up his own car and he'd driven himself back out to Wellington Drive. The first thing Jacobson did once he was through the door was to undress and take a good, long shower. The shower back at his ex-family home had been a dreary affair, an ineffectual rubber tube gizmo connected to the bath taps. This on the other hand was the genuine article. A deluxe shower unit, powerful, efficient. He turned the pressure up to the max, bright jets of water pummelling his back like a thousand eager fingers. He dried himself, changed into fresh clothes, poured out the magic formula of ice and Glenfiddich into a perfectly clean tumbler.

Back on his balcony, back in his lounger, he picked up *Pagans and Christians*. He read three or four pages but for some reason he couldn't settle. For one thing, a big black fly had taken a liking to his whisky glass. Every time Jacobson leant out from the lounger and put it down on the table, the fly landed on it. For another, his body felt refreshed but his mind didn't, insisted on replaying the sights and sounds of the day in rapid, unpleasant succession. He'd been calm, almost content, sitting out here last night. But twenty-four hours was a long time in policing. After a few minutes, he gave up and moved back inside.

His flat, like the rest of the block, came supplied with cable whether you wanted it or not. So now he could spend ten minutes – instead of two – flicking through thirty channels – instead of five – for the confirmation that there was nothing remotely worth watching. The Shopping Channel grabbed his attention for a moment as – bizarrely – it often did. Somebody, somewhere, thought their life would be improved by a Robbie Williams charm bracelet in rolled gold. They must do, he reasoned, otherwise they wouldn't make them, wouldn't advertise them. He tried to focus on the gravelly assurance in the presenter's voice: everything – yes, everything – in the world was fine, OK, hunky-dory. But what he kept seeing in his mind – Jenny Mortimer, battered and unlawfully dead – told him otherwise, told him what he already knew. That it bloody wasn't. Nothing like.

He pressed *off* on the remote control, drained the whisky in one, decided that a murder investigation entitled him to another one, maybe more than one, before bedtime. He padded through to the kitchen, glass in hand. At first glance Gus Mortimer had everything that Robert Johnson didn't. Wealth, success, status, competence. Yet Mortimer looked to have gone a step beyond even Johnson, looked to have murdered as well as raped. He thought there was some Bombay mix somewhere in one of the cupboards. He thought he fancied a bit of snacking as well as another drink. But Johnson hadn't been a typecast suspect either, not at first. He'd come from Manchester – up north as far as Crowby was concerned – from an ordinary lower-middle-class family: the kind that politicians and tabloid newspapers liked to call decent and/or normal. Johnson and his sister plus mum and dad. Dad was a senior clerk at the Inland Revenue, his mother was a doctor's receptionist. Half a dozen psychiatrists had failed to pronounce them anything other than emotionally balanced, effective parents. He'd got on well enough at school, performed above the average academically though he hadn't been a high flyer. There'd been no reports of bullying or of being bullied. No tying fireworks to the tails of old ladies' cats or strangling rabbits. He'd had a modest series of steady girlfriends since he'd been fifteen. The last one, the one he'd been with when they'd caught him, had said she'd stick by him – until she took in what he'd actually done.

Jacobson poured the whisky over the ice, found a plate for the Bombay mix. Yet the iron must be somewhere in Robert Johnson's soul. He'd gone to one of the new universities for a year after school – Derby, maybe – and then he'd kind of drifted. His ambition had been to deejay but he hadn't seemed to get anywhere with it. Mainly he'd done bar work in clubs, later a bit of bouncing. He'd been working the door at a club in Crowby when Jacobson's team had finally come calling. The only other thing that had seemed to motivate him had been martial arts, kickboxing. The Midlands Counties champion had been a reluctant character witness during the mitigation phase of the trial.

Back in the lounge, Jacobson tried to stem the futile tide of memory. None of that mattered a fuck now, he told himself. The court had believed the psychiatrists' claim that Johnson had a mental illness, albeit one they couldn't define, couldn't trace the development of. So what? Leave it and move on. He sank into his armchair, thought maybe he'd try Radio Four rather than the bollocks on the television. He took another mouthful, paying conscious attention this time, actually savouring the taste as it went down.

All Men Are Rapists, a feminist sociologist had sloganised once to him at an OU summer school. He'd agreed with her sarcastically, added on robbery, murder, torture, any bloody evil thing they thought they could get away with. Then – his *coup de théâtre* – he'd told her how the lesson from history and the newspapers, from Dachau and Srebrenica, was that women weren't any better when they got the chance. But he'd still taken her point, had never forgotten it in fact. What the court hadn't faced, what the courts rarely faced, was the possibility that Johnson had just *enjoyed* what he did, had got a taste for inflicting terror, for putting women in their place. Which brought his darkening thoughts back full circle: to the red, gravel driveway and Jenny Mortimer's bulging, dead eyes.

Chapter Eleven

Sunday 19 August   **fifty pence**   weather: hot tv/radio: page six
BRITAIN'S NEWEST, LIVELIEST SUNDAY

THE SUNDAY UPDATE

COMPANY DIRECTOR'S WIFE STRANGLED IN
MURDER TOWN AS ANGRY LOCALS DEMAND

WHERE IS PERVERT?

EXCLUSIVE REPORT BY MADDY TAYLOR

While elsewhere Britain basks in the record temperatures, anger and terror have
descended on the Midlands town of Crowby. Police confirmed last night that the
death of Mrs Jennifer Mortimer, 36, attractive second wife of local company boss,
Gus Mortimer, was being treated as **murder**. Mrs Mortimer was found dead at
their millionaire-style residence yesterday morning. A post-mortem showed that
she had been **strangled**. Police inquiries continue but the Sunday Update can
exclusively reveal that a notorious **sex offender** has been at large in the area
since Friday. Robert Johnson, better known as the Crowby Crawler, carried out a
reign of terror involving **drugs** and black magic and subjected women ranging in
age from seventeen to seventy-three to what the trial judge branded 'appalling
and atrocious acts'. DCI Frank Jacobson who brought Johnson to justice eight
years ago is thought to be heading the investigation into Mrs Mortimer's

Main Report Continued Page Three
Crawler's Catalogue of Terror Page Four
My Anguish by Mother of Victim Page Five
Keep Them Locked Up: Update Opinion Page Eleven

109

DC Mick Hume called Jacobson at home to let him know. Predictably, Hume had seen the report first, had apparently recently added the *Update* to his normal Sunday diet of the *Sport* and the *News of the World*. Jacobson abandoned his coffee in mid-cup, nipped down to the nearest newsagent, the one next to the Chinese take-away. He glanced at the headline as he handed over his fifty pence but by an effort of will he managed not to look again until he was safely back in his flat. On the whole, he thought, he'd rather not be seen swearing and spluttering to himself in public.

He poured the unfinished coffee into a small pan over a low gas. There was no problem with re-heating as long as you were careful not to let it reach boiling point. Monday to Friday, he put up with instant. Saturdays and Sundays – even if he was working on a case – he insisted on the real stuff, had recently traded up to using proper beans which he stored in the freezer, had bought himself a nice little electric grinder. Might as well be good to yourself, old son: if nobody else can be arsed. He spread the *Update* out on his kitchen table, took a fresh sip of Sainsbury's finest arabica. Imperfectly, he recalled a remark attributed to Hegel: *reading the morning paper is the unbeliever's morning prayer*. Somehow he didn't think this was what the great man had in mind.

The fact that Gus Mortimer was helping with their inquiries had been buried towards the end of the report. Instead the unsubtle insinuation, never actually stated, was that Robert Johnson might be the killer. For the rest it was pretty much the standard tabloid package. Johnson's 'reign of terror' was pruriently recycled. A clichéd editorial demanded that all keys everywhere be instantly thrown away. Linda Barnfield told the story she'd always told. Jacobson could see how it sold papers. But sad and tragic as it certainly was, Jacobson couldn't see what good its constant retelling was doing for the Barnfield family. He studied the photograph above the *Mother's Anguish* spread: John and Linda Barnfield in their front garden, *talking to top, investigative reporter, Maddy Taylor.* Only the fact that he was determined to finish his coffee dissuaded Jacobson from banging his fist down hard on the table. Shit! To judge by the light, the newspaper must have called on the Barnfields sometime yesterday afternoon. Sometime after Chivers and Salter had helpfully called off the surveillance on them. But frankly that was the least of it. The most of it – blushingly – was that Maddy Taylor, Hack of the Year or whatever, was also quite clearly – quite definitely – the woman he'd leered at in the Brewer's Rest, Friday lunchtime: the one with the legs as he'd so elegantly thought it at the time.

Driving over to the Divi, he made a point of catching the eight thirty bulletin on Crowby FM. The Mortimer case was the top story but only in the officially sanctioned version that the wife had been strangled, that the husband was helping inquiries. So far, at any rate, there was no mention of Robert Johnson. But the local radio reporters had to live here, he thought, relied on some kind of working relationship with the force all year round. Leggy Maddy on the other hand could breeze in, write what she liked and then bugger off back to London. The lights at the Flowers Street junction turned to red as Jacobson drew near them. As they always did: weekday or weekend, heavy traffic or light. As if there was a special Jacobson-Approaching setting somewhere in the circuitry.

It wasn't totally bad news, he reflected. Item one: the national press had been here since Friday but still hadn't discovered Johnson's precise whereabouts – all they seemed to know was that he was in the area. Item two: Johnson's mush was all over the *Update* but they evidently had no photographs more recent than his arrest. Any vigilantes out looking for a sicko with a mullet haircut and a moustache were likely to be disappointed.

The car park for police personal use at the rear of the Divisional building lay behind a high wall and was accessed via a heavy duty barrier. Jacobson shoved his ID in front of

111

the electronic eye and waited for the barrier to lift. The wall and the barrier were security measures that had followed in the wake of an embarrassing escape from police custody a while back. The problem was that the eye was unreliable to say the least. Half a dozen times a day, it would fail to recognise someone's ID. A lot of the uniformeds had given up on it, had taken to parking in the nearby NCP instead, 'adding' the charges on somewhere in their overtime claims. A car he'd never noticed before, some kind of expensive, sporty Lexus in a foul purple colour, was parked next to Chivers' Range Rover. He locked his own car, crossed the car park to the rear entrance. Thinking: Greg Salter's penis extension or my name isn't Frank Jacobson.

He caught up with them in the canteen of all places, took it as another sign of the Detective Chief Super's sudden nostalgia for his vanishing lifetime as a policeman. He carried a glass of milk over to their table, wasn't about to succumb this early in the day to a cup of canteen 'coffee'. Salter gave him a wary smile and a textbook demonstration of modern management techniques: never apologise, never accept responsibility, spin everything on its head. It was good that the press interest in Robert Johnson had been flushed out, great that the Chief Constable had spoken already to the *Sunday Update*'s editor, terrific that DCS Chivers and himself would soon be meeting with the *Update*'s reporter, would be encouraging her towards a more responsible line.

'Maybe, Frank, you'd like to become more operationally involved again yourself,' he suggested finally.

Jacobson wiped a film of milk from his top lip, declined the offer firmly. He'd never played at office politics, regarded it as a game beneath contempt. But he *did* understand basic organisational survival: Salter had grabbed the can – he could effing well carry it.

Kerr, Mick Hume, Williams and Emma Smith were already present in the incident room when Jacobson got there. So was DC Barber, looking tanned after his holiday.

'Listen up,' Jacobson said. 'As far as we're concerned the Sunday Scumbag can write whatever bollocks it likes. We *know* Robert Johnson's not in the frame. End of. That said, it would be nice to be in the position to charge hubbie sooner rather than later.'

He set Smith and Williams on the track of the Planet Avionics workforce. Particularly the key players from the inquiry point of view. Which meant anyone who would have close or regular contact with Mortimer, who might have been on the receiving end of his bad temper – or worse. Hume and Barber could start their day with a slice of fun. Pick up something fast and upmarket from the police garage and check out the journey times between Mortimer's house and the Business Park. Mortimer had said he'd taken half an hour, Kerr had made it inside twenty minutes. Jacobson wanted some maximum, minimum and average timings. But then he wanted them to repeat yesterday's door to door exercise around the Mortimers' neighbourhood. When potential witnesses didn't want to speak, he reminded them, sometimes you just had to keep at it: until they were sick of the sight of you, told you what you wanted to know just to get rid.

'Stalemate then, Frank?' Kerr stated/asked after the others had left the room.

'As obvious as that was it, old son?'

Kerr nodded. He knew Jacobson was right to shore up the case as far as he could, no question. But it was all looking like more of the same, more of what they already knew; circumstance not substance. They looked at each other in gloomy silence for a moment. Jacobson produced the inevitable B and H packet from his pocket. He'd got as far as removing a cigarette but had yet to put it to his lips, had yet to light it, when Sergeant Ince showed an unexpected visitor into the incident room.

Peter Robinson, Crowby's Assistant Pathologist, stooped in, a bundle of papers under his right arm.

'Inspector, Sergeant. Glad I caught you. What I've got here is too complicated to explain over the phone.'

Jacobson watched him sit down, stick the wad of data on a nearby table. He was unshaven, his eyes were bloodshot, his crudely cut ginger hair resembled a badly built crows' nest.

'Been up most of the night,' he said. 'But I think I've cracked it.'

He showed them stills of the corpse in situ, stills of the corpse on the mortuary table, photocopied extracts from textbooks and learned journals, a mass of photographs, diagrams and densely packed sentences. Finally, he handed over a dozen A4 sides which had been stapled together. Jacobson noticed a familiar looking candle and barbed wire logo on the top sheet.

'I pulled this off the Internet for you,' Robinson said. 'Explains it pretty well in, eh, layman's terms.'

Jacobson scanned the table of contents in the Amnesty International report. *The spread of modern electro-shock weapons, Actual and intended use, The difficulty of detection, Appendix One: Countries where electro-shock torture has been reported.* He passed the sheets to Kerr, lit his cigarette, held it away from both their faces while Kerr glanced his way through.

'You're sure about this?' Jacobson asked.

'Ninety-nine per cent anyway,' Robinson replied. 'There's a guy I know in Oxford, an old university friend, a specialist. I've asked him to check for me just to be on the safe side.'

Electro-shock batons, stun guns and tasers, Kerr read, had a wide variety of uses: all of them bad. Crowd control was one option. Bring out the batons and your demonstrators were running, no longer wanted to be anywhere near your embassy or your official palace. Actually prod with them and they weren't going anywhere, had just been zapped by 50,000 volts, were unable to move, except to shake, urinate and defecate uncontrollably. *The current*

*moves along low resistance routes within the human body,
for example blood channels and nerve pathways. For each
pulse received there is likely to be a rapid shock extending
throughout the body including the brain and central
nervous system.*

Brutal treatment of prisoners was another. Shocks to the
testicles, mouth, tongue – any damn place you wanted.
Compared to the *bastado* or other traditional methods, it
seemed that electric batons appealed to the modern, clued-
in, switched-on torturer for one, simple reason: they left
relatively little signs of use on the body of the victim,
making it hard to prove that they *had* been used. Kerr put
the report down on the table and felt sick. When there *were*
signs they often faded after only a few days. But Jenny
Mortimer was barely more than twenty-four hours dead.
The characteristic tiny red scars which were precisely
indicative of electro-shock torture, Robinson had just told
them, could still be seen on the breasts, back and thighs of
her trashed, defiled body.

In the breakfast room of the Riverside Hotel, Maddy Taylor
ate a bowl of muesli mixed with fresh fruit and plain
yoghurt, washed it down with a glass of grapefruit juice and
a cup of black, unsweetened coffee. Mutt and Jeff in
contrast tucked into a full English each and drank their tea
sweetened. Mutt, the *Update*'s chief photographer, had
been christened Matthew Summers, was only known as
Mutt on the occasions he worked with Jeff. Jeff was really
Geoff Clarke, the older of the two and a freelance.
Ostensibly he was also a photographer but at six feet two
and a muscled fourteen stone he was really the *Update*'s
minder, sent out with the journos on gigs like this one
where there was a distinct possibility of physical aggro.

Maddy sipped her coffee and smiled.

'Looking good, guys,' she said.

Mutt and Jeff nodded, carried on pigging. The call from
Crowby CID had been a godsend, a completely unexpected

little pressie. Their top detective guy had invited Maddy in for a chat and she'd accepted the offer fulsomely. Quite what would happen when she tried to gain access to the cop shop along with Mutt and Jeff and Mr and Mrs Barnfield was anybody's guess, she thought. But it would certainly be fun finding out.

After they'd eaten, Jeff brought the car round to the front of the hotel. Maddy got in the back and Mutt rode shotgun, peering at the Crowby *A to Z* through his retro John Lennon specs. They found the area itself without too much difficulty, finding particular streets and specific addresses took a little longer. The Woodlands estate was the usual poverty line disaster zone. Despite the name, there wasn't a tree in sight except on some long-neglected planner's drawing board. The local police called it the Son of the Bronx to distinguish it from the Bronx itself, a couple of miles further out of town. An informal competition existed between the two over which one provided the crappiest, most hope-abandoned environment. History and precedence were on the side of the Bronx but the Woodlands was increasingly giving it a bloody good run for its money.

They drove past the row of steel shuttered shops in the centre of the estate. Next came The Poets, the only pub. The window of the main lounge had been freshly boarded up after another typical Saturday night of bad pills, bad beer and bad feeling. In the corner of the pot-holed pub car park, three or four eight-year-olds were playing a game comprehensible only to themselves which mainly seemed to involve repeated diving from the end of a burnt-out sofa on to the remains of a burnt-out mattress and back again. Maddy glanced at the printout from John Barnfield's pc. Barnfield had put together a home-made database with the details of what he and his wife called their supporters. *Anyone prepared to put their money where their mouth is, love*, he'd told her. Barnfield had produced over a hundred names from the Woodlands but Maddy had questioned him about each one until she'd refined the list down to the

116

twenty or so who were the most committed and the best connected. If you want to reach the masses, first reach the leaders of the masses: she'd been in the SWP for a year or so at university and hadn't wasted the experience.

Jeff pulled up the car outside William Blake House, checked with Mutt that he had his mobile properly switched on. Mutt would stay with the car, Jeff would mind Maddy on her housecalls. The lift stank of urine the way they always did. But at least it was working. Jeff went in after Maddy, pressed the button for the eighth floor. Maddy smoothed her ringlets, checked her make-up. The lift climbed shakily upwards. In her mind she rehearsed the bare bones of her pitch. *Hi, I'm Maddy Taylor. From the* Sunday Update? *I'm speaking to local people about how they feel living next to a convicted rapist? You hadn't heard? Nobody seems to be sure exactly where. The latest I'm hearing is there's some kind of protest demonstration being organised?*

Chapter Twelve

Jacobson accepted a call from Bill Dyson with a mixture of reluctance and curiosity. Dyson was the company solicitor for Planet Avionics, was inquiring after the health of his Managing Director.

'Mr Mortimer is still helping with our inquiries. That's all I can say,' Jacobson told him, staring out of the incident room window into the Sunday morning quiet of the pedestrian precinct.

Dyson was concerned about the practicalities. The other directors were either sleeping partners – whose sole concern with the company was to check their twice yearly rake off – or they were London-based wheelers and dealers with other high earning commitments to juggle. From what Dyson was saying, it sounded like Mortimer *was* Planet Avionics as far as any hands-on top management went.

'If he's going to be out of the picture for – ah – some time, the board will need to think about a stand-in PDQ,' Dyson said.

Like Jacobson could care less.

'You'd have known both the Mortimers well then?' he asked.

'Not on a personal level, Inspector. I see Gus every week but only for business reasons. His wife I've met on a few company social occasions but I couldn't offer any opinion about their relationship or anything like that.'

'So how is he from the *business* point of view then?'

Jacobson managed to make the word sound like a smelly dishcloth.

'Best MD in the history of the company, Inspector.'

Dyson proceeded to give Mortimer a glowing job reference. Planet Avionics had been looking decidedly shaky when Mortimer took over but he'd turned things around, put it firmly back on its feet, had all kinds of expansion plans lined up. Too bad he'd just tortured, raped and strangled his wife then, Jacobson thought.

'Five years he's been with you, is it?'

'Five years, yes. He'd MD'd an electronics company in Birmingham before he joined us. Came highly recommended and more than lived up to his reputation. That's why I'm hoping—'

Jacobson cut in, thinking that Dyson's call had outlived its usefulness by at least two minutes. It was either true or untrue that he knew nothing about Mortimer's personal affairs. He was down on Smith and Williams' interview list anyway. They could figure out which it was face to face when they got to him.

'He's helping our inquiries. We'll let you know if there's any change in the situation.'

He put the phone down and headed upstairs to his own office leaving Sergeant Ince alone in the incident room, busily summarising and cross-referencing tasks to be done and tasks accomplished on the white board. Ince had already entered exactly the same data on the inquiry database but – like Jacobson – had yet to fully abandon his old reliance on non-computer methods.

Jacobson thumbed through the Amnesty report for a second time. Stun guns and batons were illegal in Britain. Vaguely he thought he remembered a rumour that the Metropolitan police had considered using them at one time, that they still occasionally played around with them on training courses. But as far as civilian use went, they were out and out unlawful. If one had turned up at the

Mortimers' place it would have been flagged up and bagged immediately. It was the normal routine with a murder case search. You had a large amount of discretion with any other offences you might uncover. But you certainly wanted to *know* about them, certainly wanted to log any illegal object or substance. That was why the cocaine from the Mortimers' mantelpiece had been relocated to MIU storage and from there to the incident room. Even so, he thought, *chez* Mortimer was a sizeable search area – and overworked socos were only human. Kerr was having a shifty out at the Science and Business Park and he'd planned to join him. But now he decided instead to give the Mortimers' house and gardens another once-over. Hume and Barber could meet him there, give him a hand once they were done with their boy racer stint.

Barber was leaning against the bonnet of a police BMW when Jacobson drove up to the line of police tape which still stretched across the driveway in front of the MIU. Mick Hume was behind the wheel, the seat shoved comfortably back. According to Barber, the engine and torque were practically identical to Mortimer's merc.

'Fifteen minutes when Mick drove at his usual speed, guv. Averaging ninety, taking the bends like a nutter, I mean. The other times we got were twenty, twenty-five, thirty-five.'

Hume grinned, adjusting the seat forward then getting out.

'Looks to me like Mortimer did it at a normal cruising speed if he's not lying,' he said.

There were two plods on guard duty. Jacobson recruited one of them and organised two teams. Himself and Barber for the house; Hume and the uniformed for the gardens and outhouses. He told them what they were looking for and why. Life must have been much easier for the murder squad, he thought, in the days before budgeting and Best Value audits. What he really needed was twenty or so plods going over the property inch by inch and back again. It was something he might still end up requisitioning. But only if he could prove to the CID resource manager that he'd at least *tried* to do it the cheap, inefficient and time-wasting way first.

The watchman from the morning before was positively keen to let Kerr in this time, handed over the keys to Mortimer's office with a look that could easily have been mistaken for cheerfulness.

'Anything I can do just give me a shout, mate,' he said.

The world was full of guys who wanted to murder their boss, Kerr thought. Having him *done* for murder must be pretty much the next best thing. He unlocked the doors to Mortimer's outer and inner offices in turn, sat down in Mortimer's chair behind Mortimer's desk. It was as good a place to start as any: looking out at the world the way the suspect had done.

Mortimer, they'd established, was forty-six. He'd been born and grown up down in Luton where his dad had been a foreman at the Vauxhall plant. After school it had been Electronic Engineering at Imperial and then straight into a fast-moving career in industrial management. He'd landed his first MD slot by twenty-eight, had worked his way through half a dozen others – each with a bigger slice of cash action – until he'd finally fetched up in Crowby. Kerr fished in the desk drawers but failed to find anything remarkable. He pulled out a copy of the Planet Avionics Products Guide. He put his feet up on the desk – wondering if it was something that Mortimer himself had liked to do – and flicked through the pages. Precision measurement and tracking instrumentation for the aircraft industry seemed to be what they were into. The kind of thing, Kerr supposed, which kept planes and helicopters in the sky rather than plastered messily all over the runway or the departure lounge. He stood up and walked over to the filing cabinet near the window. It wasn't locked so the chances weren't high that it contained anything of interest. Not that Kerr had any clear idea what *would* interest him – apart obviously from an electric stun baton with Jenny Mortimer's DNA all over the coil. In your dreams, mate, he thought, thumbing through invoices, copies of tax returns, detailed specs of tachometers and altimeters.

Unlike the laptop in his lounge at home, the computer in Mortimer's outer office booted up straight away, didn't pester him for a login. There could be anything hidden on it of course but at first glance the contents were predictable, ordinary, tedious. Lists of suppliers, memos to this department, memos to that department. He couldn't get into either the spreadsheet or the database programs – which *had* wanted passwords – but probably there was nothing more interesting on either than sales figures and personnel records. On a whim, he clicked on the Internet Explorer icon. Kerr had done the Computer Assisted Detection course at the Met the previous summer. Partly because it slightly interested him but mainly because it had meant five nights in a London hotel with Rachel. He keyed in the *Financial Times* URL and did a search on Planet Avionics. Everything that came up confirmed the claims in the brochure: a go-ahead company with a go-ahead boss. He was about to close the browser when it occurred to him to do a query specifically on Gus Mortimer himself. The FT's search engine returned six items. Kerr had already looked at four of them: pieces about Planet Avionics which named Mortimer in passing as the MD. Item five listed him as a delegate at some regional CBI junket out at the Belfry golf complex. Nice work if you can get it, he thought.

But it was the oldest item, number six, which caused Kerr to utter a loud '*YES*' and to execute several mental cartwheels across the floor.

Robert Johnson jogged down Mill Street as far as Hayle Close and then on to the scraggy wasteground that formed a barrier to the inner ring road. Mostly it was just furrowed mud and litter but Johnson managed to find a level patch of grass that was relatively free of dog shit. He did a hundred press ups in quick succession, then a hundred more. Hayle Close was a derelict row of terraced houses that even squatters had become sniffy about using. The council had slapped a condemned notice on it a year and a half ago but hadn't yet been arsed to actually demolish it. DC Aston crouched behind what was left of the back wall at the end of the row. He told himself he'd stop counting at three hundred but Johnson stopped at two hundred and fifty anyway, bounced back to his feet like he was barely out of breath, started into some kind of slow *kata* between the dog turds and the rusted tins of super lager. Lovely mover for a sick bastard, Aston thought. Then he was running again, headed back towards the houses. Aston ducked beneath the wall and paged Dennett.

They tailed him in turn back to Mill Street, into the Londis shop and finally into the public bar of the Bricklayer's Arms. Johnson complained to the barman about the restricted choice of lagers on sale but ordered a pint of Kronenbourg all the same. He settled into a table near the window and wiped a light band of sweat from his forehead. In the Londis shop he'd bought another packet of Marlboro and two newspapers. He put the *Sunday Times* next to himself on the bench where it partially obscured a deep slash mark on the red plastic seat covering. He unfolded the front page of the *Sunday Update* on the table, drank an inch off the top of his beer, didn't know whether to laugh or cry.

The search for a stun weapon had been fruitless. If Gus Mortimer had used one on his wife, he hadn't left it conveniently hidden in a flower bed or behind a wine rack. Jacobson hadn't completely wasted his time though. Back in the kitchen, he'd found a photograph of Kevin Holland and a couple of letters he'd written to Jenny Mortimer which made the nature of their relationship graphically clear. They'd been inexpertly concealed inside a spice drawer which Jacobson and Kerr had neglected to rifle through the night before. Maybe Gus Mortimer had never had his hands in the drawer either, he thought, bagging the photo and the letters carefully. Or maybe he had – furious at first but then cooling down: putting them scrupulously back in place, saying nothing, nursing a cold, vengeful anger.

He crossed out of the porch and stood under the shade of the English oak. He tried Aston and Dennett on his mobile but the number was busy. Hume and Barber drove off to make their door to door housecalls, the back wheels of the BMW spraying red gravel in the wake of Hume's lunatic foot on the pedal. He'd only got so far as thinking about a cigarette when the second plod emerged from the nearest portacabin.

'There's an email just arrived from DS Kerr, guv. The attachment's for you. He's marked it urgent.'

Jacobson followed him inside, sat down at the computer terminal. He tried twice – failed twice – to open the document before he finally let the plod do it for him. Even then it took him a minute or two to get the hang of the mouse and stop the words scrolling up and down the screen too quickly for him to read them:

Frank. This is from the FT. Five years ago. Why IS the PNC so crap?

'Stun Baton' Director is Guilty

By our Midlands correspondent

A British company director made legal history yesterday when he pleaded guilty to offences under the Firearms Act at Birmingham Crown Court. Angus Anthony Mortimer, 41, a director of CentroTech Ltd, told the court that allegations made last year in a Channel Four documentary were 'substantially true'. The court was shown video footage in which Mr Mortimer had boasted to undercover reporters posing as overseas customers that his company could supply as many electric stun batons 'as they needed. Anytime, anywhere' and 'at a knock down price.' In the UK, manufacture, sale or export of these products without authorisation carries a maximum penalty of five years imprisonment under Section 5(1)(b) of the

It turned out afterwards that the coaches had been hired under a phoney name, had been paid for up front in cash. The surveillance cars, one each on the Bronx and the Son of the Bronx, hadn't twigged what was up until too late either. As one DC put it, *even low-life scumbags deserve a day at the seaside now and then*. Which was what it had looked like at first: teenagers, mums and dads, toddlers even, piling into the bus outside The Poets. Maybe they'd seemed a bit glum for a Sunday outing. *But who wouldn't look glum, living in a shit heap like the Woodlands?*'

By twelve o'clock there was a mob of at least two hundred gathered illegally in the pedestrian precinct. The numbers swelled by the minute: the bussed-in hardcore, contacts who'd got the call by mobile and text message, casual strollers who'd stopped out of curiosity and had rapidly been converted to the cause. Down the front they even had placards to wave. NO SEX PESTS HERE. CASTRAIT THEM. KILL CRAWLER, INNIT? In the middle of the crowd, a stocky youth ladled into a battered old drum, beat out the rhythm: Da. Da. Da-Da. Da-Da. *Where, Where, Where is Pervert?* A dozen uniformeds stood, their arms folded, on the steps of the Divisional building. So far no official decision had been reached about a police response. So far nothing had been said to the crowd. Da. Da. Da-Da. Da-Da. *Where, Where, Where is Pervert?* Da. Da. Da-Da. Da-Da. *Where, Where, Where is Pervert?*

Jeff locked the car, kept up the rear. John and Linda Barnfield walked in front, then Maddy, then Mutt, his camcorder already rolling for sound and vision. They'd parked on the third level, took the lift down to the exit. Apart from Jeff, who rarely let his thoughts show on his face, they all looked well pleased as they crossed the precinct. Maddy especially perhaps. If she couldn't sell this to *Sky News*, the Pope wasn't a Catholic. They made their way to the front of the crowd except for Mutt who stopped half a dozen rows back, making it harder for the boys in blue if they decided to nab his equipment. John Barnfield produced a megaphone from the Homebase carrier bag he'd been carrying and passed it to his wife.

'Thank you all for coming,' she said, speaking in to it, waiting to be heard over the chanting.

'I think we all know why we're here—'

Yes. Too fucking right.

'We want answers—'

We want him. We want him out.

'And we want action—'

By Christ we do. You tell them. Da-Da-Da, briskly on the drum.

'We have one simple question—'

Da. Da. Da-Da. Da-Da. *Where, Where, Where is Pervert?*

Maddy Taylor took a deep breath, then walked slowly towards the centre of the line of copers, Jeff beside her, John and Linda Barnfield just behind.

'Hi,' she said. 'I'm Maddy Taylor from the *Sunday Update*. I have an appointment with Chief Superintendent Chivers?'

Da. Da. Da-Da. Da-Da. *Where, Where, Where is Pervert?*

The constable she'd spoken to deferred to his sergeant.

'I'm instructed to let you through, miss. But nobody else.'

'You don't think these parents whose daughter was the victim of a horrific attack have a right to be consulted on—'

'It's not for me to comment, miss,' the sergeant said.

Like Maddy didn't know that. Like she wasn't playing to the camera. Mrs Barnfield turned back to the crowd, bellowed into the megaphone.

'They won't let us in. They won't even talk to us.'

Da. Da. Da. *Let Them In*. Da. Da. Da. *Let Them In*. Da. Da. Da. *Let Them In*.

The sergeant spoke into his radio, watched the white riot van pull out from the side exit at the far end of the Divi, drive into the middle of the pedestrian precinct, draw up about fifty yards from the nearest protester. The crowd saw it too. There were another dozen coppers inside, hastily kitted into riot gear, smiling at the thought of unexpected action, psyching themselves up for it. PC Barry Sheldon sat nearest the rear door, would be the first out on the pavement if it went off. You could see their point, he was thinking, even agree with it. But that didn't mean he wouldn't put the boot in if the opportunity presented itself.

Linda Barnfield thrust herself between the constable and the sergeant, trying to break through. One on each arm, they held her in place just as Detective Chief Superintendent Chivers came through the revolving doors behind them. He walked punctiliously down the steps towards the police line, a megaphone of his own tucked under his arm.

Da. Da. Da. *Let Them In*. Da. Da. Da. *Let Them In*. Da. Da. Da. *Let Them In*.

'I know why you're here,' he shouted, his voice distorted but still stentorian. 'I share your concerns—'

Tell us where he is then. Yeah, where's the fucker at?

'Robert Johnson has been lawfully released. The proper authorities are fully informed of his activities and whereabouts. There is no need for alarm. I repeat: there is no need for alarm—'

He ain't living next door to your wife, mate.

It had probably been about then, Maddy decided later, that somebody at the back of the crowd had thrown the first bottle: hard and fast.

Chapter Thirteen

The Chief Constable, Dudley 'Dud' Bentham, led them down the neat, straight path between his alpine rock feature and his carp pond. A tent-like white canopy had been erected next to the pond. It struck Jacobson as improbably Arabian, exotic, in the context of the CC's back garden. But a domestic pine table and comfy, cushioned chairs were set out shadily inside, immediately overwriting the momentary illusion of Eastern promise. Apart of course from the view of Mrs Bentham's ample backside as she stuck a jug of fruit juice and a jug of iced water in the centre of the table.

'Thank you, dear,' said Bentham, his eyes – to Jacobson's mind – following her waddling retreat with undisguised uxorious pleasure. There was nothing resembling an ashtray in sight but he lit up a B and H regardless. If Napoleon wanted to get close to the troops then he'd have to endure their uncouth ways for the duration. Bentham poured himself a glass of water and took a thoughtful sip.

'Sundays in August are supposed to be off-peak budget wise,' he said. 'Overtime at a minimum, shifts at three-quarter strength. I'm supposed to *save* resources at this time of the year not stretch them to the hilt.'

DCS Chivers and DCS-in-waiting Salter nodded eloquent agreement. Jacobson tapped his ash on to an Italian paving slab. Bentham wasn't wrong but there didn't seem much purpose in wailing about it. For one thing, the kind of Sunday the Chief Constable had in mind didn't feature riots in the town centre, didn't finally need fifty uniformeds – thirty of them called in from off-duty on double pay – to restore order. Six officers had needed hospital attention, eighteen arrestees were clogging up the cells. They'd need feeding overnight, transporting to the court in the morning. For another, the scaled-down Crawler surveillance would have to be scaled back up again. And then some: as well as keeping a covert CID eye on potential hotheads, now they were also going to need uniformed deterrence patrols in the Woodlands area, the Bronx and at a couple of other potential sink estate flashpoints. For a third, after Kerr's email there was no longer any option but to put full-scale search teams into action – and quickly. One *chez* Mortimer, one out at Planet Avionics.

Bentham took another sip.

'All quiet now at any rate?' he asked.

Chivers and Salter nodded in unison again.

'As far as we know, sir,' Salter replied.

He was wearing a crisp blue shirt, smartly pressed white trousers. Sheltered by the canopy, he'd taken off the blue matching cap which Jacobson supposed he wore to protect his balding pate from the sun. Or maybe just to hide it. Salter emphasised that they wouldn't be taking any more chances. Anyone who'd ever issued a threat against Johnson was back under watch, would remain so round the clock if necessary. He was sure the Chief would appreciate that the budgetary implications had been uppermost in their thinking when they'd eased off a bit yesterday. Especially with the unexpected pressure put on resources from Jacobson's murder inquiry. He didn't exactly lie outright, didn't deny that there had been what he called significant senior management input. But a careless listener might still have formed the impression that Jacobson had been a third party to the ill-fated decision.

Jacobson decided to say nothing, let it go. He hoped

Salter had the brains to realise that it was a matter of showing CID solidarity, wasn't stupid enough to think he was toadying to a new boss. He told Bentham the story about the electric baton and why a heavy-duty search was necessary. Bentham scarcely argued, instructed Chivers to authorise it. Jacobson pondered whether he'd grasped the point at last – if you're going to go over-budget, you might as well do it in style – or whether he just wanted to get back on with his Sunday afternoon at home.

'We'll try to claim some of the cost of the Robert Johnson operation back from the Home Office anyway. With the usual sleight of hand and a bit of luck, we might be able to inflate the bill enough to cover some of Frank's outlay too. I'll get a couple of the ACs on the case in the morning.'

So that's what an Assistant Chief Constable was *for*, Jacobson thought. I've always wondered.

'Dud' Bentham stood up, indicating that the audience was over. They followed him back up the path.

'Nice pond, sir,' Salter said. 'Lovely gardens all round if I may say so.'

Jacobson and Kerr met up outside the MIU, had driven back to the Mortimers' property within minutes of each other. Kerr had Steve Horton, the civilian computer officer, with him.

'Tell me that we *did* check Gus Mortimer on the PNC, Ian, old son.'

'Emma Smith did it herself, Frank. Yesterday afternoon before the briefing. Worked through every single name that had come up so far. Mortimer was clean as a whistle. Not even a speeding ticket.'

Kerr adjusted his baseball cap, tried to avoid the glare of the sun. The thing about crime was that it usually involved other crime: checking anyone associated with the victim against police records was standard murder squad routine. Computerisation had brought speed to the process but it hadn't yet brought reliability. GIGO – garbage in, garbage out – was how the instructor had put it on Kerr's computer course. He'd also told them about the internal audit of the PNC. The one they'd tried to keep out of the papers. The one that had put the current error rate as high as eighty-six per cent.

Horton said pretty much the same thing now. He was twenty-five, tall, blond, muscular. With his brain drastically lobotomised, he would've been a natural lead singer for a boy band. No one ever believed he worked with computers.

'There's villains out there with whole strings of convictions that don't show up, Mr Jacobson,' he said.

'Plus maiden aunts and vicars who're down as armed robbers,' Kerr added.

Kerr and Horton walked on into the house. Jacobson frowned. Another one of those problems for the service that needed non-existent time and money to put right. He made for the portacabins. The coffee from the drinks dispenser would taste like shit. But at least it would be wet shit. His mobile rang just as he was removing the brown plastic cup from the machine: DCS Chivers. The full-scale searches were definitely on but there was no possibility of them happening today. The way things were they'd have to draft in extra officers from Coventry or Leicester or somewhere. First thing Monday was the best case scenario. Chivers had left it with Sergeant Ince to organise the details.

Horton had volunteered – for the price of half a day's overtime – to investigate the laptop in the Mortimers' lounge. Kerr had offered to bring it back to the Divi first. But for some technical reason or other, Horton had said it would be better to take a look in situ. Just in case, he'd said. But hadn't explained further. He sat down on the sofa, checked the power lead and the modem cable, switched the machine on.

'I couldn't get past the login,' Kerr said.

Horton switched the machine back off, switched it on

again, executed a few high speed keystrokes too quickly for Kerr to follow.

'What's one of those?' he asked with geek sarcasm, disabling the password utility and booting the machine cleanly up. He gave the directories a quick once-over.

'I reckon he's mainly used it to access his email away from the office. Not much else in the way of data on there.'

Kerr took a look himself. Inbox, Outbox, Sent Items: more dreary communications about orders, sales figures, production targets. What *was* immediately different was the sheer volume of mail stored. There had been nothing on the office machine more than a couple of weeks old. Horton suggested it had probably been set up to automatically delete every ten days or so.

'So why's he left mail on here that goes back more than a year?' Kerr asked.

'A lot of people do that,' Horton replied, professionally condescending, utterly non-stumped. 'Use their laptop as much for backup storage as anything else.'

Kerr scrolled down through the message headings in the Inbox. *Re your order. Production Bonus. June Sales Drive.* Fascinating stuff: *We Will Kill You*, as Jacobson might have said, stood out like a twelve-inch prick in a harem.

Faith Lawson, Gus Mortimer's temporary secretary, shared a flat in Longtown with a boyfriend who liked to be called Snake but whose real name was Mark Jones. Second floor: a cramped kitchen, a tiny bathroom and a lounge which doubled as a bedroom and everything else. Its best feature on a summer Sunday afternoon was the fact that the bottom pane of the old-fashioned sash window could be slid all the way up, letting maximum amounts of air and sunshine in. Despite this the room was still clouded in a blue funk haze; Faith and Snake/Mark's idea of fun appeared to revolve around their sofa, their cd player and a home-made water pipe of skunk weed which Emma Smith was sisterly enough not to mention. For one thing it made the both of them carelessly talkative once they'd got over their two minutes of paranoia.

DC Williams turned the volume down without being asked: Ozric Tentacles, not his kind of thing even if he'd known who it was.

'I've been there a fortnight. 'Sposed to be there for another week,' Faith said. 'But I wasn't sure about going in again now that—'

'Phone the agency in the morning. Get some other gig,' Snake advised, trying to pull her back into their interrupted stoned clinch. She moved away, sat up on the edge of the couch, smoothed her jet black hair. Emma Smith asked her what Mortimer had been like to work for.

'Averagely creepy. No worse than that. I'd sense him staring at me when I was working sometimes. But he never said anything, tried anything. I've known worse. Handsome I suppose' – she aimed a lurid green cushion at her boyfriend's head – 'I'm not into handsome.'

'What about the full-timers? Was he liked? Disliked?'

'I don't mix much with them usually. Why I prefer temping. Babies, holidays, getting a new washing machine – they never talk about anything real, anything worth talking about.'

'Brain dead isn't it?' Snake offered distantly, hugging the cushion to his chest, still stretched out supine:

'Work. Consume. Work. The Barmy Army.'

'And what do *you* do, sonny?' asked DC Williams.

Snake was concentrating on the space between objects, how it wasn't really space at all, more a kind of underlying substance. A residual survival instinct focused his brain on the question.

'College isn't it? Off for the summer.'

'So no gossip about the managing director then?' Emma Smith asked, getting back to the point.

'Some old dear told me to watch myself the first day I was there. Like he had a reputation for trying it on. But he didn't. Not his type maybe.'

'Any contact with his wife?'

'She phoned a few times or he'd phone her. Not every day though. All I did was put through the calls. Reckoned he was too boring to be worth listening to.'

Snake finally lifted his head a few inches.

'Rather spend all day in chat rooms. Wouldn't you love?'

The girl tried to pull the cushion out of his hands but he held it tight. She fell on top of him, giggling. Williams nodded towards the door and Emma Smith nodded back.

She left them a card just in case.

Jacobson, Kerr and Steve Horton were hunched over the computer terminal in the MIU. Someone – one of the plods – had brought an electric fan in from home. Definite promotion material, Jacobson thought, turning it on full. Horton had copied the contents of the laptop's hard disk on to something he called a zip drive, now he was uploading the data on to the inquiry's system.

There had been six emails in total, posted at regular monthly intervals. The first one had been sent in February, the most recent one in the middle of July, barely a month ago.

'All done,' Horton said.

He put the latest one on the screen for Jacobson's benefit.

'They're pretty much all the same, Frank,' Kerr said.

To: G_Mortimer@PlanAvi.co.uk
From: Action And Resistance
Subject: We Will Kill You

Do you know what electric torture feels like? You soon will. And then we'll kill you. We take no pleasure in doing what is necessary to rid the world of its parasites. It is your greed condemned you.

Judicial committee
Action and Resistance
www.ARR.org

'Are these for real?' Jacobson asked.

'Looks like it,' Horton said. 'And probably untraceable.'

He explained that the six emails had been sent from anomiser sites, a different one each time.

'There's dozens on the net now if you know where to find 'em. Set up by libertarian groups, cyber anarchists and what have you. Normally if you're determined to trace who it was really sent you an email – or anything else – you can. All the way back to the specific machine or terminal they used *and* its physical location. With anomised mail, you don't get further than the mail server. Hence the name. Keep Big Brother from snooping and all that.'

Jacobson hated the way his investigations kept running in to computer-speak these days. It was probably only a matter of time before they chucked him out on his ear and replaced him with RoboCop.

'But at least you could physically locate the, eh, anomising server?' Kerr asked.

Jacobson glanced at him. Thank fuck somebody understood what Horton was on about. Maybe he could get Kerr to explain it all in plain English later.

'I doubt it,' Horton said. 'They tend to use mirror sites, constantly on the move from one country's network to another. Before you can get an angle on the current location, they've re-routed elsewhere. Cyberspace is a big place.'

'What about www.arr.org then?'

'Exactly the same if whoever it is knows what they're doing.'

Horton brought up the web browser, keyed in the address. Arr. org looked nothing like any web site Jacobson had ever seen in his admittedly limited experience. There were no sounds, no animations, no colourful graphics. Just pages and pages of ordinary typescript set against a white background.

'Welcome to the Internet underground, Mr Jacobson,' Horton said, offering Jacobson the chair in front of the keyboard and wasting on him the kind of perfectly white smile best suited to shifting a few million cds and product tie-ins. Jacobson read just enough for now to get the flavour.

ACTION AND RESISTANCE
COMMUNIQUE 12

Communism is dead. Liberalism wrings its ineffectual hands and weeps while hunger, greed and oppression stalk the Earth. Humanity will never be free until all are free. No more hierarchies. No more bosses. No more rich. Only decentralised leaderless resistance can make the transition happen. Who is Spartacus? I am Spartacus. Who is Che? I am Che. Who makes the revolution? You make the revolution. Sweep Away the Old. Bring in the New.

WHY? BECAUSE IT IS NECESSARY.

For this issue we have completely updated and expanded our LIST OF SHAME based on latest research and investigation. ALL names on the list are verified as legitimate targets against whom ANY action is justified.

This is war.

These are the footsoldiers of the enemy.

Draw Your Own Conclusions.

THINK FOR YOURSELF. ACT FOR THE WORLD.

The meat of the site was a list of a hundred or so named 'enemies', mostly UK-based. As well as a name, each entry gave business and private addresses, telephone and fax numbers, email details. They also came with brief 'CVs', outlining the reasons for inclusion: 'broker for weapons of repression' was the category they'd applied to Gus Mortimer.

Chapter Fourteen

Jacobson carried a pint of lager away from the bar of the Brewer's Rest and found a seat in a secluded corner. He'd glanced in the beer garden but it had been chocker, every table taken. Some of the hooligans who'd escaped arrest in the precinct riot were out there. Sunning themselves, sinking beers, re-telling their exploits with Homeric exaggeration.

'Any trouble just phone for the cavalry,' he'd advised the bar staff.

He did nothing for a moment then lit up a cigarette. Amazingly it was only his third of the day. He'd called a briefing for four o'clock and he wanted to get everything clear in his head first, concentrate on what was fundamental, separate the wheat from the chaff. Gus Mortimer had attacked his wife publicly – had practically abducted her – when she'd told him she'd been fucking someone else, that she was planning to leave him. That was what mattered. Plus that Jenny Mortimer had been killed in her own home the next morning. Plus that the only person known to have been on the premises was her husband. The possibility that she'd been murdered after he'd left for work existed as a kind of theoretical abstraction. But so did the possibility that there was life on Mars: there was absolutely no sign of a break-in, no one else remotely in the frame. Mortimer was denying it of course but then he obviously wasn't stupid. Even without Alan Slingsby's coaching, he would've worked out for himself that the burden was ultimately on the prosecution to prove guilt, not for the suspect to prove innocence. It was a pity Robertson couldn't be certain that Mrs Mortimer had been raped. But Jacobson was confident that the DNA results would at least show that it was Gus – and only Gus – who'd had sex with her in the last few hours of her life.

He still hadn't touched the beer. As if he was waiting for his thirst to reach the breaking point where he would no longer be able to endure it. The prisons were full of murderers who'd been convicted on this level of evidence – or less. Everything else – the emails, the nutter web site, Mortimer's dodgy deals with brutal foreign governments – was bollocks. Extraneous information. A waste of time. Effluent muddying the water. The only thing useful from all of that was the stun baton – if they could find it. Mortimer would have kept one as a souvenir from his last job. Might have fantasised for years about using it on her. *It was a spur of the moment thing. I just flipped*: the kind of thing you heard everyday from domestic killers. A crime of passion. It was still a special defence in France. But then you went into the background, uncovered their past histories of violence, their track records of bullying, of arguing with their fists. He was ready at last, put the cigarette down on the groove in the side of the ashtray, lifted the cool beer to his lips. *She was asking for it*, they sometimes said. Even now. And wankers like Gus Mortimer couldn't wait to give it.

He was halfway through his pint when John and Linda Barnfield walked in. The woman journalist was with them and so was one of the men he'd seen her meet at the railway station the other afternoon. The big one. The one who looked a bit like Popeye's adversary Bluto. John Barnfield clocked Jacobson immediately, walked straight over.

'Inspector Jacobson. Mind if we join you?'

Jacobson didn't mind one bit. But probably not for the

reasons that Barnfield thought. The big guy got the round in, brought their drinks over on a tray.

'This is Inspector Jacobson,' Barnfield told Maddy Taylor, making the introductions. 'If men like him were in charge higher up, we wouldn't be having any of this nonsense.'

Maddy flashed Jacobson a smile, held out her hand. Jacobson shook it, caught a cool whiff of expensive perfume, resisted an impulse to raise her fingers to his mouth, continental style.

'I hear one of your colleagues is enjoying the local hospitality,' he said.

Matthew 'Mutt' Summers had put up a brave attempt to keep PC Barry Sheldon off his camcorder, had been nicked for resisting arrest. The charges would be dropped later, Jacobson knew, provided the paper didn't make a stink about the dangerous, supposedly prohibited necklock Sheldon had put him in. One of these days Sheldon would go too far. Fortunately, it wasn't in Jacobson's job spec to worry about it.

'But not his camera equipment, Inspector.'

Jacobson half smiled, took another mouthful of beer. Despite being very nearly strangled by Sheldon, Mutt had managed to pass his camcorder on to some kid in the crowd. The video footage would be halfway to London by now via motorbike courier. She let her hand linger in his for a moment.

'I suppose an interview's out the question?'

'My very presence in this pub is one hundred per cent out of the question as far as reporters go,' Jacobson answered, getting halfway out of his chair for emphasis.

'Fine. Fine. Absolutely,' Maddy said quickly. 'We've got enough of a story to be going on with anyway.'

'You've got complete bollocks to be going on with,' Jacobson replied, sitting back down, remanding the perfume, the ringlets and the sea-blue eyes to the back of his mind. He turned his gaze to the Barnfields.

'It's not doing any good this, is it?' he asked.

John Barnfield kept his voice even with evident difficulty.

'So – what – we're just supposed to let him wander around Crowby like he's a normal person?'

'He won't stay,' Jacobson said. 'He's making some daft point. He'll move on soon.'

'That's just it, Inspector. He'll move on. After what he's done to our daughter. I'd cut his balls off personally if I had the chance. Stick them down his throat and choke him.'

'You know I could charge you for saying that in public, Mr Barnfield?'

Barnfield held his hands out, wrists together, across the table: cuff me. Jacobson shook his head, took another deep mouthful of beer. Barnfield came as close to being a solid citizen as anyone did these days. Strong marriage. Probably kind to dogs. Doing his best. He'd struggled a bit after his stint in the army. But then he'd started an adventure company a dozen years ago ahead of a trend, had gone on to make a good living persuading well-heeled thirty somethings that blisters and dysentery meant you were seeing the real Peru or wherever. The attack on his daughter had torn him to bits. He didn't lead 'expeditions' any more, confined himself purely to the business end.

'How is she?' Jacobson asked.

'Quiet,' Linda Barnfield said. 'Like a zombie. They've got her drugged up to the eyeballs in there.'

Caroline Barnfield had been sectioned after her last suicide bid, was now officially diagnosed as having had a psychotic breakdown.

'Any time. Day or night, Inspector,' John Barnfield said.

Jacobson knew the Barnfields thought he was on their side. He was the policeman who'd put Robert Johnson away. He was their age, their generation. He had a daughter of his own.

'Just say where he is. We'll do the rest.'

Jacobson polished off the rest of his lager. There were

140

police who'd do just that in his position. Make it so that Johnson got what was coming to him; justify it as defending Law and Order. His own problem was that he actually understood what those two little words meant. How fragile. How easily broken. How difficult to live by.

'Go home, John,' he said. 'Or go and see Caroline.'

He glanced at Maddy Taylor as he stood up.

'And stay away from hyenas.'

Kerr gave Steve Horton a lift home on his way back to the Divi, quizzed him about politics on the Internet. He knew hazily that extremists had taken to it like ducks to water. Horton filled in the details for him. The net had arrived like Xmas for anyone on the margins, anyone outside the mainstream; far left, far right, lunatic cults of every sort. Out of the millions who used it daily, you could connect up with like minds, exchange information, preach to potential converts. Unless they came to attention some other way, whoever was behind the Action and Resistance site would be likely to keep their anonymity. Worse – once they'd posted their list of 'enemies', anyone who read it could take a pop: what they meant by *decentralised leaderless resistance*.

He dropped Horton off at his front door, headed downtown. Jacobson had suggested he call into the Brewer's Rest for a quick one before the briefing. But the detour to Horton's place had taken longer than he'd expected and now there wasn't time. He took the lift to save another couple of minutes. Sergeant Ince had booked them into one of the proper meeting rooms on the third floor. Cool and spacious in comparison to the incident room. Weekdays they were the province of senior management, used to discuss operationally vital issues like who would get the laundry contract. But they usually sat idle at the weekends. The meeting rooms too.

Emma Smith and DC Williams reported back first. They'd taken a couple of statements from Planet Avionics staff which pointed to Gus Mortimer as a low-level sexual harasser. But nothing that the women involved had felt they couldn't deal with for themselves. They'd also found two or three who'd seemed positively happy with Mortimer's suggestive attentions.

'Bit of a fan club, sounds like,' DC Williams said.

According to the company lawyer, Bill Dyson, Mortimer had been an old-style, top-down decision-maker. He issued orders not suggestions, only took yes for an answer. But he hadn't seemed to be any more unpopular than the average boss. *'He always treated you straight, you always knew where you stood'* was a typical comment. Bob Hicks, the storeman who'd acted as Mortimer's chauffeur on Friday night, had been gobsmacked by the Boden Hall incident: *'He's always seemed a decent enough bloke in the past.'* Murderers often did, Jacobson pointed out. Wife beaters too: he'd worked himself for a DCI at one time who'd been the most popular detective on the force until his wife had divorced him, citing years of mental and physical abuse.

Mick Hume and DC Barber seemed to have run into the same brick wall as the day before. Either the Mortimers' neighbours knew nothing at all about them or they claimed that they had been absolutely normal, everyday, unremarkable. Jacobson thanked them for their efforts anyway. *Déjà vu*. There were no fresh leads for them to follow. There would be overtime on the Crawler surveillance if they wanted it. Otherwise they were through for the day. Otherwise he'd see them in the morning.

Kerr held his fire until the others had filed out.

'What about the hate mail then, Frank?' he asked.

Jacobson pretended to look thoughtful.

'What about it, old son? Let's see. A lunatic terrorist gains access to the house without breaking in. Then he mistakes an attractive blonde woman for a six foot hulk, attacks and murders Mrs Mortimer without disturbing hubbie.'

When you put it like that, Kerr thought.

'Not exactly. I'm just curious as to why he never seems to have reported it, that's all.'

Jacobson stood up and started towards the door.

'Probably didn't take it seriously. Probably didn't think we would either. Look if you and Horton want to look into it as a technical exercise, be my guests. But let it wait till *after* we've booked Mortimer for the murder, OK?'

Kerr nodded. Sure. No problem. Why he liked working with Jacobson: he was the first boss he'd ever had who was at least as intelligent as himself.

The same interview room again. The same plastic chairs and pockmarked table. Mortimer sat next to Slingsby, drinking stewed tea from a plastic cup: a passenger stranded in a railway platform waiting room. Slingsby explained to him that the police had extended his detention to the full thirty-six hours. They had up until a quarter to midnight. Then they'd either have to charge him with something or let him go.

'You've made your statement, Gus. The best thing now is to stick to it. I'm guessing they've got no more today than they did yesterday.'

The custody sergeant rattled the door open and Jacobson and Kerr came in, sat down opposite. Jacobson ran through a précis of Mortimer's statement.

'This still your version of events, Gus? Or is there something more you want to tell us now you'd had time to think about it?'

Mortimer put the plastic cup down on the table, said nothing.

'My client has nothing to add to his statement. When do you intend to end this farce and let him go?' Slingsby asked.

Jacobson ignored him.

'Where did you hide the electric baton you tortured your wife with, Gus?'

Mortimer stayed silent.

'Wha—?' Slingsby.

Jacobson told them about Robinson's discovery of the marks on the corpse. Then about Mortimer's conviction. Slingsby recovered quickly, showed why he was worth his top of the scale fees.

'But no sign of this alleged weapon so far. And only the judgement of a distinctly junior pathologist to say that it exists at all.'

It was Jacobson's turn to say nothing.

'Where's the baton, Gus?' Kerr asked.

Mortimer gazed at the ceiling. A tourist in the Sistine Chapel.

'Only way you could get her to scream, was it?'

Michelangelo's biggest, mutest fan.

Jacobson rested his elbows on the table for a moment, his chin on his hands. Then he leant back in his chair, his fingers clasped comfily together behind his neck.

'I've seen some real excrement sat where you're sat over the years, Gus. But as a piece of complete shit, you're up there with the best of them. For the record, Mr Mortimer appears to have nothing to say about his former involvement in the illegal exportation of torture implements. Nor about the torture and subsequent murder of his wife. A trial jury, as Mr Slingsby knows very well, will be entitled to draw their own conclusions—'

Mortimer slapped the table loudly with his right palm.

'All right. All right. So we cut a few corners at CentroTech. So fucking what? If they don't get them from Britain they get them from somewhere else. So how does that help anybody? They're perfectly *legal* in the States. Stun guns, tasers, prods, you name it. Buy 'em mail order for ninety dollars. Probably throw in a free T-shirt for all I know.'

Frying murderers was popular over there too, Jacobson thought.

'You'd have kept hold of a few samples then, Gus?'

The ghost of his lizard smile crossed Mortimer's face.

'I'm not a total idiot. I did no such thing. We forfeited our stock to Her Majesty's Government after the court case. I expect they have records somewhere.'

'What about the marks on your wife's body?' Kerr asked.

'You're the policeman. You tell me. Mr Slingsby here seems to be saying your pathologist might have got it wrong anyway.'

'So you only raped and strangled her. No torture involved.'

But Mortimer had drawn a deep breath after his outburst, was back with Michelangelo again. Jacobson waited a minute then pressed the button for the custody team. One step at a time, he thought. Quit while you're ahead.

Jacobson and Kerr took the stairs up from the custody area and emerged on to the ground floor. Jacobson told Kerr to knock it on the head for the rest of the day. Whatever else needed doing, he could do it himself. He took the lift to the canteen, convinced himself that baked beans on the side plus a glass of orange juice virtually turned chips and a scotch egg into health food. The desk sergeant phoned him halfway through his meal, connected him to an outside caller. Apart from the forensic operation out at the house, the Jenny Mortimer case was officially classified as medium resourced. Which meant amongst other things that there was no cash for a dedicated public phone line. Any calls went to the main desk number in the first instance, took their turn with the nuisance neighbours and the stolen car hi-fis. A woman's voice identified herself as Sheila Hunter. She claimed she was a friend of Jenny Mortimer's, had only just heard what had happened, had always known something like this *could* happen. Jacobson took her details, said he'd get to her inside the hour or maybe just a bit less. *Couldn't they just talk on the phone?* No they couldn't, he told her. No, that wasn't possible. He cut her off more abruptly than she'd probably cared for. She was probably genuine, was probably worth talking to.

But she could just as easily be one of Maddy Taylor's stooges: angling for an unguarded comment, tape recorder at the ready.

He cleared his plate and then drank the orange juice which he'd saved till last. Back in his office on the fifth floor, he allowed himself the luxury of a fifteen minute snooze; jacket off, feet up on the desk. Janice, his ex-wife, had been into meditation for a while. Whether it was before jogging or after macramé and Indian needlework he couldn't remember any more. The thing was she'd persuaded him along to a few classes himself. He'd never got the hang of it properly but the experience *had* left him with an enhanced ability to take forty winks whenever he needed them. Now for example. *Everyone gets some kind of blessing*, as the ageing hippy who'd taught them had put it.

When he woke up, he took his shaving gear to the gents, freshened up, kept his face under the bliss of the cold tap for a good three minutes. He was better than his word; he was pulling up outside the address less than twenty minutes after that. Six forty-two pm to be precise. Sheila Hunter lived in classic Wynarth. A discreetly modernised terraced house, a ginger tom cat lazily asleep outside the front door, a wall-sized poster of Mongolian dancers in the hall. She was a tall woman in her thirties. Older but not unlike his daughter Sally in appearance. They talked in her front room. She told him she was an aromatherapist but that she'd used to be a teacher, had worked at Simon de Montfort at the same time as Eric Brown and Jenny Mortimer. Jenny and her had got on so they'd kept in touch. She'd seen her as recently as last month. Jenny had told her about Kevin Holland and that she'd planned on leaving her husband.

'Good for you I said. She should never have moved in with him in the first place. Certainly never married him.'

'So why did she?' Jacobson asked.

'Glamour in a word. Eric and her were living life on the small scale. Back street house. Rickety old car. Two

146

meagre junior teaching salaries. Plus Eric started talking about starting a family. I think Jenny saw her life stalling somewhere she didn't really want to be. Gus was supposed to be her ticket to broader horizons. Pots of money. Handsome. Always jetting off here or there.'

The cat had roused itself from its slumbers, slunk in from the hall, was quietly sniffing Jacobson's right shoe.

'But you didn't think it could work out?'

'He tried it on with me the very first time I met him. At least six months before they got married. Not exactly a hopeful sign for a long-term relationship.'

'Did you tell her?'

'I attempted to. But she wouldn't listen. Said I must have misread the situation.'

Jacobson scratched the top of the cat's head with his forefinger. Where he'd read their pleasure receptors were located.

'You said on the phone you thought something like this could happen?'

'I knew he hit her. She told me herself, didn't really try to hide it. But she didn't do anything sensible about it either. Like give the creep his marching orders via a good lawyer. Once you let a man do that to you, there's no telling where it's going to end.'

Jacobson asked her about Kevin Holland. She said she'd never met him, only knew what Jenny had told her.

'Sounded like another hare-brained relationship, to be honest with you. But at least it would have got her away from Gus. Some women, Mr Jacobson, are under the illusion that all the available options for happiness revolve around men. Jenny is – was – a case in point.'

She offered him a cup of tea, said she had real as well as herbal. He apologised for his rudeness on the phone, explained non-specifically about why. She was the nicest member of the public he'd encountered all day. Not just that she reminded him of his daughter: she actually seemed to have a brain on her shoulders. All the same he didn't

147

have time. And besides he never drank any kind of tea. Only coffee.

The cat followed him all the way to the doorway. She picked it up quickly.

'Otherwise he'll follow you,' she said.

Jacobson thanked her for getting in touch, headed back to his car. He'd always laughed at those cat food ads on TV. The ones where independent single women shared contented lives with sleek-looking, male-substitute felines. But Sheila Hunter was alive and well on a summer's Sunday evening; her petless friend, Jenny Mortimer, was the one whose dead body was lying in the morgue.

Kerr had been back in time for tea. Back in time to play Bob the Builder with the Lego set. Back in time for bath-time and bedtime. Afterwards, Cathy opened a bottle of Tesco's Pinot Noir and the two of them sat out in the patio, the sky still light, the temperature still warm. The Kerrs' house was at the very back of the estate. Beyond the hedge and the fence at the bottom of their garden you looked out on to abandoned farmland. It wouldn't last for ever, Kerr knew. The developers already had their planning permission for a second estate. But so far the bulldozers had remained elsewhere and the field beyond had become a temporary haven for field mice, rabbits, birds.

Cathy was talking to him about nursery schools, the pros and cons of starting early. He lifted the glass to his lips, made an effort to concentrate on what she was saying. To be a successful cheat, he realised, you had to be a little bit schizoid. Able to move at will from one specific view of the world to another and opposite one. *I know your work's important to you*, she was saying now. *But you're important to us too*. She leant closer to him, nestled her head on his chest. She could be like this sometimes. Sulk one day, act as if everything was fine between them the next. He put his free arm around her shoulder, rested his hand lightly across her breasts through her T-shirt. His wife beside him, his children safely asleep. Only a fool, he thought, would risk all this solidity, all this real feeling, for something as fleeting as a love affair. The trouble with life was that you only got to live it once. There were no alternate takes, no rewinds. Another one of God's little jokes: infinite possibilities but strictly limited choices.

Jacobson needed to speak to DCS Chivers, needed to reach a decision on whether they were booking Mortimer and, if so, when. The problem was that Chivers wasn't on his home number, wasn't answering his mobile. Which meant only one thing. Jacobson bit the bullet, got the address from the desk sergeant, turned his car back towards Crowby. As he neared the town centre, he could see his destination looming up just past Flowers Street: white and pristine, faintly unreal.

The Palace of Varieties tried hard to transubstantiate itself before its ghost was finally laid to rest. Cinema, bingo hall, failed night club. Jimi Hendrix had caused a sensation there back in the sixties during his first ever British tour. Bottom of the bill, almost unbelievably now, to Lulu and a forgotten band called Amen Corner. Jacobson had missed the rock god, had taken Janice to see the new James Bond at the Odeon on the same night. Sometimes he felt he'd missed the sixties all together. The seventies too most probably. They'd finally knocked the building down in 1990. The site had functioned as an overspill car park until the Millennium Apartment Complex had come along, opening its doors for business on the first working week of the new century. Projects like the Millennium were the latest flavour of the month. Upmarket town house style accommodation. Reclaiming the streets for the successful. Mackeson, the property speculator who Janice had left him for, was funding a rival development over at the old hat factory.

He crossed the mezzanine, took the shiny lift speedily to the top access level. Christine Salter herself opened the door, ushered him in. At first he thought gratifyingly that Schmoozing Greg had called a party but no one had come. In the light, immaculate rooms even the furniture seemed lonely.

'Everyone's up in the roof garden. Just follow me,' Mrs Salter said, smiling like an overstuffed hawk. 'Frank, isn't it?'

She was an imposing presence. A little bit more weight on her part and the Salters would be a McGill seaside post-card couple come to life. Greg with the bottle of brown ale, Christine – *Chrissie* – with the rolling pin. Up the danger-ously polished spiral wooden staircase and out on to the roof, Jacobson found himself incongenially sandwiched between one of the Assistant Chiefs and the Superintendent of the Traffic Division. He was probably the lowest ranker there, was probably supposed to have been flattered by the invitation card he'd binned contemptuously the other morning. But he was *police*, a detective, not some back-slapping company man. Even if the Veuve de Vernay *was* chilled to perfection, it was still Crowby down there; not Covent Garden or Park Avenue.

He spotted Chivers over by the barbecue, extricated himself in that direction. Fortunately, Greg Salter wasn't in the vicinity. Jacobson had last spotted him near the stair-well, smarming Dud Bentham's wife – or trying to. The way Jacobson saw it they had two choices: charge Mortimer tonight or kick him out for now, wait till the DNA results came in. For Chivers, the PR factor would be uppermost. Maybe even more so than usual. After the town centre riot, two fuck-ups in the final week of your career would start to look careless. When Jacobson got near to him, he was waving about a skin-blackened sausage on a stick, trying to get it cool enough to eat.

'If we charge him and then the DNA lets us down, Frank, we'll have size A eggs all over our faces,' he said. 'We might even get Slingsby mouthing about wrongful arrest.'

Let him mouth, Jacobson thought.

'On the other hand, a definite arrest will kill the bollocks in the press,' he replied. 'All that guff about Robert Johnson being a suspect.'

Chivers bit hesitantly into the sausage. Off duty in August, he was an unlikely looking chief of detectives. Shorts, old-fashioned leather sandals, a blue and white matelot shirt, short-sleeved. The outfit struck Jacobson as ludicrously nautical for a gathering on the roof of a building a hundred miles from the nearest salt water. He drank down the last of his glass of sparkly, waited for the great man's verdict. Chivers wiped his bottom lip with the side of his hand before speaking.

'Good point, Frank, good point. Let's have the courage of our convictions, eh?'

The argument from PR. How to play with the hierarchy and win.

PC Ogden watched the brown liquid pouring into the plastic cup, filling it to the brim and then spilling copiously over the sides into the drip tray of the MIU drinks dispenser. Extra strong, extra white, extra sugar: he'd decided he needed the lot. He'd read somewhere that sleep deprivation could be more useful than torture as an interrogation technique. Eventually the guy tells you whatever you want to hear – says whatever you want him to say – just to get his head down, just to close his eyes and dream. After a weekend like this one, he didn't find it difficult to believe. He'd spent ten days solid on the late shift, he should have been off duty from Saturday morning till Tuesday. But the fact of the matter was he needed the overtime and he needed it badly. His fiancée Becky had set her heart on a four bedroom semi with a garden. What was the point of something smaller, she'd said, something that they'd only have to move out of when they started making babies? Great: but with the deposit for the mortgage *and* the honeymoon in Thailand, the money had to come from somewhere. So he'd put in a full extra shift yesterday, had even answered the call-out for the town centre disturbance this afternoon. He lifted the cup out of the machine, coffee spilling down his hand. Fortunately, it wasn't that hot. He should have gone back home to bed then really. But seeing how he was up and about, the chance of the overnight police watch out here had seemed like a good idea at the time. It was a piece of piss after all: one constable covering the grounds, the other stationed comfily inside the MIU. Every two hours, you changed over. While you were doing the portacabin stint, you could more or less nod off anyway – as long as you kept your radio handy.

He tried a mouthful of the coffee. All you could really taste was the sugar. Probably just as well. He put the cup down on the table and yawned. When he'd made his first walkabout earlier, he'd noticed a nice little workman's hut over where they'd been landscaping. It hadn't been locked and there wasn't much of value inside. Spades, rakes, a hosepipe. An old wooden chair in the corner. Even when it was his turn to patrol the grounds again, he thought dozily, there was sod all to stop him grabbing the odd forty winks inside.

Alan Slingsby had long since gone home. Gus Mortimer was alone in his cell. The custody sergeant had brought him a cup of tea an hour ago, had told him he was lucky they hadn't put one of the toerags from the Son of the Bronx in beside him for a bit of company. He was stretched out on the narrow, uncomfortable bench when he heard two sets of footsteps drawing near, followed by a pair of eyes staring through the peephole in the door that the police called the wicket.

Jacobson had detoured to Wellington Drive, had showered, changed, watered his cheese plant, read for a while, tried – unsuccessfully – to phone his daughter. He'd long ago learnt the value of keeping a suspect waiting, letting them sweat. He glanced at his watch: eleven thirty pm. The custody sergeant opened the door. Jacobson stepped into the cell.

'No need to get up, Gus,' he said. 'No hurry. Stay right where you are if you like.'

Mortimer got up anyway, sat on the edge of the bench, stretching his shoulders, hands under his thighs. Jacobson coughed, cleared his throat. It was as close as the job came to theatre. You didn't want to fluff your lines.

'Angus Anthony Mortimer. It is my duty to arrest you for the murder of Mrs Jennifer Mortimer. You do not have to say anything. But it may harm your defence if you do not mention now something which you later rely on in court.'

Chapter Fifteen

Monday morning. Jacobson and Kerr stood outside the portacabins watching the search party organise itself. Jacobson was wearing his lightweight linen suit and a white shirt. His daughter Sally had helped him pick the suit in Next at the beginning of the summer; the fruit of one of her sudden, unpredictable trips to see him. At least, he told himself, it was still recognisably a *suit*. Most of the force's detectives were going round in shirt sleeves or T-shirts, looked like they were ready for the beach at Waikiki. Even Kerr appeared to have ditched his regulation leather bomber jacket for the duration, had turned up for the second day running with a black baseball cap pulled down on his forehead. Like a desperate politician on walkabout. Jacobson knew he could never be that casual, had no intention of trying. A detective should wear a suit. End of.

The plods started to fan out on either side of the house. The outhouses and grounds would be searched first, then the interior. It made better sense that way: do the open air work in the coolest part of the day while the sun was still low. They'd managed to pull in around fifty uniformeds all told, were using the old Crimestoppers single-decker to ferry them around. If *chez* Mortimer yielded sod all, they'd decamp over to Planet Avionics. Mick Hume and DC Barber were over there already with Sergeant Ince. Making sure nothing got moved or disturbed in the interim.

Jacobson called Emma Smith back at the incident room on his mobile. Smith and Williams were collating statements and generally cross-referencing the inquiry's documentation. Jacobson had also asked them to chase up the DNA results.

'Any news, lass?'

'They're promising to fax us something by twelve noon, guv. Earlier if they possibly can.'

He asked her to let him know just as soon as. DNA testing was outsourced nowadays to a commercial forensic laboratory in Birmingham. You Can't Fit Up Quicker: DS Kerr's suggestion for a promotional slogan. Your money back if not entirely satisfied. But in point of fact they were just as slow as the old Home Office lab had been. Performance-related bonuses notwithstanding.

Jacobson shoved the phone back in his pocket. It was a bit of a pig really. Mortimer's court appearance was scheduled for eleven o'clock, was likely to be over and done with before they knew for certain whether he'd raped or rough sexed his wife in the run up to her murder. Technically, the strength of the case against Mortimer wouldn't be an issue. Ultimately the police could charge anyone with anything: it was for the Crown Prosecution Service to decide afterwards whether the charge would stick, whether the case was worth taking to trial. But in Jacobson's experience, denial of bail and the suggestion that the police were in possession of cast-iron evidence had a strange mutual tendency to follow each other around the courts.

Robert Johnson drank a cup of tea and studied the Picasso print on the wall. A woman with her bits all over the place. Nose here, tits there. The guy had made millions apparently, was still shagging them on his death bed. Maybe nobody had ever checked the quicklime down in his cellar. The secretary on reception was the usual probation service cow. Probably employed the ugliest old bats they could find in case some nutter tried to jump them. The door to her left

opened. *Come in, Mr Johnson*. He left the tea unfinished –
cat's piss anyway – and walked through. Marshall, the top
man, the beardy git who'd booked him into the hostel, had
taken on his case personally. Very flattering. Until further
notice, he had to get here, nine thirty sharp, six days a
week. Otherwise it was straight back to the looney bin.

'Settled in all right?'

Johnson took a seat, nodded. There was another Picasso
on the wall behind Marshall's desk. The famous one.
Guernica.

Marshall offered him a cigarette. *No thanks*. Marshall
put the pack away before he spoke again, didn't take one
himself either. What was it they called the technique?
Mirroring. That was it. If the client smokes, you smoke. If
he crosses his legs, stretches his arms, *you* cross your legs,
stretch *your* arms. The usual phoney baloney.

'I take it you've seen your press coverage?'

Johnson nodded again.

'No – ehm – identity problems at the hostel?'

'Nope. Keeping myself to myself, isn't it? Low profile.'

Always say the minimum, make like you're as thick as
they think you are.

'I had a couple of job possibilities lined up for you,
Robert, eh, Robbie.'

Correct first name. Well done. We *have* been reading the
jolly old case notes. He crossed his hands behind his neck,
leant back in his chair, watched Marshall do the same.

'But I think we'll have to cool that idea for a week or so
under the circumstances. Wait till the papers lose interest.
Too risky otherwise. The question is what are you going to
do all day in the meantime?'

'There's always the library, Mr Marshall. I've been
thinking of taking up the OU, see if I can get credits for the
year I did at Derby.'

Like I want to get screwed around in some Macjob or
other. When I could be ogling blondie, getting to know her
a bit better.

156

Johnson left the building the way he'd come in. Via the rear entrance and out through the service alley at the side of Morricone's Trattoria. It paid to be careful with the media snooping around, Marshall had said when he'd made the arrangements. Across the street, a scruffy looking geezer was reading the small ads in the window of a newsagents. The guy who was hanging around the library the other day, the one who seemed to live somewhere around Mill Street. If that's not the tail, he thought, then I'm not the real Shady and Miyamoto Musashi wasn't a real warrior.

Kevin Holland, Chris Parr and Wendy Pelham were sitting round the kitchen table. Parr had made a pot of tea, Wendy Pelham had rustled up scrambled eggs on toast. Kevin Holland ate what was put in front of him without really noticing. It was the first thing he'd eaten in twenty-four hours. He rarely drank alcohol but he'd sat up late last night again with Parr. Between them they'd got through the best part of three litres of Bell's since Saturday.

'I should have been there,' he said for the thousandth time.

It had been his constant refrain all the way through. In between the reminiscences, the recounted hopes, plans and dreams. *I should have been there. I should have realised. If only.*

'Jesus, Kevin,' Parr said, slurping his way through his second cuppa, his eyes bleary. 'Nobody could have predicted this. None of us saw it coming.'

Wendy Pelham shoved another piece of toast on to Holland's plate.

'What Chris says is right, Kevin. You've got to stop blaming yourself. Jenny wouldn't have wanted—'

But she left the cliché to hang in the air unfinished. As if ashamed by her words, their banality, their total, useless inadequacy. She tried again: 'At least you'll be able to see her properly today.'

'I'll come with you if you like,' Parr said. 'I don't feel like opening up the shop anyway.'

157

'Thanks Chris,' Holland managed to reply.

The pathology department had released the corpse to the undertakers the previous evening. When he next saw Jenny she would be in the funeral parlour. Her eyes closed, her hair combed, her face restored to a ghastly kind of beauty by the mortician's skill. He knew he should try to remember her alive. Smiling, laughing, inviting him to come to her. But all he could see in his head – all he'd ever see maybe – was the twisted, battered body he'd glimpsed for a few seconds before the coppers had dragged him away.

Nothing new at the Mortimers' residence. Inside or out. Jacobson decided that Hume and Barber could supervise the Planet Avionics search without his assistance. He cadged a lift back to Crowby with Kerr, got himself dropped off outside the Magistrates Court. Mortimer's actual trial would be scheduled for a Crown Court venue. Not necessarily in Crowby. The defence might argue his chances for a fairer trial elsewhere: Coventry maybe or Leicester. If the case got that far of course, if the underachievers and incompetents at the CPS didn't lose their court materials in a wine bar or the back of a taxi. But the Magistrates Court was good enough for now. Jacobson struggled his way upstairs against a sea of humanity headed in the opposite direction. He assumed at first they had something to do with the Sunday riot but it turned out that the rioters had already been dealt with. What had actually happened was that Alan Slingsby had asked for a private hearing on Mortimer's behalf and the solicitor acting for the police had failed to sustain his objection. The stipendiary magistrate, District Judge Holmes, had just this minute obliged by ordering the public out. Jacobson showed his ID to a harassed usher and slid into a pew in the empty gallery.

The clerk of the court read out the murder charge in a flat, clipped voice that would have been dull by the standards of the shipping forecast. Mortimer, standing four square in the dock, was asked to plead.

'Not guilty. I'm an innocent man. I—'

Holmes looked down from the bench wearily.

'A simple not guilty will suffice.'

Jacobson checked his pager discreetly. Still no word on the DNA. Still no word on the baton. Alan Slingsby moved predictably for bail. Holmes asked if there were police objections. *There were m'lud*, the police solicitor replied, proceeded to itemise them. He was inexperienced, nearly inaudible; the best they could find at short notice in the middle of August maybe. It was just as well Jacobson knew what the grounds were already because he found he was only catching one word in ten. What it amounted to – scantily – was that murder was a serious business. Anyone of us might wish to avoid its consequences if we should be unfortunate enough to commit it. Mr Mortimer after all was a wealthy man, with property and connections abroad.

Slingsby waited until his opponent sat down, returned unflappably to the fray. 'M'lud. My client isn't going anywhere. He has an important business to run here in Crowby. Many local people – whole families – are dependent on that business for their livelihood. The charge against him is a serious one, yes. But so are the consequences in financial ruination if he is remanded in custody for a substantial period of time. The presumption of innocence—'

Holmes gave a practised, professional cough.

'Thank you, Mr Slingsby. I think the court gets the point. Let us – if we can – leave the pudding under-egged.'

Slingsby's ineffectual adversary muttered something by way of a counter response but Jacobson wondered whether Holmes even heard him at all this time. His voice trailed off and silence ensued while the stipe deliberated. Jacobson played with the cuff of his left sleeve. If you came from the Bronx or the Son of the Bronx, you could get banged up on remand just for shoplifting: Whispering Willie – by appointment to the taxpayer – had most likely just failed to keep a murderer, albeit a Captain of Industry, off the sunny summer streets. Holmes scribbled something in a notepad then put his pen down forcefully. The noise of it echoed upwards: as close as a British judge got to banging a gavel.

'Bail at seventy thousand pounds. Surrender of passport. To report to the police twice daily by their arrangement. Good morning, gentlemen.'

Jacobson made his exit while the principals were still collecting their papers together, while Mortimer was taken back down to the holding cells. He had no intention of running into a triumphal Slingsby in the foyer. The only consolations were the stringent bail conditions. That plus the immediate fact that Mortimer wasn't out of doors quite yet. There were still the surety arrangements, the paperwork; a couple of hours spent cooling his well-shod heels.

The DNA results spluttered out of the incident room fax machine five minutes after Jacobson got back there. They were followed by a summary which came impressively close to English. It looked like the chances of a positive DNA match between the semen removed from Jenny Mortimer and the swab taken from her husband's mouth were stacking up nicely: odds of less than one in twelve thousand that Gus hadn't done the dirty deed. Jacobson knew it was nothing to get too cock-a-hoop about. What they'd sent was little more than a snapshot, a preliminary indicator to get the customer off your back. The full RFLP analysis – rigorous and thorough enough to put before a court – would take two or even three weeks' work to complete. But this was a lot better than nothing. A lot better for instance than saying it definitely *wasn't* him, that it couldn't be him in a billion chromosomes. He phoned Mick Hume: they were about halfway through the search but so far they'd found bugger all. Across the pedestrian precinct, the clock on the white tower of the town hall chimed noon. At their desks, Emma Smith stifled a yawn, DC Williams didn't bother. Synchronised boredom.

'Come on then,' Jacobson said. 'No canteen lunch today. The poppadoms are on me.'

Mr Behar's, his favourite Indian restaurant, had undergone a refitting. White pine everywhere, less cluttered, more light, more space. Predictably, Jacobson had preferred it the way it had been before. But at least the painting of Ganesha was still on the wall, newly supplemented in fact by a shiny brass statue of the elephant god atop the bar in front of the Kingfisher and Stella Artois taps. Emma Smith went for a mixed tikka with salad. Williams, a curry novice, stuck with the chicken biryani. Jacobson ordered a lamb dansak, hot and sour.

'You reckon we've got him then, guv?' Emma Smith asked.

'I'll be happier when this sodding baton thing turns up, lass. But yes. I'd say we're nearly there.'

'Back to the thrill of car thefts and teenage burglars then, Em,' commented DC Williams.

Emma Smith rolled her eyes at the prospect, took a sip of the house white Jacobson had persuaded on to her.

Like most of the rest of the country, Crowby had no permanent murder squad: officers were transferred away from other duties purely as and when the need arose. Jacobson had been lucky. Also shrewd. Over several years, he'd built up a decent pool of experienced investigators more or less on the quiet. Kerr, Hume and Barber were his oldest hands but even Smith and Williams had half a dozen cases under their belts now. The A team that dare not speak its name: they'd all be sentenced to five years in traffic if the hierarchy so much as sniffed the possibility of somebody getting good at something. What they called an unhealthy culture of elitism and exclusion. Except for themselves, of course.

'Heat like this, Emma,' he said after a moment. 'Who knows. Might make murder contagious.'

Chapter Sixteen

Kerr and Steve Horton skipped a proper lunch, made do with sandwiches from the canteen, carried them back with them to Horton's cramped, dangerous-looking office. Brave New World, Kerr always thought when he came here – the machines are finally taking over. He'd cleared various hard drives, motherboards, modem cables and a couple of broken keyboards out of the way, had managed to create just about enough desk space to perch on. Horton occupied the only chair, had it jammed up close in front of his terminal, probably risked unconsciousness or death if he was kept away from a computer screen for too long. He'd spent the morning searching the net for everything he could find which had any kind of link to the Action and Resistance web site, had spent the last hour clicking Kerr through the data.

The earliest traces of the site itself turned out to be about two and a half years old, since when it seemed to have functioned steadily but intermittently. The self-styled 'list of shame' had been updated equally sporadically and Gus Mortimer looked to have been one of its most recent additions: January 21st this year if Horton's search results were accurate. Which meant there was less than a fortnight between the initial posting of Mortimer's name on the list and the first of the hate mail reaching his inbox.

Kerr separated one of his sandwiches, a BLT, from its clingfilm.

'A bit weird that, don't you think, Steve?' he asked. 'I mean why this year? Why now? The CentroTech case is five years old. The TV documentary that did for them is even older. The whole thing's a matter of public record for anybody who's interested. Which you'd think would include whoever's behind this little caper.'

Horton was ahead of Kerr, already had two sandwiches stripped bare.

'God knows who decides, Mr Kerr – or how. Probably if you researched all the names, there'd be some kind of pattern. Particular kinds of companies they don't like, or involvements with specific governments.'

He squeezed the two pieces of clingfilm together into a ball, threw it in a flawless arc towards the wastepaper basket.

'Then again maybe they just ran out of new intelligence, decided recycling some stale news was better than no news at all.'

'As likely as anything. I suppose,' Kerr replied, chewing through a recalcitrant slice of steel-strengthened tomato and struck by a new thought.

'What about CentroTech then? Is there much on them in cyberspace?'

It was a whim really. But it was also where Mortimer had been before Crowby; it was background, pertinent. Even Jacobson would have to admit that much.

Horton put down his sandwiches and beamed.

'What d'you want? Accounts, founder shareholders, later shareholders, directorships, other directorships held by directors? As of this week, we've got a direct dial-in to Companies House. The actual database. Not the poxy public subscription access.'

His fingers blurred the keyboard. He was downloading and printing out before Kerr got started on sandwich number two. Welcome to Cyborg Central. Humans at the back please, next to the dodo.

Kerr ran his eyes down the sheet on which Horton had

163

listed anyone who'd ever been a director of the company in neat, alphabetical order together with their addresses as most recently known to the Companies House computer. He supposed he'd been hoping for something or someone with an obvious local connection. Result: nothing. London. Glasgow. Birmingham. Mustique. Anywhere and everywhere but Crowby. Horton said he could run more checks if Kerr wanted. Cross reference to voters' rolls, credit agencies, whatever.

'That would be great if you can spare the time, Steve,' he said.

Thinking: no point discouraging keenness, blind alley or not.

Jacobson drove over to Planet Avionics to witness the last stages of the search. While the police moved systematically through the premises, the work force were making the most of their enforced idleness; sunbathing on the grass outside the building or swelling the afternoon takings over at the pub next to the artificial lake. Faith Lawson, dressed in a black T-shirt and black jeans, was sitting on a low wall near the front entrance, her face buried in a battered copy of *Interview With The Vampire*.

Hume and Barber were ensconced behind the reception desk, monitoring the progress of the search via the CCTV security cameras. On one of the six screens, they were also replaying the video footage from Saturday morning: Gus Mortimer breezing in, waving to the security guard, the timestamp clear and unambiguous: 08-00-04-16 AM. Jacobson had already seen it, had already ordered a copy to be made for forensic examination. You could doctor video easily enough if you knew what you were doing. All it took was a bit of judicious cutting and splicing. He didn't think it was likely in this case but he preferred certainty over probability every time.

'Still nowt then?'

Barber looked up from the screens.

164

'Jar full of speed in some unlucky sod's locker. Otherwise clean as a whistle.'

Outside in the sunshine, a tall figure was walking towards the glass doors. A man about Jacobson's age in an impeccable business suit. They watched him run a swipe card through the appropriate slot and step in.

'Bill Dyson,' he said, introducing himself. Jacobson retrieved the name from his crowded memory banks. The Planet Avionics' company solicitor. He'd spoken to him on the phone yesterday. He sounded out of breath, looked worse: as if a nervous breakdown was an imminent possibility.

'Problems, Mr Dyson?' Jacobson asked.

Dyson helped himself to a drink from the water cooler which stood behind the indoor palm trees, took a couple of mouthfuls before he spoke again.

'It's Gus, Inspector. The company has no problem acting as his guarantor. No problem at all. Only he's insisting on coming back to work, wants to carry on like nothing's happened.'

'Where is he now?'

Dyson looked warily outside.

'On his way over here unfortunately. Stomped out of the Magistrates Court in high dudgeon as soon as the formalities were taken care of. I'm going to go home, take a bath, get rid of the – ehm – police stink and then it's business as usual. Those were more or less his exact words.'

'He wouldn't be doing anything illegal if he—'

'Illegal or not, the board doesn't want it, Mr Jacobson. The managing director – the company's figurehead – awaiting trial for murder but still making decisions, running the show. The shareholders would go apeshit. So would a lot of the staff, one imagines.'

It wasn't a police matter as such, Jacobson thought. He had more important things to worry about. But then he saw the taxi pulling up outside and Gus Mortimer getting out, striding towards the entrance. He was still in the clothes

165

they'd arrested him in, had evidently decided that bathtime could wait. Dyson went behind the reception desk, activated some kind of emergency lock on the doors.

'Let me in Dyson!' Mortimer roared through the plate glass. 'You spineless, fucking moron!'

Jacobson managed to catch Dyson's attention, asked him how far he was empowered to act on behalf of the company.

'Fully. Fully,' he replied, repeating the adverb, clinging on to it like a comforter. 'As of this morning's board meeting, I have complete executive powers pro tem until they get rid of – until the situation resolves itself.'

'In that case I suggest you let him in,' Jacobson said, nodding to Barber and Hume.

Dyson gaped at him, a picture of doubt, puzzlement and work-related stress. It was maybe a whole half a minute later before he undid the locking mechanism and the doors slid open.

'What the hell d'you think you're playing at, Dyson?' Mortimer bawled, throwing himself inside.

He shoved Barber out of the way but he was no match for Mick Hume, ten heavy duty seasons in the police first fifteen. Hume sidestepped behind him, grabbed him in a classic arm lock, forced his head down to ground level.

Jacobson thought about booking him for assault on a police officer, banging him back up again. But there was always the risk that doing so could be made to look malicious in court, might end up donating sympathy points to the defence. He walked over to the doorway. Hume had Mortimer in a different hold now. It looked just as uncomfortable as the first one.

'This is private property, Gus,' Jacobson said. 'The legal owners thereof tell me that you're no longer welcome. If I were you I'd go home and enjoy my delightful and spacious gardens while I still had the chance.'

DC Aston had known instantly that he'd been rumbled. An

unmistakable sliver of eye contact when Johnson had emerged on to the other side of the street, loping out of the alley between the Probation Service offices and the Italian restaurant next door. No more than a split second. But more than enough: he might just as well have gone straight up to him, shaken his hand. You are the Crowby Crawler and I claim my fifty quid. He'd followed him back into the centre of town anyway, keeping his distance, maintaining the pretence. It wasn't necessarily a bad thing, he told himself. This kind of surveillance was as much about deterrence as anything else: Johnson was bound to behave himself if he knew he was being watched. Plus if he still hadn't clocked Dennett, the covert option wasn't completely blown. Not yet anyway. Johnson spent an aimless couple of hours prowling the town centre. Just another underoccupied, unemployed male. He'd browsed the cds in Virgin then HMV, studied form in Ladbrokes without actually getting so far as placing a bet. Lunchtime he'd revisited the Market Tavern; same corner as Saturday, same unappetising cod and chips. Afterwards he'd made his way back to the public library, headed upstairs to the reference section again.

Johnson contemplated *The Book of Five Rings* for an hour or so and then browsed in the Criminology section. It was stuff you could study, learn from. But somehow he wasn't in the mood. At the end of the day, he thought, other people's crimes just weren't as interesting as your own. Along the far wall, for the benefit of idlers, dossers and OAPs, there were half a dozen TV monitors complete with vcrs and head sets. He decided he wanted to see the video of an old BBC TV series, *The Way of The Warrior*; the one where they'd gone out to the Far East, filmed the masters of different styles in Japan, Korea, Taiwan. According to the catalogue, the library still had a copy.

He waited till the old cow of a librarian was busy elsewhere, then approached the inquiry desk. Jaunty. Jack-the-Lad. Give it some. Blondie had a name. Julie

Myers: printed helpfully on a badge just above her left tit. She said the video would be in something she called the back cache. She'd dig it out and bring it over to him if he wanted to take a seat. *That would be terrific, Julie.* Smiling. Remembering to look her straight in the eyes. Treating her to the hint of a wink. *You're a star, a real star. Thanks, Julie.*

PC Ogden was finally on a day off. He drove into the car park in the woodland clearing at the foot of Crow Hill, made sure that he parked well away from the entrance, well back off the road. He recognised the red convertible straight away from the reg number she'd given him on the phone an hour earlier. Also because there were three of them in it. Two men and a woman. Again just like she'd said. He noticed that the guy in the back was big, a bruiser, the kind you didn't want to run into when you were clearing the Bricklayer's Arms after closing time. Maybe agreeing to meet them out here alone hadn't been all that clever, he thought. But then he told himself not be so stupid: they were journos that was all, not the bloody mafia. He did a final visual check before he pushed the door open. Nine cars all told, all the others empty. Picnickers, dog walkers, couples. All out and about in the fresh air. All up the hill or in the woods. He jumped out, walked over quickly, got in the back beside the big guy.

Maddy Taylor was sitting in the front passenger seat.

'Three thousand,' she said, passing back the brown envelope. 'All in hundreds.'

She turned around as she spoke, wanting to see the expression on his face.

He'd asked for eight thousand at first but she'd talked him down, lied that he might not be their only potential source, that they could probably find out cheaper. Investigative journalism my arse, she thought. Mostly – like this one – they just came to you, nervously dialling the contact number the paper carried on page two. Mostly all you did was haggle, fix the price of whatever sell-out was in the offing.

Ogden glanced in the envelope but didn't actually count the dosh. They didn't usually. Either they wanted you to think they trusted you or they were just too embarrassed, too awkward about the transaction.

'The Mill Street probation hostel,' he said quietly. 'CID's got it under surveillance round the clock.'

Maddy said thanks, treated him to her best public interest rap. There was no point leaving him with useless guilt: he was just some ordinary young bloke, not bad looking in an average kind of way. So he'd spent a bit over the odds. Foreign holidays he couldn't afford maybe, or a wife or a girlfriend with a bad credit card habit. Why the hell not? Who wouldn't stuck in a town like this? The beginning and end of nowhere.

Ogden nodded, said he had to be going, beat it back to his car. The reporter was right what she'd said, he told himself. The bastard had it coming anyway. The press would be on to him sooner or later – with or without inside help. Somebody might as well get some benefit out of it. That somebody might as well be him. He shoved the envelope in the glove compartment, turned the ignition. If upstairs didn't want this kind of thing occurring then they should pay decent wages. Not fucking pin money.

Kerr twiddled his thumbs in the incident room. Sergeant Ince phoned him, told him about Mortimer's run in with Mick Hume and that the search was being wound up. Four hours they'd been at the Planet Avionics site but no electric baton anywhere. He put the phone down, mooched down the stairs to the second floor: Steve Horton's office again.

Horton looked up from his computer screen.

'Mr Kerr. I was about to call you. I've just found you a nice juicy Crowby connection to CentroTech.'

Kerr parked himself on the same narrow band of desk space as before.

'London European Technology Holdings,' Horton intoned.

He had the air of a magician pulling the rabbit out of the hat. Kerr looked at him blankly.

'London European Technology Holdings,' Horton repeated. 'I didn't twig it at first since I was concentrating on the names of the individual directors. 'Cept of course they'd never been directly represented on the CentroTech board, had they? Pretty much your typical investment company – take a back seat and watch the profits roll in. Anyway when I pulled up the detailed accounts, I found they had a twenty per cent interest in CentroTech at the time of the Channel Four documentary. By the time of Gus Mortimer's court case, they'd sold it on. They made a fair old loss on the deal – but I expect they thought it was worth it to avoid the bad publicity.'

Kerr watched Horton's fingers flashing across the keyboard. There was always the possibility that eventually he'd grasp whatever it was he was supposed to be grasping.

Horton tapped the middle of the screen with his index finger.

'Take a look at that,' he said. 'London European Technology Holdings was a subsidiary of GT EnVision. Still is as a matter of fact.'

Kerr stared over Horton's shoulder at the mass of financial and legal detail. And your point is?

'GT EnVision is the main company in Geoffrey Trayner's financial empire. You know the guy? Boden Hall? MEP? All that?'

Kerr nodded. Finally. At last. Abracadabra.

'What it all means in effect, Mr Kerr, is that Trayner was footing twenty per cent of the bill while CentroTech was illegally manufacturing and exporting stun weapon technology.'

Chapter Seventeen

Julie Myers left the library as usual at five thirty. She crossed the pedestrian precinct, walked along the High Street as far as Boots and then turned right into Holt's Way.

The S Bar was less than a year old, had opened up inside the gutted skeleton of the long abandoned Workingmen's College building. The bar shared the ground floor with Zola's Brasserie, the upstairs floors had been taken over by Club Zoo. Her friend Olivia was already there, had already bought her a Red Bull and vodka, plenty of ice. Julie felt she needed it.

'Cheers Ollie. That's better,' she said after two rapid mouthfuls.

She liked to unwind here at the end of the day. Where everything seemed bright, modern, new: where mostly the customers were young people, smartly dressed, going somewhere. Julie had split up with her boyfriend over the weekend – again. She told Olivia the news.

'Permanent this time, is it?' Olivia asked.

Julie said it was. Absolutely. Definitely.

'This time I mean it, Ollie. I really do. I'm sick of the serious relationship bit. Commitments, plans, doing his laundry for God's sake. From now on it's mindless sex for me. No strings attached.'

'That's my girl,' Olivia said. 'Fuck 'em and forget 'em.'

They both laughed. They talked about what else had

happened over the weekend, who was seeing who, who wasn't, what they might do for the bank holiday. Olivia said her sister and her mates were thinking about hiring a minibus, heading down to Newquay.

'Bloody long way to go for a shag,' Julie said, cracking up again.

It wasn't until they were ready for more drinks, until she went up to the bar herself, that she noticed him. Standing over at the far end, near the expresso machine, clasping a bottled lager to his chest, left leg crossed over right below his knee; that cocky way lads had. Not that he *was* a lad. Thirty if he was a day. She wondered how long he'd been there. Whether he'd followed her from the library. He was standing next to her before she had time to deal with her change, scraping all of it out of the tiny plastic plate, seeing no reason to leave a tip for the snooty, anorexic barmaid. *Julie*, he was saying, *so this is where you go when the library closes.*

'And what if it is? What's it got to do with you?'

Julie, Julie. I'm just making conservation. I'm new in town. Smiling like a shark fin.

He's not bad looking I suppose. Not very well dressed though. Still in that fake Nike vest. Surprised they let him in really. They wouldn't usually. Because of the hot weather maybe. *Your friend a librarian too, is it?*

'No she isn't. As if it's any of your business.'

Maybe he just likes to show off those muscles.

People don't realise how important libraries are, don't you think, Julie?

'And you do I suppose? Expert are you? No job to go to. Nothing better to do all day.'

He was confident. She had to give him that. Probably didn't want to marry her either. Or meet her mother.

'Well if you're determined to follow me around like a sick puppy, you might as well give me a hand with the drinks.'

My pleasure, Julie. My pleasure.

*

Jacobson's briefings in the Jenny Mortimer case were starting to live up to the dictionary definition: a short statement of any kind. Gus Mortimer would be reporting to the Divisional building twice daily, he told them: nine thirty am and seven thirty pm. When he came in tonight, Mick Hume would quiz him on the itinerary of his journey from home to work on Saturday morning. Mick seemed to have built up a bit of a rapport with Mr Mortimer. Laughter. DC Barber would be the second interviewer; the others could go home. The uniformeds would do a sweep search of Mortimer's alleged route tomorrow am. He'd also authorised a public appeal – asking the residents en route to take a close look around their patios and water features. It should make the TV news programmes tonight, especially as it meant they'd be able to report the electro-shock torture angle.

'I don't see it as vital anyway,' Jacobson concluded. 'As long as the DNA results hold up, I think there's a strong enough circumstantial case. We've done just about everything we can. It's up to the CPS to make the decision to prosecute or not.'

Kerr accepted Jacobson's invitation over to the Brewer's Rest afterwards. They found themselves a shaded table out in the beer garden. Jacobson supped a third of his pint down then lit up a B and H. Kerr tackled him about Geoffrey Trayner's financial link to Mortimer's old company.

'Looks like he was less than straight with you Frank,' he said.

'Par for the course with these fat cat bastards, old son,' Jacobson replied. 'Only not necessarily true in this case. Who's to say how much Trayner knew in detail about where one of his subsidiary companies was putting its money? And even if he did, what bearing has it really got on the case? Suppose Trayner and Mortimer *do* go further back than Trayner's letting on. So bloody what?'

Kerr pulled his chair back, avoiding the blue wisps of Jacobson's cigarette smoke.

'So maybe he owes Mortimer something for carrying the can. For keeping Trayner's name and reputation out of the court case.'

It sounded weak even as he said it. What exactly did he have in mind? That Trayner had disposed of the electric baton for Mortimer maybe? In all probability, the worst Geoffrey Trayner MEP had done – assuming he and Mortimer *were* more closely connected than Trayner had let on – was to deny any personal knowledge of the problems in the Mortimers' marriage. He was about to change the subject when Jacobson surprised him, very nearly astonished him.

'Drink up then, Ian,' he said. 'Better get a move on if we're calling in on Boden Hall. You're off message. Your dad's the one who's supposed to find capitalist conspiracies everywhere, not you. But I must admit I like to see the sweat on a rich man's face when he realises he's not completely above the law.'

Kevin Holland had been at the funeral parlour most of the day, had stayed on into the evening. Chris Parr had hung around for an hour or so then driven back to Longtown. He'd said just to call him when he was ready. He'd drive back over and fetch him. The woman in the office had said take as long he liked. There was always someone on duty here round the clock anyway. It wasn't unusual. He shouldn't worry about it.

The room was small, cell-like. There was an arrangement of dead flowers in front of the frosted window. There was the coffin resting on a table, a single chair in front. The coffin lid was propped up against the wall with the name plate visible: Jennifer Mortimer. When he'd first known her, first loved her, just the saying of her name held magic. *Jennifer. Jenny. Jen.* Now the two stark words had been rendered terrible by context. The first shock had been how small she looked lying there. As if death had already diminished her. He'd found himself checking for her feet, suddenly panicked that they weren't there – that they'd been cut off in some grisly, unauthorised medical experiment. He cried for a long time and then he talked to her. Then he cried again, talked again. He couldn't have said how long for. When he was talking to her, he didn't know if he was speaking out loud or not. Mostly he said sorry. Sorry he hadn't been there. Sorry he hadn't thought it through. Sorry he hadn't taken her with him to Wiltshire. Sorry he hadn't come back sooner. Sorry he hadn't met her years ago. Before Mortimer. Before even Eric Brown. Before any of it. Sorry and sorry and sorry.

They'd painted her face, put her into some kind of pale-coloured gown. Her hands were clasped in front of her. They'd combed her hair forward, made her like a blonde version of that old Victorian painting. *Ophelia.* But the painting had lied, had failed to conceal the presence of the living woman within the pose of the corpse. This was the real, terrible, empty thing. There was no life in it, no Jenny in it. He'd taken hold of the cold hands, kissed the cold lips, had never known the full, awful meaning of coldness before. He'd brought roses with him. Red. And his Kahlil Gibran. The burial, the public ritual, would be the afterthought. This was *his* ceremony.

When he was finally ready to leave he scattered the roses over her body, read from the book. He still didn't know if his words were out there in his mouth – or held captive inside his brain.

> Only when you drink from the river of silence shall
> you indeed sing.
> And when you have reached the mountain top, then
> shall you begin to climb.
> And when the earth shall claim your limbs, then shall
> you truly dance.

At the rear end of Boden Hall, the cottage garden had been ripped up and replaced by a small but deep and perfectly blue

175

swimming pool. Elaine Trayner performed a perfect scissor dive from the springboard and swam to the side. In reaction to the sudden appearance of Kerr and Jacobson she reached out of the water and retrieved her bikini top. Geoffrey Trayner was stretched out in a sun lounger, a jug of something sangria-like by his side, a copy of Zadie Smith folded cover-upwards over his stomach. The Scandinavian au pair who'd shown them through the labyrinth of the Hall itself, reappeared with a couple of extra glasses.

'Thanks but no thanks,' said Jacobson.

He told Trayner the outline of what Kerr and Steve Horton had uncovered.

Trayner removed *White Teeth* from his midriff, sat up in the lounger. As Jacobson had predicted, he went for the easy explanation.

'Sorry,' he said. 'To be honest, it never really entered my head when I spoke to you yesterday. It's stale news after all. Must've been, what, five years ago? I'm sure you'll appreciate that neither myself nor my senior executives are in a position to micro-manage every single transaction of the subsidiaries. Whenever we got wind of the allegations in the television documentary, the instructions went straight out from head office – sell, sell, sell.'

Kerr's eyes were involuntarily full of Mrs Trayner, climbing silkily out of the pool, then reclining on to a giant green towel, adjusting the straps of her bikini. He forced himself to concentrate on what Trayner was saying. You heard a lot about ethical business these days. A contradiction in terms was what his father called the idea.

'So Gus Mortimer wasn't personally known to you at the time?' Jacobson asked.

'No he wasn't. And I still wouldn't say that I know him "personally" now.'

'Bit of a coincidence though surely. He takes the rap for CentroTech in court – admits full personal responsibility – and a couple of months later he waltzes into Crowby, still a top dog. I'm surprised he got another job so easily.'

Trayner was off the lounger now and on his feet. Defending his territory. Keep your hands off my stash. He waved his arms in front of him as he spoke.

'Nothing whatsoever to do with me. Planet Avionics is one company we've never been involved with. Check the records—'

'We're checking,' said Kerr, his eyes back on duty.

'As for how Gus Mortimer was able to walk into another directorship, it's like I said yesterday – he's a highly competent player with a top-notch track record. Anyone can make an error of judgement—'

It was Jacobson's turn to shift his eyes away from the fleshy delights of Trayner's trophy wife.

'An error of judgement, Mr Trayner,' he interrupted. 'Is that what it was? Selling the tools of the trade to torturers.'

Trayner bridled.

'Now hold on, Chief Inspector. I'm not sure I like your tone. It's always easy to criticise from the outside looking in. When you've no responsibility to shareholders. When the taxpayer coughs up your salary every month—'

Trayner was standing with his back to the pool. One hefty shove and he'd be in there, Jacobson thought, getting his shorts wet, enjoying a chlorine aperitif.

'I don't give a fuck *what* you like, Mr Trayner. But the next time I need to talk to you about the background to a serious arrestable offence, I want the full card, not the edited highlights.'

Trayner's jaw gaped wide enough for the *Titanic* to berth in his hygienised mouth.

'Enjoy your evening, *sir*,' Jacobson added. 'We'll see ourselves out.'

DCs Aston and Dennett couldn't choose between an ancient episode of *Frasier* and a programme about the building of the Egyptian pyramids that Dennett reckoned he'd seen before. In the end they watched neither, started half-heartedly on a gloomy game of chess.

'There are times when this job's not worth a jot,' Dennett said. 'Stood in a bar, watching a sexual pervert chatting up two young lasses. And not allowed to lift a finger.'

Aston had tailed Robert Johnson openly to the S Bar, had hung blatantly around outside. Only Dennett had been able to risk actually going in. As far as they could work out, although Johnson had sussed Aston he was still unaware of Dennett. Seven twenty he'd finally left the bar, had made it back to the hostel in time for his eight o'clock curfew with barely minutes to spare.

Aston castled.

'That's the trouble with this whole operation, mate. Unless or until he does something illegal, it's strictly hands off.'

Dennett fingered a pawn but didn't move it.

'Wish I could say the same for Sick Boy. Practically had *his* up her skirt.'

Aston stood up, walked over to the fridge.

'Same thing applies. He can *shag* her so long as it's by mutual consent. So long as it's not in the hostel. So long as it's not between the hours of eight and eight.'

He threw Dennett a can of Stella Artois, took another one out for himself.

'If it was me, I'd be looking for a bird who works nights.'

For once Dennett didn't laugh, didn't seem to be in the mood to see any kind of funny side. He caught the can deftly, pulled on the ring top, still didn't move the pawn.

'It if was me,' he said, 'I'd top myself for what I'd bloody done.'

Gus Mortimer had driven back from his interview with Hume and Barber in time to see the MIU being towed off his property. The police forensic team had completed their tests and the police watch was no longer necessary. He stood in the porch watching until both the lorry and the

178

trailer had disappeared completely through his gateway. On the way over, he'd thought about visiting the funeral parlour but had decided against it for tonight. He hadn't wanted to risk running into one of her friends or – worse still – her lover. He'd phone them in the morning, make a specific time for him to see her.

It was starting to get dark but the evening was still warm. He stepped out of the porch and turned leftwards, his shoes scrunching heavily on the gravelled drive. It was ridiculous, he knew, but somehow he couldn't face being inside the house on his own. Not just yet anyway. It hadn't bothered him earlier when he'd come home, washed, changed out of the clothes they'd arrested him in. But there'd still been a couple of uniformed police around then, keeping an eye on things. They'd seemed civil enough. Just doing their jobs. It was the CID you had to watch out for, he'd realised. Slimy. Devious. Out to trip you up the whole time. Now there was only himself here. Monarch of all he surveyed. It occurred to him to drive over to Birmingham, book into a hotel, pick up some tart, put his problems on hold. But he knew it would be a bad move. From now on he'd have to think before he acted, try to weigh everything up in the balance. Anything that smacked of callousness – that didn't look like remorse or regret – could end up being used against him in the trial.

He walked round the side of the house to the start of the gardens behind. He wondered what his chances in court really were. Alan Slingsby had already started talking about trading down to manslaughter, pleading guilty to lesser charges. *With good behaviour and a strong plea in mitigation, you could serve less than five years*, Slingsby had argued. Brilliant! But Slingsby wouldn't be doing the time, wouldn't have his career falling about his ears, wouldn't be slopping out his piss in a bucket.

He crossed the top lawn to the start of Kevin Holland's Arabic garden or whatever the hell it was supposed to be. It was just like Jenny to take up with the hired help, he

179

thought. Once a bleeding-heart *Guardian*-reading school-teacher, always one. That had been the problem really. Nothing in common apart from screwing. Which hadn't lasted. Which never did. And to think he hadn't even kicked her out once he'd got sick of her. He'd let her stop on, hang around, discover herself or whatever it was she did all day, her handbag conveniently full of the credit cards he paid for. All he'd asked in return had been for her to look decorative on the odd social occasion; to act with a bit of bloody decorum.

He turned his head and looked behind him. A couple of bats were swooping over the canopy of the swimming pool building. They were only just visible against the darkening sky. When he did finally go indoors, he'd need to check that the security lighting system was still set properly. It was going to be another mild night. He might come back out again later – take the midnight air – if he couldn't sleep, if he still couldn't get on with being there on his own.

At least keep her fucking legs shut.

Chapter Eighteen

Tuesday 21 August **thirty pence** weather: still hot tv/radio: page eight
BRITAIN'S BRIGHTEST DAILY

THE DAILY UPDATE

Exclusive: <u>Update</u> reporters in riot town track down pervert

<u>Update</u> memo to Crowby Crawler: WE KNOW WHERE YOU LIVE

SPECIAL REPORT BY MADDY TAYLOR – see pages 3, 4, 5
Is This The Face of Evil? – see page 2

<u>Update</u> **front page Opinion**

Today inside this special edition, the Daily Update exclusively reveals the address where serial rapist Robert Johnson is living at your expense. The Daily <u>Update</u> believes that **you** – the great decent British public – have a **right** to this information. We are also publishing exclusive **photo** images, using the latest computer technology, which show how the Crowby **Crawler** may have changed his appearance to escape public attention. The Daily <u>Update</u> believes in responsible journalism. Yesterday we condemned the Sunday **rioting** in Crowby. But we also understand the **anger** of local people in the fear-stricken Midlands town. In his notorious reign of terror, Robert Johnson committed eight brutal **rapes**. The question that we believe must now be answered by those responsible for setting him free is whether <u>cont'd page six</u>

The first editions of the *Daily Update* rolled off the presses at midnight. The story was picked up by the national radio and television news networks barely minutes later. By six am, Maddy Taylor had been speedily chauffeured back to London, was flirting idly with a premier league footballer as she waited to make her appearance on BBC Breakfast TV. She would be debating issues of press freedom with a junior minister from the Home Office and the editor of *The Times* just as soon as the latter made it to the studio through the morning traffic chaos. Result with a capital R, she thought, feigning an interest in the footballer's holiday experiences in the Dominican Republic.

An hour later, the first protesters started to arrive in Mill Street. Outside the bail hostel they were met by two full lines of riot-kitted police. DCI Chivers was on megaphone duty again.

'Go home or go about your business. Robert Johnson is not here. I say again – Robert Johnson is no longer at this address. You must clear the area or face arrest.'

His words were difficult to hear above the drone of the ITN helicopter overhead. The police had denied the press direct access to Mill Street at ground level but the sky was more difficult for them to control.

DC Aston stared down at the unfolding scene from the window of the stakeout flat above the Atlantis laundrette. He was starting to wish he'd never had anything to do with this particular operation. Behind him, sitting on an old chair and on the grubby sofa respectively, DC Dennett and Robert Johnson were watching the aerial view from the helicopter as it was transmitted live on to the TV screen.

'All this fuss for a waste of space like Sick Boy here,' Dennett said.

Aston didn't bother to reply, kept his eyes on the street outside. In the span of a few hours they'd gone from monitoring Johnson – the job he'd signed on for – to *minding* the bastard for his own protection: the one he most definitely hadn't.

'If there was any justice, we'd chuck him out there, let him take his chances with the rabble,' Dennett tried again.

Aston still didn't answer. Surely the fucker would see sense now, he was thinking. Surely he'd fuck off somewhere else so that he – Aston – could fuck off himself. Back to good old Brum. There was an operation against one of the city's big crack and heroin cartels in the offing. That was a lot more his style than nannying an out and out scumbag, a piece of pure human detritus. Johnson said nothing either, just stared intently at the television, his eyes barely seeming to blink.

Colin Marshall, the Chief Probation Officer, emerged from the front door of the hostel. He was a bulky figure to Aston but only a jerky dot on the screen for Dennett and Johnson. A thinner looking man in a T-shirt and jeans emerged with him. Aston clocked him as the warden of the hostel. Another scruffy looking do-gooder, he thought. Marshall took the megaphone from Chivers, repeated the same message the DCI had already given.

'The police are telling you the truth. Robert Johnson is no longer here,' he barked distortedly. 'Please respect the residents' privacy and leave.'

The crowd was less than fifty strong. Most of Sunday's hardcore hotheads were still banged up. Either they'd been sentenced to ten or fourteen days for their part in the disturbance or they'd been remanded for Crown Court trials on more serious charges. Also, unlike Sunday, there'd been no luxury coaches laid on this time. They'd had to make their own way there, risked making themselves late for work if they happened to be in jobs. After some token heckling, they began to drift away. There was nothing thrown this time, no diehards launching themselves at the police lines. Not even John and Linda Barnfield stayed for long. Barnfield had banged the door of his Audi loudly shut as they'd driven off. Before that, he'd contemptuously torn up the parking ticket that PC Barry Sheldon – exhibiting his customary sensitivity – had stuck under the wiper blade for parking on double yellow. By seven forty the numbers remaining had shrunk to no more than half a dozen or so bored-looking youths.

Chivers threatened them with arrest via megaphone again.

'No need to shout mate,' one of them answered back.

The others laughed but their hearts weren't really in it. Soon they were out of there, shuffling around the corner, seeking diversion elsewhere. Aston watched the helicopter do a final swoop above the area and then head away. On the TV screen, Dennett and Johnson saw the programme cut back to the studio and then on to a fashion feature: fantastic new ideas in beachwear. Dennett switched the set off, got up and boiled the kettle. Pointedly, he only made two mugs of tea, carried one of them over to Aston, still at the window. They gave it another half an hour and then Aston called the cab company.

Ten minutes later, three men, one of them gripping an Adidas holdall in his left hand, piled into the yellow CrowbyCab which had pulled up outside the laundrette. Dodgy geezers up to no good: Robert Johnson was the least scruffy looking of the three. The taxi executed a U-turn and drove off unnoticed and undetected by the small huddle of reporters still on the corner, Mutt and Jeff amongst them, still scratching their heads, still wondering where next for their story.

In his fifth floor office, Jacobson spread the *Update* out on his desk and studied the report in detail. They'd uncovered the address all right but the computer-generated photo images were well wide of the mark. There were four of them leering out of the second page. Although one had Johnson's close cropped hairstyle to a T, none of them gave a good likeness of his features. Certainly not good enough to single him out on the street. Jacobson rubbed his hands along the wooden arms of the ageing, creaking chair which had followed his career around the building, enjoyed the brief sensation of coolness on his palms. The chair had survived two office furniture upgrades in recent years. It was unlikely to survive a third, he thought gloomily. From sheer habit he checked down the latest Incident Sheet and then listened to his voicemail: nothing pertinent in either case. He was thinking about fishing out his kettle, making himself an unpalatable cup of black instant coffee when DCS Chivers phoned through. They were ready. He swivelled himself out of the chair, decided to take the lift down, save his legs for later.

Dud Bentham, Chivers and Colin Marshall were already in the meeting room. Bentham at the top of the table, Chivers and Marshall to his left and right. Jacobson sat down next to Marshall. At least, he thought, he still had a long way to go before he would be as overweight as 'Santa', a man for whom a six-course lunch allegedly constituted a diet. Greg Salter came in last, took the chair next to Chivers, gave profuse apologies for lateness that nobody had actually asked for. Bentham himself started the case conference, outlining the hastily agreed plan personally – as if to give it the ultimate seal of official approval.

A space had been found for Johnson in a bail hostel in Manchester, his home area, and the Probation Service up there had agreed to supervise him.

'As of this morning, gentlemen, he's off our patch and out of our hair,' he said.

'Happy to go is he, sir?' Jacobson asked.

'He's no choice in the matter, Frank,' Bentham answered. 'Under licence means under licence. Crowby has become an untenable location for the time being so he *has* to agree to move on. It's really as simple as that.'

'*For the time being*, sir? You mean we might be facing this whole pantomime again in six months or a year?'

'It can't be ruled out Frank. But Colin here thinks it's unlikely.'

Well that's reassuring then, Jacobson thought.

'Once he's settled in back there—'

Marshall started to speak but Jacobson cut across him.

'And you don't think we're just giving in to mob rule then, sir?'

Bentham gave a weary shrug. The force's Atlas, burdened with all its cares.

'In an ideal world, Frank, with infinite time and resources, then another outcome might have been possible.'

Chivers tried out the PR angle he'd probably be selling for public consumption later in the day.

'Giving in? Certainly not. Achieving only a partial success? Regrettably yes.'

The plan was as much news to Greg Salter as it was to Jacobson but that wasn't about to stop him nodding enthusiastically in support.

'Plus Johnson himself has had to recognise that Crowby may not be a suitable environment for his rehabilitation. That in itself must be some kind of an achievement surely.'

'Surely,' Jacobson repeated ambiguously.

Salter was possibly more adept than even Chivers at putting an instant spin on unforeseen developments: without a doubt the old boy's worthy successor. He decided to stop arguing. He had more immediate tasks to worry about anyway. Wrapping up the Jenny Mortimer case for example.

'And the timescale?' he asked.

'DCs Aston and Dennett are with him at the railway station right now,' Chivers replied. 'They'll take the ten thirty train, travelling incognito, deliver him personally to the Manchester force. I'd rather he was going by official police transport of course. But the fewer who know the better. Apart from our two Brummie colleagues, no one outside this room knows what the arrangements are *or* the destination.'

It was Jacobson's turn to nod. He was with the hierarchy on this one at least. Maddy Taylor was smart but she wasn't psychic. Someone on the force must have blabbed. Someone who would most likely get away with blabbing. This time anyway.

After the meeting broke up, Jacobson made his way down to the custody area where he'd arranged to meet DS Kerr. He'd scheduled the morning briefing for ten o'clock, untypically late. But – the stun baton search apart – the case was winding down to the paperwork stage anyway; somehow it had seemed to make more sense to do it after Mortimer's morning check-in than before. Once Mortimer clocked in, he'd be brought to one of the interview rooms for another quizzing. They had no new questions to put to him but in Jacobson's experience it never did any harm to go on putting the same old questions whenever you got the chance. Even the most skilled liars sometimes contradicted themselves at the fifth or sixth or seventh attempt to keep their stories straight.

Kerr was standing next to the custody sergeant's desk. So, unbidden by Jacobson, was Alan Slingsby. He certainly worked for his money, you had to give him that. Slingsby chanced his arm and asked what was happening in the Crawler situation.

'None of your business, old son,' Jacobson told him.

'As bad as that,' Slingsby replied, smiling blandly. 'Never *was* my business, fortunately.'

Slingsby and Associates had declined to take on Robert Johnson as a client at the time of his original arrest. The only instance Jacobson could recall of Slingsby turning down a high-profile case. He was well off out of it as far as Jacobson could see but he kept the thought to himself. Kerr checked his watch: nine thirty on the dot. After a minute or two of mildly awkward silence, the custody sergeant phoned up to his counterpart on the main desk, announced that so far Mortimer hadn't entered the building. Jacobson waited until exactly nine forty then asked him to check again. A moment later the sergeant put the phone down frowning.

'Still no sign, guv,' he said.

Jacobson looked in his notebook. Mortimer had given the police two land line numbers at his home address as well as his mobile. The sergeant dialled each one in turn. Jacobson, Kerr and Slingsby watched his face intently as he did so. So far nobody was answering.

'Better get a patrol car over there pronto, old son,' Jacobson ordered.

In the railway station concourse, Johnson and Dennett sat at the back of the Costa coffee franchise while DC Aston bought three tickets to Manchester Piccadilly. One single, two Super Saver returns. Dennett dunked a chocolate croissant incongruously into a cup of Twining's English Breakfast Tea. Johnson stared at a large size cappuccino he'd yet to lift to his lips. Dennett seemed to have got fed up with taunting him, had finally ran out of insults maybe. Aston came back via WH Smiths, a *Mirror* and a *Telegraph* under his arm as well as the *Update*. He kept the *Telegraph* to himself, put the others down on the table. Dennett picked up the *Mirror*, turned to the sports pages.

Johnson continued to stare at the cappuccino, left the *Update* where it was. He knew what it was they wanted to see, precisely what they were after: the pervo reading his press, salivating at his latest coverage. No way he'd give them that – or any other – pleasure. He looked at his watch with infinite slowness. Nine thirty-five. Fifty-five minutes until the train was due. Time to go all the way into the mountain, he thought. Time to come all the way back out again.

Chapter Nineteen

As luck would have it, there had already been a patrol car in the area, less than three minutes away from the scene and able to set everything quickly in motion. Jacobson and Kerr got there in Kerr's Peugeot only minutes ahead of the first forensic contingent. Robinson – with a much shorter drive from the hospital – had already performed a swift initial examination, was waiting for them in front of the house. It would have been quicker to go round by the left-hand side, out past the conservatory. But somehow Jacobson felt more natural taking the path in the opposite direction: along the gravel driveway to the far end of the house and then crossing the lawns behind. The same way they'd done on the first morning of the inquiry.

Gus Mortimer's dead body lay face down on the winding but incomplete pathway behind the swimming pool building. The watering can that Jacobson had kicked over on that first morning lay lopsided only a few feet away on a caked mound of dug-over earth. Mortimer's corpse was sprawled and twisted. One hand was parallel to his left ear, the other stretched out in front of his head. Both palms were flat to the ground. His left leg was bent high and sideways at the knee. The effect was of a sniper crawling under barbed wire or of a swimmer weirdly stranded on dry land. His trousers and underpants had been pulled down to his knees and the backs of his legs were a dark welter of bruises.

When Jacobson and Kerr bent down to take a closer look, they saw that the face was a mess too, the eyes bulging and bloodshot, the lips split and swollen, the nose savagely broken. Next to the body on the edge of the path was something they'd only seen in photographs until that precise moment. An electric stun baton. The full monty version, a foot and a half long, a leather wrist strap handily attached at the user's end.

Jacobson and Kerr moved out of the way, stood over beside Robinson. Most of the socos were still clambering into their space suits, getting themselves ready for business. But one of them was already in action, had grabbed the camera and started making the video record. Jacobson watched him filming as he spoke to Robinson.

'They say first impressions count for a lot, old son.'

Robinson seemed to be watching the soco with the camera too.

'Early days, Inspector, as Professor Merchant would no doubt tell you—'

'But?'

'But as follows – probably. One: a complete surprise attack. Almost certainly from behind. Almost certainly out here in the garden. Almost certainly using the stun baton to subdue the victim and get him quickly, helplessly, to the ground. Not a difficult thing to do with fifty thousand volts to play with. Two: once down, the assailant's given him a fair old kicking, especially around the head and face.'

Kerr asked him about the undone trousers and pants. Robinson paused not quite imperceptibly before he answered.

'My guess is that at some point the stun baton was used on the anus and genitals. Whether before or after death, it's probably impossible to say.'

Jacobson felt a sudden stab of pity, even for Gus Mortimer.

'So what did for him then? The shocks or the kicking?'

Robinson strove for matter-of-factness – for the non-melodramatic – but didn't entirely succeed.

'Neither actually, Inspector. I'm virtually certain the specific cause of death was asphyxia due to strangulation. Exactly as per Mrs Mortimer.'

Talk about overkill, Jacobson thought. After a moment, he asked – inevitably – about the time of death.

'Full rigor. Areas of permanent lividity. Subject to the post-mortem, we could be looking at an elapse of as much as twelve hours.'

Robinson glanced at his watch as he answered.

'As a first stab, I'd say somewhere between ten o'clock and midnight last night.'

Jacobson dabbed his forehead with his handkerchief. It was going to be another hot, August day. He called up Mick Hume on his mobile. Hume and Barber were en route to the crime scene in Hume's car.

'Change of plan, Mick,' he said. 'Get over to Kevin Holland's gaff. Make sure he's there. If he is make sure he stays there. DS Kerr and myself are on our way over.'

'Kevin Holland,' Kerr said. 'You don't think that—'

Jacobson had already started walking back towards the house.

'Know anyone else with a bigger king-size motive, Ian?' he asked.

Kerr considered reviving the debate about the Action and Resistance web site, considered querying where the hell Kevin Holland was supposed to have got a stun gun from. But for the moment at least he decided to let it go.

'You're the boss, Frank,' he said: uncharacteristically – fooling no one.

Wendy Pelham and Mick Hume were matter and anti-matter. If even their fingertips ever accidentally came into contact, whole galaxies would implode, the known universe would find itself short of a couple of million stars.

'They've no right to be here,' she said for the fifth or sixth time, staring malevolently up at Hume from the white sofa.

'I thought I told you to button it,' Hume said, filling the lounge doorway with his bulk.

According to her probation report, her father was a surgeon somewhere, had forked out for an education at Harrogate Ladies College. She'd cut herself off from privilege: Hume had never enjoyed the pleasure of the option.

'Leave it, Wendy,' Chris Parr said from the big cushion next to the big rubber plant. 'They'll be gone soon enough.'

Kevin Holland sat next to her. So far he'd said nothing at all.

DC Barber was over by the window.

'It's like I say,' he said, trying to restore diplomatic relations. 'There's been developments in the case. DCI Jacobson needs to speak to Mr Holland. Nobody's forcing anybody else to hang around if they don't want to.'

He glanced behind him, saw Kerr's car pulling up in front of Chris Parr's dayglo ambulance.

'Anyway he's here now.'

Hume went out into the hall, let them in.

'Make yourself at home, why don't you?' Wendy Pelham called after him, 'Fascist bastard.'

Jacobson got straight to the point, asked Kevin Holland what he'd been doing and where he'd been the night before.

'I was with Jenny until around nine,' Holland said.

He was holding a snapshot-sized photograph of Mrs Mortimer in front of him with both hands, never took his eyes away from it.

Jacobson stared at him, nonplussed.

'Kevin means he was over at the funeral parlour,' Chris Parr explained.

Kerr noticed that Parr was still wearing the same red T-shirt as he had on Saturday afternoon.

'I drove him over there in the afternoon, picked him back up later. Well, he was in no state to be driving himself, was he? Afterwards, we came back here. Sat up talking for another couple of hours—'

'More than a couple of hours, Chris. Must've been after midnight anyway before we called it a night,' Wendy Pelham interjected.

Parr glanced at her for a moment then turned to Jacobson.

'Yeah. That'll be it then. We've been hitting the whisky a bit, Kevin and me.'

Jacobson asked her if she'd been here when Parr and Holland had returned from the funeral parlour.

'Yes I was if it's any of your business,' she answered. 'Why are you harassing us? Why do you need to know?'

But Jacobson had already moved on to his next question.

'Is there anyone who doesn't live here who can confirm any of this?'

'There was some lady on duty at the funeral parlour,' Parr said. 'She was still there when we left. What's it all about, mate?'

Without going into the details, Jacobson told them that Gus Mortimer had been found murdered at his home.

'You mean he's dead?' Holland asked, looking up for the first time, letting the photograph drop through his fingers.

The two states are usually connected, Kerr thought. He was leaving the questioning to Jacobson but he was following every expression on every face.

'I mean somebody murdered him, Kevin,' Jacobson said.

Holland grabbed both of Wendy Pelham's hands as if he was about to pull her to her feet for a dance.

'He's dead,' he said. Then: 'He's dead. He's dead. He's fucking dead.'

They brought Holland down to the Divisional building once he'd calmed down, let Chris Parr go with him. It was in his own interests to let them have a DNA mouth swab, Jacobson had argued. He wasn't being arrested. Nothing like. It would help eliminate him. That was the thing. Besides, if their story checked out, he had nothing to worry about anyway. Absolutely nothing. They waited until he'd changed his clothes first. They needed to examine whatever

193

he'd been wearing last night. Same reason, Jacobson told them. But Wendy Pelham had still thrown a wobbly as they'd driven off. ACAB, ACAB, she'd chanted from the doorstep. All Coppers Are Bastards. Holland and Parr had gone in the back of Hume's car. Kerr and Jacobson had followed behind. Kerr lost them in the traffic at one point, didn't share Hume's disregard for a red light. But are all bastards coppers? Jacobson had wondered idly. No, he'd thought. The world was in a much more parlous mess than that.

Chapter Twenty

The incident room. Eleven am. Jacobson parked his arse on a bench next to the photocopier and defied the No Smoking ban which extended throughout the building with the sole exceptions of the cells and the interview rooms.

'A revenge killing then?' DC Williams asked.

'It's the only obvious motive we've got,' Jacobson said. 'Why we need to go over Holland's story with a fine-tooth comb.'

'But if he did it, guv, there'll be forensic indications all over the crime scene anyway. Whatever yarn he's spinning,' suggested DC Barber.

Jacobson lit his B and H, put the precious silver lighter back in his pocket.

'By forensics, I expect you mean DNA evidence, old son. Ian, care to explain?'

'Benign Transference is the technical term,' Kerr said. 'The problem with DNA evidence in this case is that Kevin Holland has been a frequent visitor at the Mortimers' place over a period of months. Dropping skin cells, hairs, fibres of clothing every single time. It's totally in keeping with him being completely innocent if somehow some of that stuff found its way on to Gus Mortimer's body or his clothes.'

'Especially as he was shagging old Mortie's wife on a regular basis,' Mick Hume added, evidently relishing the

195

crudity of the remark. Not to mention the scoring of a considerable point over Barber.

'So why bother with the mouth swab and his clothes at all then?' Emma Smith asked.

Before he answered, Jacobson inhaled, exhaled, tipped his ash in the wastepaper bin.

'It's still the standard procedure regardless, Emma,' he said. 'Besides, it never does any harm to put the suspect under a bit of legitimate pressure. If he's – if they're – telling the truth, he'll stick to his story. If he's guilty, well, it might encourage him to fall usefully to pieces.'

Kerr watched the DCs' heads nodding in unison. Welcome to Frank Jacobson's murder squad master class, he thought.

Jacobson stood up now, getting into his stride. Barber and Hume would repeat their tour of nearby properties, he told them. Even if nobody had seen a bloody thing when Jenny Mortimer had been murdered, it was stretching credulity that a second killing had been committed without some curious neighbour noticing something out of the ordinary. Some vehicle they'd never seen before. Something that didn't look quite right. Smith and Williams would escort Kevin Holland and Parr back to Longtown, would take detailed signed statements from both of them plus from Wendy Pelham.

'Be my frigging guest,' Mick Hume muttered under his breath but still audibly.

Jacobson told them he'd be checking out the funeral parlour alibi personally.

'As for DS Kerr here. He's off to Birmingham to see the *first* Mrs Gus Mortimer. Who might – or might not – be as fair to behold as the second.'

Hume was virtually in party mode by now, started whistling an old, best forgotten tune: 'Some Guys Have all the Luck'.

The bypass was as clear of traffic as it was ever likely to

be. Provided you avoided the holiday routes and the town centres, driving on Britain's roads could sometimes turn into something very near to a tolerable experience in the summer. With a third of the working population on holiday at any one stage and the schools closed, the rush hours were less nose to tail than normal. You could even get in and out of the suburbs without the clogging presence of the four by four armies: the middle-class mums ferrying their brats to school in oversized people wagons. He shoved John Lee Hooker on the tape deck, rolled down the window, blasted 'Boom Boom' and 'Crawlin' King Snake' out into the hot air. After a while he had to cut it, realised he couldn't think deeply enough with his left foot tapping on the floor, his left hand slapping an imaginary bass.

Visiting Gus Mortimer's first wife was an idea Jacobson had cooked up the previous evening as they'd driven back from Boden Hall. An instance of his thoroughness: soaking up the background, looking at all the angles. Arguably it was a less urgent task in the light of new developments. But Kerr wasn't about to make the argument, was happy to stick to the arrangement. Birmingham was an hour's drive each way. Alone in the car. Time to think things through for himself. Sometime since Sunday afternoon, Jacobson had given the hate mail and the web site nutters serious and proper consideration – no matter what offhand impression he'd tried to create to the contrary. If he was rejecting a possible line of inquiry, it was because he'd *thought* about it, weighed up the possibilities. It was how he worked, why he was good at what he did. But for some reason – or maybe for no *reason* – Jacobson had failed to convince Kerr that they really were an irrelevance. The sick meal that someone had made of Gus Mortimer's body with the help of a stun baton hadn't been any more persuasive in that respect either.

He made good time, was clocking the M42, junction six – the NEC and the airport – barely forty minutes later. Ten minutes after that and he'd reached his turn off: junction four. To an outsider like Kerr, anywhere between the city centre and the surrounding motorways constituted the thing, the entity, called Birmingham. Yet in the redolent imagination of the locals, this area – Knowle, Hockley Heath, Eastcote – was as far removed from Handsworth or Queensway Circus as Richmond or Henley-on-Thames was from Hackney. This was where you fucked off to when you were doing all right, when you'd raked in enough from the Great Wen to fork out for a bit of upmarket leg room. Lebensraum: I have no more territorial demands. Once you were off the motorway and on to the hidden circuit of B roads which criss-crossed the green, open countryside or ran along the walled-off and fenced-off edges of wooded estate land you felt you'd travelled a long, devoutly justified road from the Bull Ring. Wherever the toiling masses were, they weren't here. Wherever they were toiling, they toiled for *you*.

Kerr pulled on to a grass verge to check his map. With the engine switched off, he could hear birdsong in the distance, listen to the fat bumble bee buzzing around his wing mirror. A horse and rider trotted past on the other side. The horse was a tall handsome bay, the horsewoman young and blonde. She smiled prettily at him as she rode past. Even though he was his father's son, he couldn't find it in himself not to smile back, not to enjoy the soft, idle clipping of the horse's hooves.

Hucklecote Cottage was a mile further on, set back from the road at the end of a narrow but strictly private lane. Who knew if sometime in the past there hadn't been a cottage here – of clay and wattles made. But if so, no longer. At the top end, the lane expanded into a neat driveway in front of a substantial, modern house. It was modest in relation to *chez* Mortimer but palatial in comparison to Kerr's own gaff. Barbara Russell – for eight years Barbara Mortimer – was watering a hydrangea, the flowers pink and fulsome. She watched Kerr getting out of his car with a non-committal eye.

They talked in the coolness of an air-conditioned kitchen, drinking Earl Grey from china cups, Brian Eno somewhere indefinably in the background. *Music for Airports*. She knew most of the story from the papers, even knew that Mortimer was dead. With the national press booking out the Crowby Riverside Hotel, even overspilling into the Travel Lodge and sundry B and Bs, it was maybe less than totally surprising that Mortimer's death had achieved a rare accolade for the provincial murder of a male victim: the Radio Four bulletin at noon.

'I can't say I'm sorry, Sergeant,' she said. 'Although maybe for her, maybe a little.'

She'd used to work as an exhibitions organiser, she told him, had taken it up again in fact since the divorce. She'd met Gus at an electronics trade fair in Stuttgart in the mid-eighties, had been involved with him for a dozen years all told. She should have known better from the start really. She'd pinched him from another woman herself. At first she'd thought Jenny was just another conquest, just another bit on the side she could turn a blind eye towards.

'The next thing I know *I'm* the one being turfed out. Surplus to requirements as they say.'

Kerr asked her about the divorce settlement.

'Generous enough in the end. The house in Crowby was only half-built at the time. He held on to that, I became the sole owner here.'

'Was he ever *violent* towards you?'

She sipped her tea before she answered.

'No. I could tell he wanted to be a couple of times. Especially after he started seeing *her*, started seeing me as in the way. It's something he has – had – in him all right. But he wouldn't have dared. My brother's firm specialises in family law. Just about the best in the country. We'd have taken him for every single last penny if he'd laid a finger.'

'You're sure about that, Barbara?'

She held the cup midway between the saucer and her lips. Her hair was auburn and she was a little taller, a little older. But she didn't look so different from Jenny Mortimer that you wondered why the same man had been attracted to both. Meet the old wife. Same as the new wife.

'Completely sure,' she said, 'Certain.'

Kerr had toyed with the idea of taking a look at the CentroTech factory, fifteen miles north west on a godforsaken industrial estate somewhere off the A34. But when it came to it, he crossed the flyover at junction four, circled the roundabout, headed back along the motorway in the direction of Crowby. He told himself he really didn't have the time, that there were more quantifiable jobs to be getting on with. But the impulse niggled at him all the way. The same urge that had caused him to kneel over Jenny Mortimer's corpse on the first morning of the inquiry. Sometimes you needed to see something to know the truth of it. Barbara Russell had claimed that she'd known completely nothing about the company's sideline in illegal exports for the torture trade until the media had got hold of the story. She'd denied ever having seen Gus bring any samples home. Which might really mean – if she was lying – that she'd rather not have seen, rather not have known. She was bitter about the break up certainly. Still. But she hadn't seemed unhinged, hadn't looked very likely to have extracted an elaborately vicious revenge five years after the fact. Besides she had an easily checkable alibi for the time frame: she was just back from the World Plastics Convention in Miami, she'd shown him the paperwork *and* her airline boarding cards. A taxi had driven her home from Birmingham International about midnight. She'd even remembered which firm.

He listened to John Lee Hooker again for a mile or so but this was upbeat blues and he had no more mood for it. He'd have put on something by Robert Johnson – the other one, the angel or demon of the dark, brooding guitar – if he'd had any in the car. Which he hadn't. Instead he drove on with only the noise of the engine for company. By all accounts CentroTech was under new management and back on the straight and narrow, had transmuted itself into the British assembler and distributor for a Japanese electronic toy company. He wondered if it mattered a fuck to the people who worked there *what* they made, what ends their labour served. The chances were the workforce didn't give a stuff so long as they got paid. His dad had spent his life – ravaged it, wasted it – in thrall to a different notion, preaching class solidarity. Kerr and his sister had imbibed the arcane language of internationalism, of the proletarian struggle, almost before they could walk. *Workers of the world unite*. But they never had done. Not really. Or not enough. When he'd glanced at the street atlas, it had looked like CentroTech was barely down the road from Hiatts. They were legit too, always had been, supplied handcuffs to bona fide police forces around the world. Yet back in the eighteenth century they'd got their big break from bashing out nigger collars for the slave trade, had carried on manu-facturing leg irons and shackles into the 1980s. His dad had got done for obstruction outside the gates one time, trying to hand out protest leaflets. Kerr smiled at the memory. His mother, the pragmatist, had done her nut when he'd eventu-ally come home, hours late, his dinner burned and ruined. *Leaflets*, she'd argued, *that'll have them quaking on Wall Street*.

There was a double line of lorries ahead as far as he could see. He signalled right, moved out into the fast lane. But if leaflets didn't do it, if the workers refused to play ball, if conventional politics was worse than useless, there had always been other – desperate – measures to hand. And always some prepared to use them. Put up or shut up. *This is war. Draw Your Own Conclusions*.

The connecting train for Manchester hadn't pulled into Crowby until quarter to eleven, hadn't pulled out again until quarter past. Robert Johnson had a window seat opposite DC Dennett. Aston sat next to Johnson, blocking

201

him in. They'd barely travelled a few miles north before they'd been shunted to an abrupt halt. There was a problem with overheating track up ahead, the guard had announced on the PA. That would be the same track, Aston thought, that gets the wrong sort of leaves to deal with in autumn, the wrong kind of snow in February. He hated trains, fucking hated them. Always late, always crowded. They weren't even safe anymore. Traffic jams weren't exactly fun but at least when you were stuck in your car you were in your own space. You could listen to the radio, play music, scratch your balls. There were no snotty-nosed kids, no whingeing businessmen. And only your own mobile would ring. He took the lid off the too-hot carton of coffee, emptied the little white bag of sugar into it. Dennett had wanted tea, Johnson hadn't wanted anything. The service trolley trundled further down the carriage, the harassed steward endlessly repeating that the delay was nothing to do with him but that he was sorry for it anyway. Truly. Madly. Deeply.

Johnson watched them sipping their drinks, reading their papers; still going through the pretence that they weren't coppers, that he wasn't their prisoner. Manchester, he was thinking. What was he going to do there, what purpose could he follow? It had begun in Crowby. Therefore it had to end there. And he'd only done eight so far. One a month, always on the thirteenth. That had been a nice embellishment, an extra little touch. But it was a detail, he realised, that might have to be ditched. As long as the sword was sharp, it didn't matter about the jewels on the handle. Successful strategy depended on change, surprise. You had to stay with the now, flow with the unexpected. It was the final tally that mattered anyway. Take away eight from thirteen and you were left with five. The number remaining until the vow was fulfilled. After that he could stop. After that there would be no need. Thirteen lessons he'd promised. Thirteen demonstrations that there was no meaning in this world. Neither sky above nor earth below, as the Zen classics taught. That suffering wasn't suffering. Only the illusion of suffering. When thirteen had come through, there would be completion. By then he wouldn't even be enjoying it, would know pleasure too as illusion, mere ego distraction. Thirteen brides. One plus three. Four. Plus himself the bridegroom. Four plus one. *Five Rings*.

The train started up again. A stupid-looking old woman, a face like a splayed fish, gaped across the aisle at them.

'Oh that's better,' she said.

As if anybody wanted to hear the demented fucking clutter in her clogged-up brain. The one called Dennett was yawning. The one called Aston was reading the stocks and shares page. Like it made any difference to him on his crap, police wages. Other than you got to put the boot in now and again or snoop around in the odd knicker drawer, being a copper made you no different to any other nine to five stooge. One of millions. A nobody. Suckered. Mired in illusion. The train picked up speed, the countryside rolling past, flat and repetitious. He'd like to go to the toilet if that was allowed. Dennett scowled. *Tuh.* Aston put his paper down, stood up to let him out. *Come on then. But don't take all fucking day.* How it was: Dennett still sitting, still yawning, Johnson standing in the aisle, Aston, having let him out, leaning back over the table, intent on taking the paper with him, reading it outside the bog while he waited.

Bang.

A dull thud really at first. Then screeching, scraping, roaring. Noise louder than noise. Glass in faces. Metal on metal, bending, buckling, breaking. The old woman thrust across Dennett's legs like a lap dancer. And the whole carriage seeming to defy gravity, de-coupling itself from the surface of the planet. Sixty seconds later Dennett was unconscious, Aston was wedged under the table, badly concussed, the old lady had several broken ribs and a fractured collar bone. But Robert Johnson barely had a scratch, felt he could have hung there all day, fingers gripped

securely round an intact support column on the opposite
luggage rack. The carriage had landed on the side where
they'd been sitting. Without thinking about it too much,
letting his body and his adrenalin deal with it, he half
swung, half clambered to the nearest door. A young lad
already had the window down, was already pulling himself
out into the sunshine.

Johnson scrambled in and out of the carriage half a
dozen times in the next half hour, carried or led half a
dozen passengers to safety. Finally, when they were
organised enough, knew what they were about, the
firemen insisted that the uninjured passengers get themselves checked out, leave the rest of the work to them.
If they weren't suffering from shock or exhaustion yet,
then they would be soon enough. The train had de-railed
itself on a part of the line which was less than a third
of a mile across the nearest field from the Crowby motorway services. The ambulance teams set up their emergency
centre in the lorry park. For some reason of efficiency
or other, they were treating the walking wounded in pairs.
Johnson found himself in a treatment cubicle with a para-
medic and the Crowby Branch Manager of the Alliance
and Leicester Building Society. It just seemed natural for
them to hang around together once they'd been given a
basic all clear. The motorway services people had set
their Happy Eater restaurant aside for the train passengers. They sat down, were brought tea. With an urgency
which was probably the first symptom of shock, the building society manager said he was keen to get back to work
if he couldn't carry on with his journey. They'd closed
the northbound carriage for the rescue vehicles but the
southbound carriage was still open – or at least one lane
was. Did he fancy a lift back to Crowby? Only he was
sure they'd be able to find some motorist willing to help
out. Damn it, he'd *pay* for it if they were too mean
spirited to offer. Well, did he fancy it? The Crowby
Crawler finished off his tea with gusto. Oh yes he fancied

it all right, mate. That would be great. That would be absolutely terrif.

The driver took them all the way into Flowers Street. Only too glad to help, he'd said, wouldn't take the twenty spot the manager had tried to press on him.

'Mind how you go,' the manager said to Johnson once they'd got out.

'Same to you, mate,' Johnson answered.

They shook hands before they set off in opposite directions. Johnson headed towards the High Street and the Shopping Centre, whistling softly under his breath. The last guy he'd helped out of the train had been as grateful as the others. Also a bit light-headed, had fainted a couple of times. He hadn't remotely noticed Johnson dipping into his inside pocket as he'd half carried, half dragged him towards the carriage door. The guy had two hundred quid in his wallet and three credit cards. Johnson had taken eighty quid. The kind of sum that made you think you'd been counting up wrong or that you must have spent more than you'd imagined. He only took one of the cards. With a bit of luck it would be several hours, maybe longer, before his rescuee discovered there'd been a fee to pay for services rendered. Half an hour and six stores later, Johnson had transformed himself. Serious trainers, decent jeans, a natty Ben Sherman half-sleeved shirt with another one nestling inside the Calvin Klein carrier bag. His Adidas holdall was somewhere back in the train. Too bad, he thought. Tough shit. He travels faster who travels light.

He made it to the S Bar more or less on time. Quarter past one: five minutes late at most. She was fussing with her make-up, looked like she's only just got there herself. She was off Tuesday and Thursday afternoons, she'd told him. The downside was she had to work Saturdays usually. He'd said in that case meet me here. We could do something with the afternoon if you liked. She'd said she'd think about it.

'You look a bit smarter today,' she said, 'giro come in has it?'

205

'Julie, Julie,' he answered, 'I'm not afraid of hard work. What do you take me for?'

I'm going to take you for everything.

Chapter Twenty-One

Two murders not one. The national press swarming on the doorstep of the Divi. And now a bloody train crash. Seven carriages flipping over in broad daylight, the roof ripped off the buffet car. No one actually killed but lots of injured. Including the two Brummies. Apparently not including Robert Johnson. Unaccounted for, scarpered, missing.

Jacobson sat in his office, tried to take stock. His phone rang: DCS Chivers. *Meeting in my office, Frank. Five minutes.* What the fuck did he want now? Jacobson washed his face in the gents, took the back stairs. Slowly.

Chivers was in his Parker Knoll, Greg Salter was leaning on the window sill. Jacobson plumped as usual for the low, comfy chair in front of Chivers' desk. For once, Chivers cut to the chase.

'Geoffrey Trayner is a prominent local citizen, Frank. His business affairs have no known bearing on your murder investigation. He's got the ear of the Chief Constable for God's sake.'

Better give it back then, Jacobson thought.

'Do I take it he's been bending said ear?' he asked rhetorically.

'Yes, Frank he has. Called your manner belligerent and aggressive.'

'There were bits and pieces of background that

legitimately needed clarifying, sir. If he'd been a less unhelpful fucker—'

'That's just it, er, Frank,' Greg Salter interjected, 'The Right Honourable Geoffrey Trayner isn't a *fucker*, he's a highly successful entrepreneur, a role-model. The force needs men like him on our side, making our case in the corridors of power.'

Jacobson pretended to mull over the point.

'Maybe he could sponsor a few patrol cars,' he said, 'Cops R Us, Old Bill U Like.'

It wasn't funny, he thought, it was already happening somewhere in the South West; Devon or Somerset or some such. And now Salter was here in Crowby. A moderniser. A zealot. From what Jacobson had seen, an arse-licking incompetent: a man destined to go far.

'OK, OK,' Chivers said, moving on, 'But Mr Trayner is off limits without my say so, yes?'

'You're in charge, sir,' Jacobson said.

Possibly it was an answer, possibly it was just an unconnected statement.

Chivers asked for an update on the case, Jacobson told him what he could. His team were doing the standard things – looking for witnesses, checking out Kevin Holland's alibi, waiting for the autopsy results. He had a question of his own. Two words: Robert Johnson.

'Every uniformed patrol's been briefed,' Chivers said, 'A 1 Priority. Plus the CID who were on estate surveillance. We're also circulating his release photographs to forces nationwide. The assumption has to be that he'll have ditched the electronic tag more or less straight away.'

Not that it would tell you bugger all if he hadn't bothered, Jacobson thought. Other than that he was nowhere near the bail hostel. Which was already more than apparent.

'It may be that he's well out of our area by now anyway,' Salter offered, 'In which case he's no longer our concern.'

Jacobson studied his face, still reddened, still pissed off

by Jacobson's sarcasm. Speak for yourself, pal. But you're wrong anyway. Not just about Johnson. Not just about policing. About everything that matters under the sun.

The meeting over, he nipped into the canteen, chose chilli con carne from the menu of daily specials, regretted not substituting chips for the over-boiled glutinous rice. He drove out to the funeral parlour in time to see a cortège setting out en route to the crematorium, the chief mourners in their Sunday best, filing out into the waiting limos, black and polished. Alice Bowlby was a small, lively woman you thought might be happier in a department store or in a noisy, busy office than behind the sombre mahogany counter. She was on what they called days today, would be able to put her feet up tonight. They worked a rota system so that it evened out over the week. One day you did normal office hours, the next you came in for the afternoon but stayed on in the evening, answered the calls from the newly bereaved, let in the mourners who wanted to spend special time with the deceased. She'd been here from two pm until midnight yesterday, had seen Kevin Holland both arrive and leave.

'What time did he get here?' Jacobson asked.

'Two thirty. I remember it clearly. I'd just taken a phone call from a lady out at the hospice whose husband had passed away. We always record the time of the initial phone call so we can track our response.'

She made it sound as if speed was of the essence. Which probably it was: for the relatives if not for the stiff.

'Alone?'

'No he had his friend with him. An older gentleman. Pony-tail and, ehm, a bit of a beer gut.'

Her eyes twinkled.

'The other thing that sticks in my mind was their vehicle I have to say.'

The upshot was that Parr and Holland had arrived in Parr's dayglo painted ambulance. Parr had hung around till about four and then driven off. Holland had been on the premises till ten past nine when Parr had come back for him and they'd both left.

'A long time staring at a coffin surely,' Jacobson commented.

'You'd be surprised, Inspector,' Alice Bowlby replied, 'most people only stay an hour or so, that's true. But every now and then there's someone wants to stay longer. We had a lovely old gentleman a week or so back. Fourteen hours he must have sat there with his wife, bless him.'

'And you're sure he was here the whole time?'

She pointed to her right: an open door and a short, red carpeted corridor.

'He was only just through there. Room three. Never stirred other than to use the gents until his friend came back for him. I offered him a cup of tea on one occasion but I'm not sure he even heard me. It hits some harder than others.'

Jacobson thanked her for her help. He'd need to send one of his officers over some time in the next day or so, take a signed statement. That would be fine she said. She had a son in the army who was thinking of the police when he came out. A good secure job, wasn't it? Jacobson agreed that it was. But not as secure as burying the dead, he thought gloomily. Some time in the globally warmed or asteroid wrecked future, it might be the last sodding occupation of all.

At the back end of the Mortimer's property, a narrow lane connected Brownlea Farm to the main road. It was the third time Hume had called round, the second time for Barber. Each time they'd been more reluctant than the time before. Most of the Mortimers' neighbours approximated in type to the Mortimers themselves. Much of a muchness: under fifty, style-conscious, glib. Whatever it was you called yuppies once they'd achieved their precious career ambitions and goals. Nouveau riche rather than the old, fuddier money you got out on the Wynarth Road. But if they were smarmy and had no very useful evidence to give, at least they were polite. You rarely got off the premises without an offer of a cup of tea or a beer or a cliché or two about what a great job the police did, how much they supported you, how much they valued you. Barber even reckoned there was one woman, her husband repairing a database in Seattle until the middle of next week, who'd taken a shine to Hume. *It's what you call a paradox, Mick,* he'd said. *Probably mistakes your trade mark rudeness for quaint, manly charm.*

The gate to the farmyard was padlocked as usual. The other times they'd called, they'd stopped here, shouted, waited for someone to answer. Now they just vaulted over, Barber swearing at the dirt cloud which enveloped his new Clarks deck shoes. The ageing, yapping collie contented itself with growling, low to the ground, as it followed their progress to the front door of the farmhouse. Yesterday it had made the mistake of snapping at Mick Hume's ankles, had benefited from a kick in the doggy tackle hard enough to dissuade it from a repeat attempt. Brownlea had been for sale, had been bankrupt and ruined, long before the foot and mouth outbreak. It had been farmed by Neville Chapman's family for nearly a hundred years, as he'd used to tell anyone who'd cared to listen. Chapman blamed the government, the EC and the supermarkets for his problems. Whispers in the local NFU were less sympathetic, blamed Chapman himself for his mismanagement, his inability with figures and accounts, his fondness for the bottle. Hume didn't give a toss either way. The scion of Yorkshire mining stock, he hadn't seen many Barbour jackets on the picket line at Orgreave, had somehow missed the farmers calling for compensation when the lifeblood of the pit villages was being sucked bone dry.

Barber thumped his fist on the door, Hume peered through the unwashed kitchen window. There would be no smiles, no welcome here. That was for sure. Chapman didn't care for visitors these days, didn't seem to care about much at all. His shotgun licence had been revoked a few

211

months back on the advice of his GP. His wife had left him, his sons wanted nothing to do with him. He was more or less squatting on the farm until the repossession and resale procedures were finally completed.

After a couple of minutes, they heard shuffling inside, what sounded like the unlocking of several chub locks, the loosening of chains and bolts. Chapman rattled his door open and stood glaring out at them. He could have been any age from forty to sixty. The details of his face were smothered by a black unkempt beard. It looked and smelt like he was accustomed to sleeping in his dishevelled navy blue jersey and torn, baggy corduroy trousers.

'You again,' he snarled, 'what is it with you people? Can't keep from gloating, is that it? Eh? Eh?'

His breath stank of cheap, blended whisky. And behind the whisky something worse: something undigested and gastric, symptomatic in all probability of incipient liver damage.

'My great grandfather came here in nineteen hundred and four. Eh? Eh? Drove a tram in the General Strike by Christ. Could still do a day's harvesting when he was eighty. Eh? Eh?'

On their previous visits, Chapman had said he knew nothing about the Mortimers: he didn't even know their names, didn't know any of those rich bastards' names. All he knew was they'd had the good sense not to be born into farming.

It hardly seemed worth it but Hume asked him about last night – Monday evening – regardless; whether he'd seen or heard anything unusual. Chapman suddenly noticed the collie which had padded cautiously forward to within a couple of feet of Barber. He took an unsteady step towards it but the dog shied nervously away from human contact, ran off, barking, towards the padlocked barn doors.

'Only you lot,' Chapman muttered, steadying himself on Barber's shoulder, then shuffling back into the doorway.

'Think I don't know. Eh? Eh? Bloody damn what d'you call it? Surveillance.'

Hume repeated the word.

'Surveillance?'

'Bloody van. Last night and the night before. Up the bloody lane.'

They asked him what time, whether he was sure. The most coherent answer they got was late – but not as late as midnight – last night, later the night before. Could he describe the van? 'Transit. Eh? Eh? Nobody in it when I looked. Don't pretend you don't know. Snooping around. Gloating.'

Could he show them exactly where?

'Come with me fine lads,' he said, some brain-alcohol interface switching his mood from paranoia to bonhomie in the space of a micro second.

'Know every inch don't we? Nearly a century. Eh? Eh?'

I See You. Someone's idea of a joke. Or more likely someone's complete lack of a sense of humour. In whatever case, ICU, Scotland Yard's Internet Crimes Unit, was less than a couple of years old. The latest attempt to promote national coordination in the investigation of a criminal growth area. Steve Horton had set up a three-way conference call. Himself, DS Kerr and Inspector Susan Gardner from the unit. On the telephone in his shared office, Kerr was the only one of the three reliant on voice alone. Gardner and Horton had patched in a video stream to their computer screens, could wave to each other, smirk from time to time at Kerr's technical blunders. The ICU's main targets were illegal net gambling, share fixing, paedophile rings: but old-fashioned subversion and terrorism also figured in their mission statement.

Gardner told them that the Action and Resistance web site had been monitored for the past twelve months, had been assessed as category six: low-level risk only.

'What that means is that the site gets spidered monthly.

213

We'd automatically log and record any changes or additions but I'm afraid that's about it,' she said.

'So you wouldn't try and trace where it was hosted, who was behind it?' Kerr asked.

She gave him the same spiel that Horton had done on Sunday afternoon about mirror sites, the difficulties involved. Remarkably, he thought, he understood some of it.

'So suppose it *had* been assessed as high risk. What then?'

'Then we'd be into an operation, Ian,' she said. 'We'd email them from an alias ourselves, feed them intelligence, try and lure them into traceable communication.'

Horton realised who it was Inspector Gardner reminded him of. PJ Harvey – but sexier. He flashed her his whitest smile, clicked her email into his address book.

'And you're sure they didn't – don't – merit the full treatment?' Kerr persisted.

'We can never be sure. But our resources are as stretched as any other police unit. We make assessments, hope we get it right.'

Horton chipped in, dressing to impress:

'And there's nothing at all on their site that's not available from public sources, yeah?'

'Steve's right,' she said, 'That's one of our major criteria obviously. The more serious the intent, the more you'd expect information that's *not* in general circulation.'

Kerr was about to hang up, about to thank her for her time, when Horton went back on the pull.

'What about emails posted *to* their mailbox though? Presumably that traffic gets spidered as well.'

'Yes it does but it usually gets an even lower-level classification. Spotty hackers in teenage bedrooms for the most part.'

'But it *would* give an idea as to who's been visiting the site?' Kerr asked, suddenly animated.

On the screen in front of her, she watched Horton giving

214

the thumbs up. Bright lad, she thought, too bad about the over-handsome face.

'Give me an hour,' she said, 'How far back do you want to go?'

Chapter Twenty-Two

Footprints and tyre tracks had nailed as many killers as fingerprinting. You could conceal your fingertips easily enough but you had to transport yourself to the scene of the crime somehow, had to move around once you got there. The socos had checked out the back wall of the Mortimers' place as a matter of standard procedure following the discovery of Jenny Mortimer's body on Saturday morning. It was the obvious point of entry for any intruder with even half a notion of what they were about. The lane behind was a twisting, bending dead-end, only ran as far as Brownlea Farm. Any averagely fit person could scramble up and over the wall. You might get a few cuts and bruises from the leylandii on the way down; nothing to go crying home about. But if they'd found nothing then they'd found something now. They'd re-scoured the area inch by inch, reckoned they'd pinpointed a fragment of tyre track. It was a good twenty yards from the spot where Neville Chapman claimed the International Anti-Farmer Conspiracy had parked their monitoring vehicle. But it had been dark and Chapman by his own admission had been dead drunk.

Jacobson, Hume and Barber stood out of their way. They'd already photographed and measured it from every angle, now they were taking a cast in quick-setting silicone.

'It's definitely something van or transit-like, guv,' Barber said. 'Not a car or a tractor anyway.'

Jacobson nodded. It would be hours before they got the initial expert analysis. Depending on the quality of the track, they could sometimes come up with the precise make and serial number. So often nowadays, his own skills seemed to be needed most in the interstice between forensic sampling and forensic conclusion: the interval where most arrests were made or failed to be made. It was no good knowing definitively who'd done something, he thought, if they'd legged it in the meantime or – worse still – had taken the opportunity to strike again.

'Farmer Giles swears he saw it twice, you say?'

'Sunday night *and* last night,' Hume answered, looking down the lane towards the heavily padlocked gate. 'Not that he'd make a very convincing witness unfortunately. Alan Slingsby'd eat him for breakfast.'

'You believe him though?'

'I believe he saw something like what he says he saw about the time he says he saw it.'

'Peter Piper picked a fucking pepper, mate,' Barber commented.

He shoved his hands in his pockets, sniffed the cool, tree-shaded air. Moments like these were why you stuck it, didn't get some easier, safer job with regular hours and BUPA.

After the S Bar, they'd taken a bus over to the Flowers Memorial Park, got off at the stop on Riverside Walk. Solid Victorian mansions on one side of the street, the walk itself on the other: a tree-lined colonnade between the two bridges which crossed the river into the park. They sat on a bench for a while. He put his arm around her shoulders, pretended to listen to her whinges about her boyfriend, her job, her life. She couldn't understand why anyone would move to Crowby if they had a choice, if they could live anywhere else.

Where would you like to live then, Julie?

'Dunno really, Los Angeles, Hollywood. Somewhere

217

exciting, somewhere really glamorous.'

Dream on Barbie, he thought. As if time passed any quicker for film stars and the glitterati. As if they didn't get old and die, never felt sick and empty. They watched some kids feeding bread to the ducks and a couple of cygnets until one of the parent swans moved in, claimed the buffet for himself. They walked along to the furthest bridge, hand in hand. She was telling him about her mother now, how she was a control freak, how she didn't know why her dad didn't just belt her one, shut the stupid cow up. A couple of middle-aged American tourists were admiring the floral clock next to the bridge. Probably lost, he told her, probably think they're in Stratford. The man gestured with his camera as they approached. He winked at her, stepping forward. *Anything to oblige, isn't it?* Somehow the photo session got extended. The Yank and his wife. The Yanks and Julie. The Yanks and himself. When they were halfway across the bridge, she stopped and turned towards him. She reached up and kissed him full on the mouth, her eyes closed, needy.

The old boating lake near to the middle of the park had been reopened the previous summer thanks to a millennium grant. The algae had been cleared out, the fish restocked, the boats made watertight, brightly repainted. The municipal tea hut had been consigned to the dustbin of history, replaced by a Pizza Express franchise with an open air terrace which extended out over the lake on wooden slats. They'd bought a couple of bottles of Smirnoff Ice and a couple of Budweisers at the Threshers off licence before they'd caught the bus. The sign on the side of the ticket kiosk reminded you that there was strictly no alcohol allowed on the boats. But the guy with the earring who sold the tickets – who didn't always give you a ticket, who pocketed every sixth or seventh admission for himself – didn't give a monkey's, wasn't going to be some killjoy, searching handbags for a living.

He rowed them out into the centre then pulled the oars

out of the water. She clambered over towards him – *mind you don't fall in, Julie* – sat between his legs, her elbows on his thighs, her head resting against his left shoulder. He bit the metal cap off an Ice with his teeth: the kind of trick he couldn't resist. He passed her the bottle, then did the same with a Bud. He sipped the beer, stroked her hair with his free hand.

One of the things he'd had to 'volunteer' for in the hospital had been group therapy. Intensive. Three hours every day, sometimes more. A female shrink had run the sessions for a while. Not old. Not gruesome. All the nutters had wanted to shag her – and worse. *Why do you hate women so much?* she'd asked them, asked him. *Why do you hate me?* Like any game, any con, you learned the rules eventually; understood finally what was necessary. *Resistance. Breakdown. Breakthrough.* That was the theory of it, the script you built the impro on. Denial followed by remorse. Denial followed by guilt. Denial followed by self-loathing. Then they could *intervene*, then they could re-build you in their own, banal image. She'd brought in big scrolls of paper one time, a yard wide. You had to spread them on the floor, write on them with marker pens. *Details*, she'd said. *Details and big writing.* Everything you'd ever really wanted to do to some slag, things that really hurt, things you really had done. Then you had to turn the sheets over, write the opposite, find a positive for every negative.

He finished the beer, opened another one. Her hair smelt of some shampoo or other. Apple or pear or something. What a joke it had all been. How easy to play them, fool them, blag them. You got so good at acting, you almost believed it yourself at the time: in the heat of the moment. Imagine *liking* women, she'd said. And being liked. Visualise it. See it.

She wanted to row them back, she said. So he let her, lying back in the little boat, cupping his eyes from the sun, feeling the rays on his face. It wasn't the first time he'd played it like this, he reminded himself. Romance: picking them up like a normal Joe, a stooge. Sometimes you did the full nut case routine. Stalking, breaking in, total stranger terror. But sometimes you wheedled your way in first, got to know them, got given a key, enjoying all the while the knowledge that you'd be back later: hooded, silent – doing stuff you knew they didn't want, doing stuff that hurt, not giving a flying fuck. It was strategy as much as anything else: why they'd taken so long to link the cases, even longer to catch him. If he hadn't made it easy for them, gifted them the thirteenth of the month scenario, they might never have nicked him at all.

They grabbed a pizza after the boat. She had Perrier with hers, he ordered orange juice. Both thinking the same thing. Neither of them wanting to be pissed, losing the memory of it. At the far end, the park turned into woodland. The approach had been developed into a picnic area. Wooden tables with benches. Litter bins. Sand pits and swings. Families with kids and dogs. She told him how boring Brian had been in the end, how men could be too considerate. With a name like Brian, he said, smiling, his arm around her waist as they walked past the picnickers into the trees. *Opposites*, she'd said. *If not hurt, if not pain.*

For a long time, he just kept it in her, not moving at all, not saying anything. Just feeling it, just watching her face. He'd never seen anyone who looked so alive. You're beautiful, he wanted to say. But he was afraid to break the spell by speaking; the deep, wooded quiet. Despite the orange juice and the Perrier, they dozed afterwards, his head on the bark of the tree, hers nestled on his chest. He was awake bolt upright when they were still two feet away. But there were three of them and it was much too late.

Chapter Twenty-Three

Four pm. Kerr took the return call from Inspector Susan Gardner in the small office he shared with DS Tyler – though rarely simultaneously since they usually worked different shifts, different cases.

'Probably not as much for you as I'd hoped,' she said. 'With category six sites, the tracking software operates more or less randomly. You set the parameters – once a day, once a month or whatever – and it takes a look whenever its little electronic brain feels like it. More of a snapshot than the full picture I'm afraid.'

She had a nice, smoky voice, Kerr thought, but I wish she'd just get on with it.

'Anyway, I'll FTP the raw data to Steve as soon as I put the phone down and he can take it from there. They've been mailed to from all over by the looks of it. Australia. Europe. Canada. The States. I've highlighted any IP addresses that are obviously UK-based. I imagine that's what you're really interested in.'

He said that it was, thanked her for helping out. FTP: how you transferred data between computer systems. IP addresses: the first step in physically locating any computer connected to the Internet. He put the phone down, realising that he must have picked up more on his computer course than he'd imagined. Even though his memory of it was mainly of daydreaming at the back of the class, wanting it to be five o'clock, wanting to be with Rachel for another evening and night time.

Trying to coax a breeze into the room, he'd opened the window, wedged the door wide to the corridor. Jacobson was standing in the doorway when he looked up. Whether for seconds or minutes he had no idea.

'Penny for them, Ian,' he said, entering the room and plonking himself into DS Tyler's chair. 'As if I didn't know.'

Kerr told him about Barbara Russell, formerly Mortimer, about the input from the Internet Crimes Unit. Jacobson grimaced inwardly at the word – *input, ugh* – but let it go, responded with Alice Bowlby, with the forensic developments *chez* Mortimer.

'The tyre angle looks hopeful then. Holland losing it, driving out there, doing the business,' Kerr said.

Jacobson fingered a new B and H packet but kept it unopened. They ought to confer in Kerr's office more often, he thought. It would help him keep the cancer sticks where they belonged: inside the cellophane.

'Which would probably mean Parr and Wendy Pelham are lying to alibi him,' he said. 'They're tight together all right but are they tight enough to cover him for murder?'

Kerr lifted the postcard from the top of his in-tray. The Duomo with a penned-on arrow pointing to the campanile. Tyler was still on holiday, off another week. He glanced at the back. *Too bloody warm, too many crowds.* What did the sod expect at this time of year?

'And how did he come by an illegal stun weapon?'

'That thing,' Jacobson said. 'Whoever's responsible wiped it clean for prints. But why leave it there in the first place?'

'If we assume for the sake of argument that there's some remote connection to the Action and Resistance propaganda, then it could be a calling card – sending the world a message.'

Jacobson put his cigarettes resolutely back in his pocket.

'Or making it look that way, old son.'

Kerr's phone rang before he could reply: Steve Horton.

'The IP addresses, Mr Kerr? I know it's a bit sad but I recognised one of them straight away. A sub-node in the allocated range for the main server at the university.'

They took Horton with them, went in Kerr's car, Kerr translating into English as he drove.

'What it means, Frank, is that somebody logged into the university's network has been mailing the web site.'

Horton sat in the back, clutching a laptop across his knees like an emergency oxygen cylinder.

'It's where I worked before I joined the force, Mr Jacobson,' he said. 'I'd know that particular range of numbers in my sleep.'

Lucky you, Jacobson thought, but kept that to himself too.

He'd expected the campus to be half-deserted in August: he was wrong. It was difficult to park. There was bunting, balloons; crowds milling around in every direction. Crowby was one of the 'new' universities, formed out of the ashes of the old College of Arts and Technology and the Teacher Training College, precariously dependent for its survival on the numbers of students it could persuade through its doors every year. While Oxbridge dons took walking tours in the Pyrenees, had languorous affairs with fresh faced Fulbright scholars from Arkansas or Milwaukee, wrote their research papers or were filmed for documentaries on BBC2, Crowby's mass-market lecturers endured the horrors of Open Day: guiding parents around the halls of residence, finding specious academic reasons why two E grade A levels equipped some embarrassed son or daughter for a university education.

Kerr and Jacobson squeezed past the jazz band in the foyer, followed Horton to the lifts. Jacobson had considered informing Vice Chancellor Croucher of their presence – the textbook procedure – but had decided against it. *No point anyway*, Horton had said, *he's probably not here*. Apparently the university's senior executive – two days a week – was now also a consultant to the board of a privatised water company – three days a week. Jacobson suddenly remembered his run-in with Croucher in the midst of the Roger Harvey case. What it is to be in demand, he thought. He'd read something in the papers about the national shortage of skilled professionals. Naively, he'd assumed they'd meant engineers, doctors, brain surgeons: not committee men with a talent for parking their arse and toadying. Horton led them to the set of open plan offices which formed the nerve centre of the computer network. His mate, Alan Hampson, still worked there, he'd told them, though he was on the look out for a better job. *Everybody there was.*

At least this one looks like a proper geek, Jacobson thought. Slightly built, spectacles, lank, greasy hair. Jacobson and Kerr left Horton and his ex-colleague to it while they went off in search of the Computer Services Manager. Snubbing the VC was one thing. But if the university's computer records turned up information which formed part of a chain of evidence subsequently put before a court, they'd need to demonstrate that it had been legally obtained with the cooperation and agreement of the university authorities.

When they returned, Horton and Hampson were crouched over the printer. Someone had emailed the Action and Resistance web site at three ten pm on the fifteenth of January, a Monday afternoon, but the audit trail had fizzled out before the point where they could finger one specific user – and the system deleted all its backup copies of email every two months. What they *had* got: a list of every user logged in between three and four pm on the day – all two hundred and six of them.

Steve Horton took the sheets of A4 out of the paper tray. They'd correlated each user's logon ID to the person details: name, address, department or course. Jacobson frowned. The ambiguities in what was now a case of double murder were such that he could no longer completely rule out the web site nutter angle. But never in the real world would upstairs authorise the scale of operation needed to *trace* every single user. Much less *establish* which one had contacted the site. Much less *prove* that the contact had been criminally malicious: even if Gus Mortimer had made his debut on the 'list of shame' barely six days later.

Chris Parr and Kevin Holland had given their signed statements at the Divisional building before Emma Smith and DC Williams had driven them back over to Longtown. The nuisance was that Wendy Pelham hadn't been there, had left her housemates a note that she was going into the town centre for the afternoon, that she'd see them later. Smith and Williams had called back at twenty past four, were sitting in the kitchen drinking tea with Parr when she'd finally returned at a quarter to five. Surprisingly, she barely made a fuss, seemed to be enjoying the fact that she was dictating to them: changing her mind over the precise form of words every now and then, watching Emma Smith hastily scrubbing a line out, having to start again. It had been five thirty before they'd finally finished, got her to sign on the dotted line.

'Fancy a quick one, Em?' Williams asked when they were back out in the street.

'Why not?' she replied, wearied by the slog of the day.

The interview had genuinely taken the best part of forty-five minutes. No one back at the Divi would be too astonished if it seemed to take a little bit longer still.

There was a tiny, local pub on the corner. A front-room sized bar and a desultory beer garden out the back. The kind of place that was dying out everywhere except on nostalgic TV soaps. Emma got the round in, watching the morose, overweight barman pulling the pints. Dust-dappled refracted sunlight fell grey-stained through the patterned glass window, making her eyes squint from the contrast when she carried the beers out into the full glare of the garden.

'D'you reckon he'll crack it then?' Williams asked after a deep rich mouthful.

'If Frank Jacobson can't crack it, it can't be cracked.'

They drank on in silence for the most part; just unwinding, taking it a little easy.

'Any plans for the weekend, Em?'

'Yep. Pig out and sleep, if this bugger's over.'

Williams mock-tutted.

'A woman your age, Em. Mid-twenties, knocking on. There should be a nice house husband at home by now. Doing the dishes, ready with the essential oils after a hard day.'

Emma snorted into her pint.

'You ever *smelt* that stuff?'

Anyone else, Mick Hume say, she'd have taken offence. But she knew Williams, worked well with him, trusted him. It was something you needed on the force – partnership, knowing that someone would go right down to the line.

Their pagers bleeped. Jacobson wanted a briefing at six thirty. They drank up. Emma returned the glasses to the bar on the way out. *Thanks*, the barman said distantly, like it had been choked out of him. They walked back up the street to where Williams had parked the car. Without really thinking about it, just a reflex of the job, she glanced at the front door again as they drove past: Wendy Pelham opening it, Faith Lawson and Snake/Mark Jones stepping in.

Chapter Twenty-Four

They'd hauled him away from her before she took in what was happening. His arms pulled behind his back, some kind of blue plastic tie on his wrists. He'd kicked and fought hard, brought the third one to his knees, winded, gasping for breath. But the two burliest ones had him locked between them now, one arm each, his feet off the ground, rushing him through the trees, the branches catching his head, scraping, striking. They were tall, all three of them, one in shorts, the two others in jog pants. That was all she would remember really. And all three with stocking masks over their faces. She struggled to her feet as if weighed by the sleep of a hundred years.

Stop. Don't. Help! What's going on?

But the third one had got to his feet too, held her by the neck, covered her mouth.

'Leave it, girl. You stay here. Stay out of it,' he said, almost gently.

She kneed him, was struggling loose. He slapped her hard, knocking her over, stunning her. *Sorry*, she thought she heard him say, falling.

When she picked herself up, she ran in the direction she thought she'd seen them take. She ran all the way to the perimeter of the trees: where the park finally ended – bordered by the roaring stretch of dual carriageway which led into town one way, out to the bypass the other. There was a white van parked dangerously on the narrow grass verge. One of the back doors was half open and she thought she could see movement inside, bodies struggling. But then the door was banged tight shut and the van roared off into the stream of traffic, was out of sight, gone. She ran back again, colliding with trees herself, cutting her cheek, not caring. In the picnic area, there was a family outing spread over two tables. Hampers, cool boxes, wine, beer. Two women, a mother and a daughter, sprinted over to her. She heard somebody, a man, shouting excitedly into a mobile.

'Police. Quickly. There's a girl been attacked.'

'*No*,' she screamed, '*No! That's not it at all.*'

The patrol car that came was from Crowby Central, so that's where they took her: the local nick on the other side of the town centre from the Divisional building. Little more than a reception area, a roster room, half a dozen holding cells. It stood at a mid-point between the main shopping streets and the night life area, was defined by its location: shoplifters and thieves by day, pub brawls and drug dealing by night. They sat her in an interview room, brought her a cup of tea. From somewhere, they'd called in a female PC. They sat down opposite: the woman cop plus one of the two male constables from the patrol car.

'Take it easy, love,' she said, 'you're safe now.'

No. No. You don't understand. They've got him. They took him.

Slowly, some of it began to click with them. Slowly, she got some of the story out. His name was Robbie Jackson. She didn't know his address actually. They'd only just met yesterday. He'd only just moved here from up north somewhere. They had to do something quickly, get people out looking, find them. He was six feet, she said, about thirty. Shaved head, gorgeous.

'*Really gorgeous and tender and—*'

'We've got a technique called an e-fit, Julie,' the police-woman said, 'After the doctor's seen you, you can help us get a good likeness of – eh – Robbie. And his attackers.'

'But I don't need to see a doctor. I've told you – I haven't been attacked. It's Robbie. They're taken him. Don't you fucking understand?'

Chapter Twenty-Five

Robinson had fitted the autopsy in around his other work, hadn't been able to schedule it before five. Jacobson had sat at the back as usual, sucking a Polo mint. It was coppers' lore that sweets helped with the smell. Nothing helped with that smell, he'd thought. But it was as good a cigarette substitute as any and the chief soco had been offering. He beat a hasty retreat afterwards, had seen rather too much of the pathology suite in the last few days. There had been nothing revelatory anyway, only the confirmation of what Robinson had already said in situ this morning. Mortimer had been attacked with the baton, kicked senseless and then strangled. It was impossible that there hadn't been some kind of forensic transfer. The attacker's shoe for instance would be a likely candidate for traces of skin fragments, even bone.

Jacobson got into his car, drove out of the hospital car park and on to the bypass. But even the most basic, the most initial, DNA results were hours away. If that. Plus if something from Kevin Holland turned up on Mortimer's body, it proved nothing. Plus if from an unknown someone else, it took them nowhere. Fuck it, he thought, switching the radio on, deciding to give himself ten minutes off from the case. There was only boring, bloody cricket on long wave though – and the fm reception from Radio Four never seemed to work properly in this part of town. He switched to Crowby FM but the drive time programme was in the middle of one of its frequent commercial segments. The first show house would be opening this weekend, he heard, at Mackeson Properties' spectacular new town house development. *That's Why They Call Us Mack The House*, drivelled the jingle. Great, he thought, another Caribbean winter in the bag for Janice, his ex-wife, or another trip to the Great Barrier Reef. She'd loved watching the sharks apparently, he'd heard via Sally, their intermediary. I'm not surprised, Jacobson had said to his daughter, she sleeps with one every night.

He got back to the Divi at six ten, ate two bacon rolls in the canteen. He nodded to young Ogden on the way out but the lad didn't seem to see him, had an altogether unhappy-looking expression on his face. Girlfriend trouble most probably, Jacobson thought, the impression barely lapping his consciousness; certainly never getting further than his short-term memory. He kicked off the briefing with a summary of what Robinson had said at the autopsy. Then he took the reports back in turn from Kerr, Barber and Hume, Smith and Williams. As they were speaking, Sergeant Ince wrote quick summaries on the white board. When they were finished, Jacobson grabbed the blue marker pen from Ince, starting drawing arrows where he saw connections: solid lines if the link was strong, dotted lines where it was tenuous, more or less speculative.

'Neville Chapman thinks he saw a transit van somewhere near the back wall of the Mortimer's place on Sunday night and again on Monday night. He'd be a fairly hopeless witness except that the socos *did* find a tyre track close enough to the spot – one which wasn't there on Saturday morning, which must have been made since. A transit van, as we all know, is what Kevin Holland drives. Alice Bowlby puts Holland and Parr leaving the funeral parlour at ten past nine last night.'

He paused, coughed, tapped the white board with the stem of the marker for effect: listen, concentrate.

'Peter Robinson's estimate of the actual time of death is between ten and midnight. Time enough to get back over to Longtown from the funeral parlour and then out to the lane behind the property. That's one side of it – I think the most important side – but there's also what Emma's just seen. Faith Lawson and her boyfriend turning up at Holland's gaff. Lawson, you'll recall, has been working as Gus Mortimer's temporary secretary for the last fortnight.'

DC Barber had a question.

'But just suppose Holland's our boy for last night. He's still placed in Wiltshire or wherever on the night *Mrs* Mortimer was killed.'

Mick Hume thought he had the answer.

'Old Morty's still the prime suspect for his wife's murder. If Holland did Mortimer, it's the revenge killing angle isn't it, guv?'

Jacobson nodded.

'Simple solutions are usually favourite,' he said. 'The problem here is the use of a blasted stun weapon in both cases. There's a plausible mechanism whereby Mortimer could have got his hands on one, though unsubstantiated of course. But Kevin Holland? That's another story altogether.'

Williams asked if it was the *same* weapon that had been used both times.

'If only we knew, old son. If it is, it might have been cleaned so thoroughly between times that we'll *never* know. The sweep search of Mortimer's route to work certainly yielded bugger all – as did the appeal to the great Crowby public.'

He gave in at last, broke open the packet, lit up, let the discussion of the known facts run on. The truth was *in* there, he thought, coining a phrase. But somehow he just wasn't seeing it yet. He took two deep drags, one after the other.

'OK. Tonight's marching orders.'

Holland would be brought down to the Divi, would be

formally interviewed by himself and Kerr. If he insisted, he could have a solicitor present. Smith and Williams would be talking to Parr and Pelham again, going over their statements inch by inch. But he wanted it doing over at Longtown, wanted it kept low key for now. For the time being, nothing was to be said to them about Faith and Snake/Mark.

'I want to keep the element of surprise on that one,' he said.

It was more than time that Hume and Barber did a deskbound stint incidentally. They were to check out the list of university computer users as far as they could. At least ensure that no one who'd figured elsewhere in the inquiry wasn't also conveniently on the list. At least look at each of the names once.

When in doubt, he thought, plod on. At least get your spadework done.

He sent a patrol car out to pick up Holland, used the twenty minutes this bought him to shave, freshen up, complete his grand evening repast with a cup of the canteen's savage coffee. At the start of the interview, he mentioned the availability of the duty solicitor. But Holland said no, said he'd rather talk for himself. He was wearing some kind of collarless flannel shirt, his dreadlocks tied back with a bright strip of red wool. His face was unshaven but he was still young: designer stubble rather than the grubby white whiskers that had started to appear on Jacobson's own chin if he left it alone for more than a few hours.

Kerr read the main points of his previous statement out aloud. Holland claimed he'd left the funeral parlour at nine, had spent the rest of Monday evening at home with Chris Parr and Wendy Pelham, same as he'd done Sunday.

'This still your version of events, Kevin?' he asked.

'Yes it is,' Holland replied.

Jacobson asked him when he'd last set foot on the Mortimers' property.

'You should know, Inspector. You were there. Saturday morning when – you know when.'

When Holland spoke, he looked them straight in the eyes. The rest of the time, he stared into space. Somewhere far away. Jacobson told him about the discovery of the tyre track, asked if he had any comment to make.

'What? You're saying it was my van?'

'I'm not in a position to say that at the moment, Kevin. I might be when the forensic checks are complete.'

'I didn't kill him. I haven't got that much honour, that much spirit.'

Jacobson leant forward, his elbows on the table, his chin arched by his hands. A thinker grappling with the truth more than an interrogator.

'Whether you killed him, that's not what I asked you, Kevin. That's not the question – yet.'

There were four other tenants in the house where Pelham, Parr and Holland lived. They'd all been checked out, talked to, dismissed as peripheral to the case. One of them, Big Bob, some kind of undefined market trader with a sideline as a guitar teacher, opened the door to DCs Smith and Williams.

'Chris and Wendy aren't here,' he said. 'Gone over to the Wynarth Arms, isn't it?'

Before they left Emma Smith asked him about the last couple of days, how much he'd seen of the trio.

'Been keeping out of their way to be honest. It's been a bad blow for Kevin all this. Obviously. Most of the time they've just been sat round in the front room. Chris and Wendy listening to him, feeding him whisky, trying to help him through it.'

'What about last night?'

Big Bob confirmed that Parr and Holland had driven back from the funeral parlour about nine thirty, thereabouts. He'd had a brief conversation with them and with Wendy Pelham, knew that the three of them were still in the front room when he'd gone up to bed an hour later.

'After that I couldn't say. I do an antiques stall over in Leicester, Tuesdays. I've got to get up and leave here at five in the morning.'

It was a forty minute drive over to Wynarth. There were no parking spaces in the market square so they parked in Thomas Holt Street, walked back round to the Wynarth Arms. Apparently, Wendy Pelham deejayed some kind of World Music night in the back lounge once a week and Parr ferried the equipment for her, lugged the decks and records over in his ambulance. They were still setting up when Smith and Williams walked in.

'Surprised you didn't cancel,' Emma Smith said.

'What's it to you?' Wendy Pelham replied, 'Life goes on. Kevin knows that. 'Sides, Chris'll collect him from the cop shop or see him back at the house once everything's underway here.'

Two youths wandered in waving bottles of lager. The first punters. Williams ushered them out firmly.

'This lounge is closed for the minute, lads,' he said.

Wendy Pelham gave them a filthy look, started to protest. Williams slid a table across the entrance to discourage any more customers, interrupted her briskly.

'Sooner you talk to us, sooner we'll be gone.'

They seemed to accept it at that point, stopped pissing about with wires, cables, the cheap-looking mixer. Smith and Williams took them through each statement line by line. Twice. Three times. But neither Parr nor Pelham wanted to change any detail, wanted to add anything new.

'I hope you know what you're doing,' Williams said finally. 'Making false statements in a murder case is serious shit, believe me.'

Parr picked up a cd from the nearest pile, held it between his thumb and forefinger as if for emphasis. Toumani Diabate.

'Life is serious shit, mate,' he said needlessly.

*

The printout from the central records of registered computer users at Crowby University had been produced in logon ID order; the lowest number first, the highest number last. Some limitation inherent in the, quote, fucking cheap software, unquote, that the university still insisted on using. Or so Steve Horton had explained to them over the phone when Mick Hume had called him up at home – interrupting his game of *Quake* – to quibble. The irritation, the problem, was that instead of an easy to follow alphabetic list, Hume and Barber had been stuck with a non-alphabetic jumble. Which was why, as Hume had just said, it had taken them the best part of an hour rather than a quick ten minute glance to get there. Never mind, Barber replied, got there they had: that was what counted surely.

Chapter Twenty-Six

They'd blindfolded him while they were still amongst the trees. After that there had been some kind of transportation. Slung on the floor, his face pressed on metal, some bastard's rubber sole heavy on his neck for most of the journey. Hard to say how long. But not very. Ten minutes maybe. They hadn't spoken, not even amongst themselves. Then he'd been booted in the arse, shoved out, his hands still behind him, his eyes still covered. They'd spun him round before they'd pushed him indoors. Till he was dizzy, his head spinning: unsure whether he was going upstairs or down, left or right.

The two biggest ones had held him while the other one punched and kicked: stomach, balls, ribs. He thought there'd been someone else there too, a fourth, who'd hit him as well. Lightweight taps that barely hurt him. But slapping his face from side to side, spitting on his mouth. Already, he realised, he longed to be back in those moments, craved them like an old man dreaming of some distant, youthful summer's day. When he was still on the outside, still able to stand up.

They'd undone whatever had been tight – cutting – round his wrists, taken the blindfold off, before they'd forced him in. Bare seconds. But time to see that there were just three of them again. The masked faces, the thrusting arms and bodies. Pushing him in backwards, forcing it tight shut.

By now his fingers had explored every inch they could reach and his mind had grasped the total fucking awfulness of it, knew it for what it was. Anyone with his interests, his obsessions, *would* know. Had they hoped otherwise maybe? Thinking that not knowing would make the terror and the panic worse. They'd got that wrong anyway if they did. He ran his hands down the surface in front of him again. The metal panels felt rough to the touch. Cold and a little bit oily, greasy. If he looked down, straining his neck beyond endurance, there was a line of holes running across the front, right at the bottom. Eight holes. Each a bright, tiny circle of light. Already he couldn't focus on them properly. Already they were dancing in front of his eyes, growing huge or shrinking small. A few seconds only. Then he had to ease his neck muscles, look away.

Darkness otherwise.

He could feel his hands if he stroked his face but he couldn't see them. The eight points of light, which it hurt his neck so much to see, were all that told him he wasn't blind. That it was where he was that kept him from seeing. That his eyes hadn't died. It would have been a trade-off for them most probably. The fraction of daylight versus the fraction of air: the longer he could breathe, the longer he could suffer. He pressed his hands forward, putting his arm muscles to work, trying to gauge the thickness of the casing, the strength of the locks and hinges. Everything felt solid, up to the job. He drew as deep a breath as he could take. Breathing from the abdomen, holding, exhaling slowly. He tried to picture his life energy, his *Chi*, flowing in its circle. Spine, head, chest, stomach. Circulating and returning. The fire in the belly. Lose that, he thought, and he was finished. If he tried to stand, his head wedged itself painfully in the apex while he was still half bent. If he lowered his head, tried for any kind of half-sitting position, his knees jammed excruciatingly into the front. You read about it in the SAS memoir books, the armchair soldier magazines. A box. A base and four sides. As old as counting. He kept on breathing, kept on thinking about breathing. Anything else and he'd be banging, screaming, clawing, begging. Anything else and he'd be fucked: stuffed, washed up, over and out. Kebabbed.

He thought he heard a door open somewhere near, thought he heard footsteps. Then there was a voice. Male. But quiet, barely audible. That might have been deliberate too – so that you weren't sure if you really *had* heard it, found yourself repeating every word, every phrase, till they were dinned into your brain, the only thoughts in your head.

'I'm off for my dinner next. Then maybe a bit of telly or a spot of gardening. I won't be back here for a good long while. No one will. They say some Vietnamese holds the record. I can't remember what side, whether he was North or South. Eight hours he lasted. Think of it. Eight hours. He survived too – if you can call crippled for life surviving. Most though, IRA, Paras, whoever: give 'em ten minutes – half an hour max – and that's it. Crying worse than babies. Tell you anything – *do* anything – just to be let out even for a few minutes.'

A hand thumped one of the side panels.

'Still. Good turnout Sunday, eh? Hanging's too good for him. That's what they were saying in the crowd. Ought to have it done to himself, what he did. That's what I heard a lot of them saying. But I don't think so. No not really. You'd like that too much, wouldn't you?'

Another echoing thump. And then there was only silence.

Eight ten pm. Jacobson smoked a cigarette in his office. Kerr was with him, drinking tea from one of Jacobson's chipped red mugs. There had been no milk as usual, just Coffeemate which had been long past its sell-by-date, which hadn't dissolved properly.

Jacobson had successfully requested a warrant in respect of Kevin Holland, had authorised overtime for a forensic search team. The main thing, he'd told them, was to remove any likely looking clothing, especially boots or shoes. Holland had already handed over what he *said* he'd been wearing last night but that didn't mean he wasn't lying. He'd sent Hume and Barber over with them in case the natives were restless. He stubbed his cigarette end out on the bottom of the wastebin, made a half-hearted attempt to conceal it under Kerr's still damp tea bag.

'Right, old son,' he said. 'Let's go party.'

They'd just finished what smelled like an Indian takeaway when Jacobson and Kerr knocked on their door. There were plates on the little table in front of their sofa, spice-stained paper bags, empty food cartons. The lad had let them in, stood with his back to the hi-fi and the TV set. The girl was still sitting on the sofa. She put one plate on top of the other, collected up the knives and forks, closed the lid on a jar of lime pickle: something to do with her hands.

Mark Edward Jones was twenty, three years younger than his girlfriend, Faith Lawson. On Sunday afternoon, he'd told Emma Smith and DC Williams that he was at college. There was nothing suspicious or out of the ordinary about that. Half of Crowby referred to the university as 'college'. Snake, it turned out, was an English and History student. That wasn't against the law either. But the records showed that he'd been logged into the university network at three ten pm on the fifteenth of January, had been logged in since two o'clock in fact, had logged out again at three twelve: scarcely two minutes after the email to the Action and Resistance web site had been sent.

Jacobson told them they'd been seen entering fifty-six Claremont Road – the address of the house where Holland, Parr and Pelham lived – earlier in the evening. What had been the purpose of their visit? Who did they know round there? *Just being sociable isn't it*? Snake said. They'd got to know Chris Parr because of his shop – *shedloads of cheap cds* – had run into him and Wendy Pelham at a couple of gigs. Yeah, they knew Kevin Holland too. But not so well.

'English and History, Mark,' Kerr said.

'Yeah. So?'

'What kind of History? Ancient? Modern? Political?'

'Load of bollocks mainly,' Jones replied, 'Too much theory. Not enough actual history, actually doing it.'

Jacobson showed him a copy of the printout, with his logon/logout details circled in red biro.

'You agree this is your, eh, user ID? You agree you were using the, eh, network at the time shown?'

'I expect it's my ID if it says so. I don't know it off by heart. You can't expect me to remember a particular day in January but.'

'OK,' Jacobson said. 'Assume for the sake of argument that the records are accurate – what kind of thing would you have been doing if you had been logged on?'

'Dunno. Research for an essay most probably. Using the Internet. We was doing a project about the legacy of 1968 back in January I think. You know – the May events and all that.'

Jacobson did know – in retrospect anyway. At the time it had just seemed like long-haired posh kids taking the piss as usual. We *were* doing, he said, unable to resist the correction. Then he put the leading question.

'The Action and Resistance web site. That one of the sites you visited for your research?'

Jones looked at the girl, then at the floor. But he met Jacobson's gaze when he answered him.

'No. I don't think I've heard of that one.'

'Sure?'

'Yeah. Definitely. Never heard of it.'

They'd driven over in Kerr's car which they did more often than not. Driving back, Jacobson said they might as well call it a day; there wasn't really anything more to be done until they got some serious forensic results in. Especially the provenance of the tyre track down the Mortimers' back lane.

'My guess the kid was lying,' Kerr said.

'Maybe. Maybe not,' Jacobson replied, rolling down the window, enjoying the first hint of evening coolness which had started to creep into the air.

The quantitative odds on Jones being the emailer were two hundred and six to one. But his girlfriend had conveniently landed the temp spot in Gus Mortimer's personal office. Plus he was personally acquainted with Kevin Holland – Jenny Mortimer's lover – and his housemates. If you looked suspiciously on these additional facts then the qualitative odds could be very much shorter. He rolled the window down further, let more of the welcome air in. Suppose Jones *was* the source who'd proposed Mortimer for the enemy of the people club: what the hell did that *prove*, what the hell did it have to do with either murder?

Chapter Twenty-Seven

He'd lose it soon. Over and out. Already he'd lost all sense of time. He could've been here hours or only minutes. Already he'd no idea. Already he thought he might have passed out, his head lolling, his mouth dribbling. You had to go into yourself. Or beyond yourself. A warrior won in battle by transcending the battle. But how did you transcend this? This not moving. This not seeing. He was finding it difficult, panicky, to breathe now. There *was* air, the holes guaranteed it, but that didn't mean your heart and lungs weren't starving. Your brain. There was no inch of him now that wasn't pain. Pain and being trapped. No turning. No standing up. No stretching out. He tried to think about her. He tried not to think about her. The girl. Julie. That had been different, hadn't it? Not like the others. Not like the others at all. The way she'd smiled, taking him in. He rubbed his hands together, trying to keep his forearms in motion, stop them cramping. It was the only real movement possible. Why they'd untied his wrists. He was sure of that now. They wanted him to keep going: the longer he took the better, the more pain the merrier. He badly needed to urinate. But he didn't want to die in piss, die breathing in the stench of it. He was sure he would die. Sure he'd never get out. Why would they come back for him? Why pity him? He'd shown none himself, spared nothing to none of them. Not one single slag. Until her. He wouldn't shout anyway. Not cry out and beg. At least he wouldn't give them that.

He was breathing as slowly as he could. Trying to make each one last. The air when it hit his lungs was hot, stale, putrid. No worst, there is none. Fuck knows where that came from. Poetry it sounded like. Something he'd heard at school, some idiot lesson he hadn't blocked out of his head quickly enough. He badly need to urinate. But he didn't want to die in piss. The warrior lived with the certainty of death, embraced it in every conscious second. How fearlessness was born. They wanted him to keep going. The more pain the merrier. He didn't want to die in piss. Taking him in. Poetry it sounded like. Already he'd no idea. Lolling, dribbling. Not stand up. Not sit down. If he thinks of the sea, attack like the mountains. He badly needed to die in piss. Pitched past pitch of grief. Fuck knows where. Not give them that. A woman with her bits all over the place. If he thinks of the sea. Soon lose it.

Chapter Twenty-Eight

Chris Parr had driven Kevin Holland home from the Divisional building then he'd gone back over to the Wynarth Arms to help Wendy Pelham with her set, pack up the decks and stuff at the end of the evening. Kevin Holland said it was all right, not to fuss, he'd be OK. He had to try and get on with things, hadn't he? He'd sat in the kitchen until the socos were finished in his room. As soon as they'd gone, he went up there himself, climbing the two flights of stairs to the attic level. Holland had the top room in the house: quiet, hidden, distant somehow from the rest of the world. Jenny had liked to stand on tiptoe at the high oval window in the middle; gazing out over the street, the roofs opposite.

They hadn't made too much mess anyway. Although they seemed to have taken away nearly half his clothes. They'd even made him change out of what he was wearing today, bagged the shirt and trousers, picked out something else for him to wear in the meantime. He rolled himself a spliff, stuck Nick Drake on the cd player. *Five Leaves Left.* Jenny's favourite. Something she'd loved years ago, she'd told him, hadn't heard for God knows how long until she'd spotted it in his collection. He stretched out on his bed, smoking, listening. He knew he was getting through it now. Getting stronger. Now that Gus was gone too. Right now he felt almost peaceful here on his own. But hot. He'd opened the window wide but it would be a while yet before the room would get cool enough to rest properly, close his eyes, maybe even sleep.

He'd liked to have gone over again tonight. But there was no question of that now. Not after what had happened. He'd been lucky enough to get away with it before. That copper: fast asleep in the tool shed, practically snoring. He'd crept past all the same, the key to the conservatory tight in his hand. She'd given him a set of keys to everything. Not just the outhouses: the swimming pool too – and the house. Now – too late – he thought he knew why. It had made her feel safer thinking that when she was locked up with him, she wasn't really locked up – she had a rescuer, a knight errant.

He'd stood outside the conservatory for a moment before he'd gone in, looked up at the harvest moon, fat and orange, through the trees. Inside, the air had been lemon-scented, humid. It hadn't bothered him. It could have been as hot as a furnace and he'd still have been there. *Meet me*. He'd heard her voice as clear as a bell. While he was sitting in the front room with Chris and Wendy. While Chris was pouring out another whisky for him. While Wendy was saying he ought to eat something. *Meet me*. And he had done. Later, after the other two had called it a night: steering the van through a whisky haze, keeping the speed down, doing fine until he'd skidded at the last minute, nearly hit the back wall. *Meet me*. Meet her where he'd first kissed her, held her, fucked her. A Tuesday afternoon. Wintry, bleak, grey outside. But warm and sumptuous amongst the lemon trees and ferns. She'd asked him something about the datura cuttings. Could he have a look? Smiling. Her eyes dancing, foxy.

He'd just sat there really. Remembering. Trying to sense some trace of her in the atmosphere, some presence. He'd nearly jumped out of his skin when he'd heard the sudden heavy footsteps, seen the light beam swaying back and forth from the swinging torch. The copper: the sod must've woken up, decided he'd better check his beat sharpish. That was when he'd flung himself flat on the floor, crawled right in next to the pipework, his heart thundering. His luck had held, the cop had only glanced through the panes on his way past, hadn't actually looked in properly, hadn't bothered to test the door. He'd listened to the footsteps drawing near and then growing distant again. Even then, he'd waited a good ten minutes before he stirred. Somehow his back foot had got wedged behind a corner pipe. He'd had to reach down with both hands to extricate it, bumping his head in the process. Which was when, wedged behind his wedged foot, he'd made his discovery.

Kerr had dropped Jacobson off at the Divi. Jacobson had decided he'd wait for Barber and Hume, maybe try and catch a word with the chief soco, before he really did pack it in for the night. He took the lift up to his office on the fifth floor. Although it was still light outside, he switched on his desk lamp. No point in straining his eyes for no reason. All his life he'd enjoyed twenty-twenty vision. Still did as far as long sight went, the optician had assured him. Except now he was supposed to use glasses for reading and for any close-up work. Another intimation of mortality, he'd thought. Another sign of the machine running down. He didn't always bother but it was a habit he was trying to establish, get into. He took his spectacles out of their case, picked up the latest Incident Sheet from his in-tray.

Burglaries, stolen cars, the usual garbage. Robert Johnson had yet to be located but the operation to do so was being personally supervised by DCS Chivers and pro-DCS Salter. That's in the bag then, Jacobson thought, reading on. A female witness, aged twenty-one, home address Crowby, had reported the possible abduction of an adult male in the Flowers Memorial Park. The alleged victim's name was Robert Jackson, known as Robbie, described as white, six foot, close-cropped hair, aged around thirty. E-fits of those involved in the alleged incident were being compiled and would be made available on the computer network ASAP. Jacobson *had* a computer terminal, every ranking officer had to have one. It sat neglected on its own neat little table in the corner of the room. He could switch it on, spend twenty minutes trying to find what he was looking for – or he could walk downstairs to the incident room.

Jackson. Close-cropped hair. The Memorial Park. Robbie for fuck's sake! Sergeant Ince was logged on to the terminal, updating the inquiry database. Barber and Hume had just got back, were writing up their reports. Ince found him the e-fits in roughly thirty seconds. Two minutes later all four of them were headed out of the building by the back stairs.

'You don't think the Super should be handling this, guv?' Hume asked, getting in behind the steering wheel.

'Of course he should,' Jacobson replied. 'I'm one hundred per cent out of order. I'm probably totally wrong and probably headed for demotion. The three of you too if you're daft enough to come with me.'

'Thought so,' Hume said, starting up the engine, accelerating swiftly out into the street.

'Ve ver only following ze orders,' Barber quipped.

There was a cobbled alley behind the houses in Riverside Avenue, wide enough for cars, even for the refuse collection lorry. As a scant precaution, they cruised along it first, pulled up outside what they hoped was the right back garden. Barber got out, squinted through the side window of the old, red-brick garage. He nodded, getting back inside the car. Yes there was some kind of van in there. Yes it had looked like just the type of thing you'd use.

Hume drove back round into the street itself, parked a couple of houses up. Even in an unmarked car, you used discretion if you could. Jacobson rang the door bell, the others standing behind him. The porch door was shut as well as the main door. Not the usual custom in the area unless you were out for the day or away on holiday. He rang the bell again, rang it a third time. Shuffling inside. Then John Barnfield in shorts and a sweatshirt, a stiff drink in his hand. A loud swell of music behind him.

'Inspector Jacobson. Now isn't really a very good time.'

'I never had you down as a rap fan, John.'

'Oh that. It's Caroline. She's with us for a couple of days. What they call home time. Part of her therapy programme.'

'I need to come in, John.'

Barnfield had his free hand on the door, ready to slam it.

'What on Earth for? Shouldn't you be out looking for that animal Johnson? According to the news he's gone missing. They're telling people to watch out for him. Broadcasting his picture. A bit bloody late—'

'I need to come in, John.'

'You can't – not without a warrant.'

'I don't have a warrant, John. But I *can* get one. I'd be stationing my colleagues here meantime – front and back – if I did have to go and fetch one.'

Partly Jacobson pushed his way in. Partly Barnfield didn't really try to stop him. Linda Barnfield and her daughter were in the front room, both sitting upright in upholstered Regency chairs, rose patterned to match the wallpaper. Snoop Dogg had never sounded more out of place. Jacobson turned the volume down but there was nothing to hear behind it anyway. Caroline Barnfield was tall and fair, blue eyed. She looked out as blankly at Jacobson as she did at everything else. John Barnfield watched her from the doorway.

'What would you have done, Inspector? Nothing?' Then: 'Come on. I'll show you.'

They followed him upstairs to a back bedroom on the second floor.

'This was where he kept her,' he told them, opening the door. 'Chained to the radiator.'

The box was in the middle of the room, buttressed by scaffolding poles which had been drilled solidly into the floor and the ceiling. The front panel was secured by half a dozen padlocked bolts. Altogether it was an impressive piece of DIY. Barnfield undid the locks, slid the bolts back. Hume and Barber lifted Johnson out, laid him down on the floor very nearly gently. He'd muttered something as they'd brought him out, then he'd fallen back into unconsciousness. Sergeant Ince was already on his radio, organising an ambulance.

'Where's your bathroom?' Mick Hume asked, his hands wet from Johnson's urine-soaked trousers.

Chapter Twenty-Nine

Wednesday morning, first thing, Chris Parr shaved, put on his cleanest shirt, his best Levis. He drove over to the Beech Park Estate in his ambulance, parked it between a shiny blue Corsa and one of the new style Fiestas.

He'd grown up in a street like this himself. The neat gardens, the cars in good nick. Everything straight as a dye. He was calling on the Swains, Jenny Mortimer's mum and dad. The murder of Gus Mortimer had thrown the arrangements for his wife's funeral into confusion. The coroner had given permission for the burial to go ahead on Friday. Even Thursday if that was what was wanted. But the funeral parlour needed a name to send the bills to. Preferably belonging to someone non-deceased. Jenny's father had stepped in, had said he'd meet the cost, that it wasn't a problem. Maybe not, Parr thought. But the sum that her husband would barely have missed would probably be a big hole in her parents' savings.

He straightened his shirt collar, rang the bell which chimed something that might have been 'Greensleeves'. Everybody in the house wanted to attend the service. They'd mostly met Jenny at one time or another. They'd liked her. They wanted to support Kevin. Parr knew the kind of people her family were, he'd told them. It would be better to let them know, clear it with them: *do the right thing*. Swain came to the door, showed him into the lounge.

His wife was on the sofa, a photographic album spread wide across her lap. They could have been his own parents, he thought. Hard working and – that dreadful, dead word – *decent*. They were probably about the same age – or would have been. His mother was still alive but his dad had died two days before his fortieth birthday. Cancer. He'd worked in the paint factory for twenty years, had probably become ill through contact with a reckless polymer process which had been prohibited – banned – later. But only probably. There had been medical doubt, room for manoeuvre. The company had never paid out a penny in compensation. But it had been steady work, regular, secure. That's what his dad had liked to say. His dad's mates too. Everybody who came round the house, everybody in the street, everybody you ever met. Forty-eight weeks out of fifty-two. Five or six days out of seven. Once, fifteen and cocky, out to change the world, he'd told the old man he'd get less of a life sentence for murder.

The father made him a cup of tea. The mother showed him the photos of Jenny toddling, walking, growing up. They'd caught his dad in the rat trap but they hadn't caught him. London, Paris, Amsterdam. Squats, communes, agit-prop. Eat the Rich. When he'd come back here a decade or two later it had been on his own terms, uncompromised. Still sussed. The record shop did OK and there were bits and bobs of politics to be done. Even here. Even now. It was grass roots work. Digging down to rich, hidden seams. Passing it on to the youth.

'I think you should know that she was happy,' he said. 'Her and Kevin. What she was looking for.'

The mother said it was good of him to come round. The father said they'd settled on Thursday, two o'clock. *The sooner it's done*, he started to say. But his voice trailed off into silence.

Parr sipped his tea, tried just for once not to slurp.

Attempting to compete with its newer, flashier rivals, the

Brewer's Rest had recently taken to opening at nine am on weekday mornings, serving up all-day breakfasts, teas, coffees, danish pastries: aiming for the non-alcoholic market. Their coffee was far from brilliant but it tasted a lot better than the re-heated paraffin derivative which was available in the police canteen. Jacobson ordered a large mug but did without the pastry, found himself a shady table in the still-quiet beer garden.

He'd just come from a meeting with the two-headed chief superintendent beast, needed to clear his mind before his nine thirty briefing. Chivers had huffed and puffed about Jacobson's highly previous intervention, his deviation from the laid-down procedures. But at least with Chivers there was still a real policeman buried somewhere beneath the layers of management speak and bullshit. He'd cranked out the standard lecture but had found time afterwards to say well done, quick work. Much more worrying, if Jacobson had cared to worry, had been the frosty reaction of Greg Salter. Salter had given him the silent treatment: before he'd even picked up the reins of office, he'd probably been thinking, he'd been upstaged, undermined, made to look a fool.

Jacobson shrugged to himself, tried not to take too much notice of the morning barmaid's lithesome figure as she cleared away the greasy remnants of an English breakfast from a nearby table. Maybe Salter was eager to make a collar, prove he could still be hands-on. If he'd wanted to start with John Barnfield, he'd have been more than effing welcome. Jacobson was for law and order every time, knew that without it everything was lost. But that didn't mean he couldn't empathise with the father of a raped, mind-fucked daughter. Barnfield had been charged with unlawful arrest and that was just for starters. He'd almost certainly make bail but his chances of a non-custodial sentence weren't high. Vigilantes were at the very top of the judiciary's hate list. Way above even yobbish rock stars and insider traders. The louder the tabloids and the hack politicians howled in

253

his support, the worse it was likely to turn out for him. He'd admitted he'd had accomplices – *good lads who could get a job done* – but he'd refused to name them. That wouldn't help him either. Then there was the whole issue of premeditation. Chance was a factor: Barnfield jogging in the park, spying his bête noir in the queue for the boating lake. *I'd know that godforsaken face anywhere, Inspector*. But he hadn't knocked the box together in a quick afternoon, must have had his heavies on pre-arranged standby for the call from his mobile which had set the kidnap in motion. As for Robert Johnson he was currently sedated in hospital with a round-the-clock guard at his bedside. The consultant had said it was too early to speculate on either his physical or mental recovery. But he'd looked more than averagely gloomy as he'd spoken – even by the rigorous gloom and pessimism standards of his profession.

Jacobson opened the little portion of cream, poured in the contents. He had a sheaf of faxes and paperwork spread out on the table: reports from the Birmingham lab and from the Divi's own socos. To an unaware bystander, he looked like any other middle-aged, middle-ranking executive or businessman sneaking half an hour out of the office. But one who'd at least taken his work with him, who certainly couldn't be accused of skiving. He had that air of concentration that instinctively led any remotely intuitive strangers not to choose a table too near or not to chatter too loudly if they did. He seemed to scan quickly through everything then go back a second time: pausing on certain items, studying the fine print. Finally, as if satisfied that he'd seen all there was to see, he bundled the papers together, concentrated on drinking his coffee in the warm summer air.

He checked his watch. Nine twenty. Just nice time to drink up then stroll back. He had two hot items to report. One: whatever the hell else had been going on, it was looking more and more certain that the last person to have sex – or force sex – with Jenny Mortimer was her husband.

The odds against it not being Gus had soared to one in two million, looked set to rise still further. Two: the tyre track behind the Mortimer's back wall might not belong to Kevin Holland's transit. But only if it belonged to someone else's. Someone else's with an identically worn cross-ply Firestone on its front wheel, passenger side.

Claremont Road, he told the briefing, would be the new focus of the investigation. The entire household at number fifty-six would have to be questioned again. Every occasion they claimed they'd seen Kevin Holland since Saturday would need to be logged and cross-checked. The operation would fan out to the rest of the street too. Neighbours would be visited, quizzed. Had they noticed Holland's van coming and going over the last few days? Could they put their finger on any actual times? He watched his expanded army file out of the room. In addition to the original team, he'd managed to borrow four extra detective constables and a couple of experienced plods. All only for the day though. All charged to his overstretched budget at the top whack rate.

At ten thirty-five Kevin Holland was brought back to the Divisional building: interview room D. He was formally cautioned this time, was told he was now officially helping the police with their inquiries. He still didn't want a lawyer but Jacobson overrode him, insisted on the duty solicitor sitting in. He got straight to the point. There was witness evidence that Holland's van had been in the vicinity of the Mortimers' property on Sunday evening and again on Monday evening. There was forensic evidence that bore the witness out.

'Come on, Kevin,' he said. 'What exactly's been going on?'

Holland looked into the eyes of the older one, glanced at the younger one: Kerr or whatever. Then he turned his head to take in the lady lawyer sitting next to him in her smart powder-blue business suit. She smelled as fresh as a plastic daisy. He asked the older one for a cigarette, stalling for a little time. What could he tell them, people like this, that they'd ever grasp, ever comprehend? Jacobson passed him a B and H, lit it, took one out for himself. Holland stared at the table for a while, passing the cigarette between the fingers of each of his hands and back again. Mulling things over.

'OK,' he said finally.

He told them he *had* driven out to the Mortimers' place Sunday night, parking in the lane, gaining access by the back wall. He told them about the conservatory, about needing to be somewhere that was special to them, somewhere where her soul might fly to. He shook his head at that point: how could these dead spirits – married to their pensions and mortgages – understand? He didn't mention the electric stun baton concealed behind the pipe work, didn't see that they'd earned the right to everything that he knew.

'What about Monday night?' Jacobson asked.

Holland shook his head emphatically.

'I was there Sunday. But not Monday. Everything I said before about Monday is true. I was at the funeral parlour till gone nine. Then Chris drove me back home. I never went out again.'

'So why lie before, Kevin?' asked Kerr.

'To keep the man off my back. To keep you off my case.'

'So why should we believe you now?'

Holland's barely touched cigarette was smouldering in the ashtray. He tipped the ash, took a deep draw.

'First up, it's true. Second – can you *prove* otherwise?'

At the end of the interview, Jacobson asked him if he wanted a word in private with the solicitor. No he didn't. No thanks.

'Suit yourself,' Jacobson said, pressing the button for the custody team.

He'd asked for Chris Parr and Wendy Pelham to be brought in too. Pelham was already in the building by the

256

time they'd finished with Holland but it took another half hour to locate Parr. His distinctive ambulance was finally spotted and intercepted en route between Beech Park and Longtown. They quizzed them separately, Pelham then Parr, were treated to the same repeat performance each time. At first, they both stuck to their original story: they'd sat up Sunday night and well into Monday, feeding Kevin Holland whisky and sympathy. Jacobson had to resort to playing each of them part of the tape of Holland's interview before they admitted they'd been lying: that they'd crawled off to bed before midnight, couldn't swear that he hadn't gone out on his own later. They'd just been trying to look out for him, they said. Losing Jenny was enough for him to cope with; without all this hassle, all this aggravation.

'But we only lied about Sunday, mate,' Parr said, giving his version. 'Monday night went off just like I said it did before.'

Chapter Thirty

Twelve noon. Kerr and Steve Horton drove over to Longtown in Kerr's Peugeot. Kerr wondered if Jacobson's holiday hadn't maybe unhinged him a little. Too much French plonk or too much travelling or too much sun. The unsanctioned raiding party on John Barnfield's place had been dangerously close to professional suicide. If it hadn't come off – if he hadn't been one hundred and ten per cent right – Jacobson would be on gardening leave by now while Chivers and Salter prepared the grounds for a terminal disciplinary hearing. Only Jacobson didn't have a garden, was one of those coppers you couldn't imagine doing any other job.

He rattled the door long enough for any reasonable person to give up whatever they were doing, at least creep up to the other side, at least sneak a butcher's through the security spy hole.

'Not at home, it looks like,' Horton said superfluously.

Kerr used his credit card, overcame the poorly fitted yale lock with minimal effort, minimal damage. He had a duly signed warrant in his pocket, was legally entitled to use reasonable force to gain access. But his name wasn't Barry Sheldon, he reminded himself: there was no need to be malicious just for the sake of it.

There was no sign either of Snake/Mark Jones or of Faith Lawson in their cramped, tiny flat. But it wasn't them they'd come looking for anyway. At least not directly. Horton had spent the morning back at the university, had failed to find anything incriminating anywhere in the drive space allocated to Jones on the student network. The hope now was that Jones might have a computer of his own at home – with something more interesting stored on it than a pirated e-text of *No Logo* and some downloaded pages from the Jesus and Mary Chain web site. Kerr pushed back the rug and the sofa, tested the floorboards with his foot then with his fingers.

'Here we go,' he said, pulling the loose one up, reaching a hand underneath.

It was an old model, Horton said a few moments later, powering up the battered looking laptop. It was a wonder that it was still working. But it was: beautifully.

Twelve ten pm. Emma Smith drank a cup of tea in the front room of the McGuire sisters' terraced house at number fifty-three Claremont Road. Siobhan was the elder of the two but more active than her sister, Kathleen, who was dozing in her armchair, occasionally snoring. There was cricket on the television, the unheeded commentary blaring. They'd lived here more than fifty years, Siobhan told her, the only way they'd be leaving now would be in a box. When it was time for them to be six feet under. Which it would be soon, she dared to say. It had been Mammy and Daddy's first home in England, when Daddy had left Donegal to find work. Either you slept all the time at their age. Which was like Kathleen. Or you hardly slept at all. Which was like herself. There weren't many like either of them round here anymore, that was for sure. All young people; students and what have you.

'I expect you think it drives me to distraction at my age, do you? Noise, parties. Well it doesn't, dear. It'll be quiet enough where I'm going. Sometimes I just sit up at night, listening and watching. The comings and goings, the chatter and the laughter. My bedroom's upstairs at the front you see. I expect they think I'm some terrible old nosey parker.'

Emma Smith ran her through the key elements again. Yes, she was certain it was Monday night. Yes she was certain it was around eleven. She'd swear it on Daddy's grave.

'The big white van. But not him. No, dear, not him. Kevin, isn't he? Oh, I know him. Helped me with Kathleen, the last time she had one of her falls. A fine-looking young man even with all that hair. No dear. It was his van all right. But not him getting in, not him driving off.'

Twelve fifty pm. The chief soco personally led the forensic team back into fifty-six Claremont Road. They had a warrant to search the entire house this time but in the event only one room seemed to interest them. Particularly the wardrobe. From which they removed very nearly the entire contents.

One pm. Wendy Pelham refused the meal brought to her cell on a plastic tray by the custody sergeant. She hadn't been fucking charged with fucking anything; she had a fucking right to fucking walk out the fucking front fucking door.

'Now that's where you don't understand the law, miss,' the sergeant told her affably. 'You and your friends are assisting Chief Inspector Jacobson's inquiries. That's assist as in he can keep you here for up to twenty-four hours without making specific charges. If I were you, I'd *want* to eat, make sure I kept my strength up.'

One fifteen pm. Interview room B this time. Jacobson, Kerr, Chris Parr and the duty solicitor. Parr had requested someone from Slingsby and Associates, preferably Alan Slingsby himself. But the firm had declined to assist for the time being. They'd just interviewed Kevin Holland again, had just sent him back to the cells. If you could call it an interview when Holland had refused point blank to answer any more questions. He had nothing more to say to Babylon, he'd said, they could do what they liked, *infer* what they liked.

Kerr ran through some relevant highlights from the data found on Mark Jones' laptop computer. They'd found copies of email correspondence with the Action and Resistance web site, he told them. Emails going back as far as January. Emails as recent as last month. Emails confirming that Jones was the source of the information about Gus Mortimer which had been posted on the site. But worse for Chris Parr was the electronic diary which Jones had maintained on his C drive. Dates of meetings between himself, Faith Lawson, Parr and Wendy Pelham plus detailed notes and comments. A regular Gang of Four, Jacobson thought, listening intently. The upshot was that Jones had sent the emails but they'd all been involved in drafting them, doing the research.

Jacobson tried to stay calm, tried to project a confidence that he didn't feel. Getting computer evidence accepted by the courts was a legal minefield with a high failure rate. Parr might not know that of course or, if he did, he might forget it under pressure. Kerr reached the end of his summary.

'Just supposing some of what you say is true, mate. I'm not entirely sure which law I'm supposed to have broken. Or what it's got to do with the murders. Not that I'm losing any sleep over the sad demise of Gus Mortimer,' Parr said.

Scotch that theory then, Jacobson thought.

'There's incitement to violence for one thing, Mr Parr,' he said. 'And that's before I even take a look at the handy little Home Office guidebook on the Terrorism Bill. But what interests me right now is the effect your, eh, propaganda had closer to home – on your housemates for example.'

Parr rubbed his neck, fingered his scraggy pony-tail.

'I've already told you. Kevin was with me on Monday

night, right up until he hit the sack. Besides – no offence to him – but Kevin hasn't got a political bone in his body. Into the mystic, isn't it? Following the spiritual path and all that.'

Jacobson pressed the button for the custody sergeant, stood up, squeezed past the solicitor, hovered over the tape machine.

'This is DCI Jacobson terminating this interview at one forty-two. Mr Parr will remain in police custody while my inquiries continue. I hope to speak to him again very shortly.'

He pressed the stop button.

'Who mentioned Kevin, Chris?' Jacobson asked rhetorically, almost in a stage whisper.

Chapter Thirty-One

Jacobson was what the textbooks called a reflective practitioner. He *thought* about policing – its scope, its nature, its value. There were countries, he believed, where the police force was the last career he would have chosen, where he would rather have starved. Countries where corruption was endemic, where fitting up was standard, where physical torture was a technique to be applied, mastered, applauded. But everything, he knew, was relative. He wasn't a social worker or a psychotherapist: his job was to catch the guilty. So he'd sent Kevin Holland and Chris Parr back to the cells after their interviews, left them there all day until nearly midnight. Wendy Pelham likewise. Who was to say what necessary inquiries he had to make in the meantime? Who was to challenge his right to speak to them again only when he was ready – only when it best served the needs of his investigation? Certain forensic facts might have first become known as early as six o'clock but it evidently takes time for a mere policeman – even an experienced one – to absorb complex scientific detail, to work out thoroughly the practical implications. Anyway, it wasn't that they were being denied their statutory phone calls, that they weren't being fed and watered, that they weren't being talked to civilly.

It was just that they were banged up, locked in, unfree. If

ten hours were like this, what would ten days be like? Or ten years? Let them stew a bit, old son, he'd said to DS Kerr. Let the buggers stew.

Chapter Thirty-Two

The custody sergeant brought Chris Parr a cup of tea about eleven twenty on that Wednesday night.

'I think he wants to talk to you again shortly,' the sergeant said.

'Ta, mate,' said Parr, sitting hunched on the edge of the bench, his thin legs dangling in front of him.

It had all been fun but now it seemed to be getting out of hand. It wasn't that Mortimer hadn't deserved it. He had, more than – a domestic bully, a cog in the global structures of oppression, an A1 shit. But maybe not at this price, this much collateral damage.

Once the police experts got their teeth properly into what they'd assumed so far must be Snake's laptop, everything would start to unravel. For the moment, the coppers thought that they could prove they'd been communicating *with* Action and Resistance. But soon they'd take a closer look, realise that to all intents and purposes they *were* Action and Resistance. They hadn't put someone else up to sending Mortimer hate mail, they'd done it themselves. At some point it would even occur to someone – Jacobson maybe, fat boy fat – to look properly into Faith Lawson's background: to discover for instance that her first class honours degree in Computer Science possibly over-qualified her as an office temp.

He took a nice, deep slurp of tea. That had been pure

chance, pure serendipity. Faith noticing the advertisement in the window of Office Angels, suggesting she put herself forward. *Infiltration, isn't it?* Snake had enthused. It had been that all right, mate, and a lot more besides. It was the get out of jail card. Although maybe not for all of them.

Chapter Thirty-Three

Eleven forty-five pm. DS Kerr and DCI Jacobson watched the custody team lead Kevin Holland out of the interview room after another non-interview. *I've nothing to say, don't you get it?* A few minutes later they came back with Chris Parr in tow. He sat down in the empty chair next to the duty solicitor, asked Jacobson for a cigarette. Jacobson passed him one, took one himself. Kerr and the non-smoking lawyer exchanged resigned glances. In America, Kerr thought, he could probably sue the force for endangering his health by making him work with Jacobson.

Parr insisted that Holland had nothing to do with the web site stuff. That was the first thing he wanted to say. It wasn't Kevin's thing, it really wasn't. All he'd done was to show them the baton. He'd found it hidden out at the Mortimers' place. If only he'd left it there, Parr said. But he hadn't – and so they'd needed to deal with it. That had been on Monday morning. It had thrown them, all three of them, he didn't mind admitting. They hadn't *known* it had anything to do with Gus Mortimer's attack on his wife – not then obviously. But somehow it had just *felt* like the kind of thing the bastard would do. They'd hung on to it all day, hidden it out of the way of everybody else in the house. Up in Wendy's room. When he and Kevin had driven back from the funeral parlour, somebody – Big Bob maybe – had mentioned hearing the police appeal on Channel Four, the seven o'clock news programme. They'd discussed it then again evidently, well of course they had, eventually come up with a plan of action. The next day – Tuesday – one of them would get rid of it discreetly, somewhere public, somewhere the police would be likely to find it. If it wasn't found, they'd think about making an anonymous tip-off. Wendy had said she'd do it. She had to go into town in the afternoon anyway, sign on. That had been it, mate. It had been gone eleven by then. They'd had a tiring few days since they'd come back from Wiltshire. They'd just hit the sack after that as far as he knew. All three of them. Yeah he knew he'd said after midnight before. But that had been stretching it a bit to be honest. And he *was* being honest now.

That's all I know, mate. But I've got something else to trade if you're interested.

Chapter Thirty-Four

Wednesday turned into Thursday morning. It was one twenty am before Jacobson was finally ready to put the charges. Go home if you like, old son, he'd said to Kerr while they waited for the lift to come up to the fifth floor. There was no need for everybody to be up all night. Especially not those with a choice of beds, a plenitude of desirable sleeping arrangements. After all, he could easily poach a DC from the regular night shift to sit in. Not a chance, Frank, Kerr had said, ignoring the innuendo, watching the numbers above the lift doors illuminate and de-illuminate: one, two, three, four, *five*.

Jacobson had carried on grinning all the way back down to the custody area. He'd just phoned Chivers and Salter from his office, had taken a particular, childish pleasure in disturbing the Salters in their town house eyrie, waking up Chrissie to wake up Greg. He'd been so sorry to phone so late. He needed to *liaise*, to keep – eh – Greg up to speed with the latest developments. But his smile had promptly vanished as they'd followed the custody sergeant along the low corridor towards the first of the interview rooms.

So far the forensics were far from conclusive. There were matching clothing fibres – yes – yet the route of transmission was deeply ambiguous. As easily brought to Gus Mortimer's garden indirectly – via Kevin Holland – as directly. The computer evidence too, even when it had been done and dusted to the nth degree, would only ever be circumstantial. Saying that you wanted to kill someone, that someone ought to be killed, wasn't very nice. In certain circumstances – probably in *these* circumstances – it was highly illegal. But it still wasn't the same as doing it. Irony, no less: forget your computers and your DNA. A sharp-eyed old lady unable to sleep, staring out at the street in the moonlight, could still be ahead of the game.

He was looking across the table at Alan Slingsby, who'd re-interested himself in the case now that it had turned out so refreshingly complex. Mortimer had killed his wife and then someone had killed Mortimer – before you even got on to all the other stuff.

Someday, Jacobson thought, I'll look back on my life and see only this. Dingy interview rooms late at night. Smug lawyers. Suspects washed up, stuffed.

He always used the standard form of words. Precise, unembellished.

'It is my duty to arrest you for the murder of Angus Anthony Mortimer.'

Slingsby reminded her that silence needn't always indicate guilt. It was shocking, even terrifying, when serious charges were put to you. The most innocent person could go to pieces, find themselves temporarily unable to think straight, give clear answers. Juries were starting to appreciate that at last, thank God. All this and more Slingsby said for the benefit of the tape, for the benefit of his client's defence.

But Wendy Pelham didn't seem to be listening to him, to any of them.

'People like Mortimer. Think they rule the world. I wiped the smile off his face all right. I'm not sorry.'

December

Chapter Thirty-Five

The Saturday before Christmas. A sleek column of invited cars bearing invited guests along the private road to Boden Hall. Lines of coloured bulbs hung in the trees. In front of the Hall itself, a giant Norwegian fir, bedecked with holly and fairy lights. The Salvation Army silver band on hand as always to greet the guests as they approached the front doors. Once inside, deferential hands taking your coat, welcoming you with punch or champagne.

Geoffrey Trayner stood on the edge of the ballroom. His left arm around his wife's thrillingly perfect waist. His right hand cupping a glass of more than decent brandy. His foot tapping. He was talking to Charlie Walsh and dear old Pamela, but paying scant attention to what he was saying. Any patronising rubbish. Walsh and his pet bat would listen anyway – smiling, nodding, agreeing – just for as long as *he* wanted them to.

'Let's dance, darling,' Elaine whispered in his ear.

If you'll excuse me? Smiling, letting her lead him forwards through the crowd. She'd wanted a sixties theme this year. Mini Skirts. Pop Art. 'Hi Ho Silver Lining'. Everywhere you looked there were kipper ties, kaftans, flared hipsters. His guests – his courtiers – as gratifyingly eager to please as ever. The lookalikes had been a nice touch. He'd spotted four of the John Lennons so far, a couple of Jaggers. Plus an attractive woman who might have been Mandy Rice Davies. Come to think of it: who might have *been* Mandy Rice Davies.

Jacobson and Kerr were in the fifth Range Rover. Observer status only. DCS Salter had angled like fuck to get the invite himself. But the NCIS team had turned out to be surprisingly resolute on that score. They wanted the lads who'd done the work – who'd given them the lead – not the local figurehead. There were eight vehicles in toto. Forty officers all told. Plus an armed response unit behind the gazebo: ready if needed.

'Think he'll give any trouble?' Jacobson asked the driver.

'Hard to say, guv. The boss thinks no. That he'll want to keep the lid on it in view of the party guests and such. But you never know with a caper like this.'

The Range Rovers taxied on to the lawn in a v formation. It *was* nice to be invited, Jacobson thought, even if it was more of a PR gesture than an operational need. He strained his ears to listen. The helicopter should get here soon. Then it would kick off.

Faith Lawson had turned out to be a formidable young woman. She'd told them everything she'd found out from her fortnight in Gus Mortimer's office, retrieved data that even Steve Horton hadn't been able to access. The quid pro quo had been lesser charges for Parr, substantially lesser charges for herself and Mark Jones. The two of them had done a runner at first but they'd eventually given themselves up to the transport police at Euston, sick of a month spent dossing and begging on the streets of London.

Hidden on the computer in Mortimer's office had been a folder of encrypted files and emails. Decoded, they'd looked innocuous at first sight: details of orders for Planet Avionics' standard product range. Tachometers, altimeters, guidance systems. The orders had been brokered by London European Technology Holdings but destined for a medium-scale civilian aircraft manufacturer in Spain. So far so legit. But several of the emails contained references to

King Midas. The first time Steve Horton keyed those two words into the PNC, a security clearance warning flashed up on his screen. Minutes later, a duty superintendent at NCIS made an urgent telephone call on a secure line to Dud Bentham. NCIS: the National Criminal Intelligence Service. AKA Supercop.

The roaring blades overhead, the sweeping searchlight. No one in or out till they were done. Everything to be catalogued, seized, removed. Computers. Documents. Banking details. Shipping arrangements. Any potential data source. Jacobson had deeply feared he might have to run at some point but steady, purposeful walking was the order of the day. The request made at the door was polite. But insistent, firm, compelling.

Trayner wasn't the major player but his involvement was deep. Trawling through his records would take them deeper, might even put Midas on hold for the time being. The idea was simple to conceive but difficult, labyrinthine, to execute. In the new caring, sharing Europe, individual governments were individually shirty about trade with overtly repressive régimes, imposed quotas, refused export licences. In the new caring, sharing Europe, all governments wanted to assist their fellow Europeans in the old eastern bloc – help them recover, help them modernise. As Jacobson understood it, Midas worked like the old lady who swallowed the fly. Parts were supplied across Europe from one legitimate company to another. Orders were combined or separated – disguised or manipulated – as suited the stage of the operation. EC incentives and tax breaks were utilised whenever possible. Eventually, somewhere near St Petersburg, fully operational military kit was assembled or completed. Dictators and rogue states for the use of. Africa, the Middle East, the Pacific, South America. Even after the Russian mafia deducted their facilitation fees, there was plenty of rich gravy left on the murderous train.

Yes, it had been *very* nice to be asked, Jacobson thought,

helping himself to a glass of nicely warmed aromatic punch. If only, two seconds ago, to watch Geoffrey Trayner taken into custody, his face white with anger, his black plastic Sergeant Pepper moustache drooping.

Author Note

The use of electro-shock batons, stun guns and tasers is increasing world-wide. As is their 'legal' and illegal manufacture inside the European Community. Excerpts from Amnesty International material in Chapter Eleven reproduced by kind permission. Amnesty International continues to monitor developments and to provide up-to-date intelligence (*www.amnesty.org*).

Official audits of the Police National Computer have repeatedly expressed concern over high error rates. Amongst numerous reports in the British trade press see, for example, *Computer Weekly*, London, 27th April 2000 (*www.cw360.com*).

Miyamoto Musashi is a real, historical figure. Direct quotations from his writings are taken from Victor Harris's translation of *A Book of Five Rings* and reprinted by kind permission of Allison & Busby, London.

Iain McDowall
www.crowby.co.uk

A Study in Death

Iain McDowall

A stylish crime debut, in the tradition of Rankin

Dr Roger Harvey, a high-flyer headed for the academic first division, has pursued his career and women with equal passion. But now he's just another murder statistic; his body has been lying in his flat for four days when a small-time burglar literally stumbles over it on his way out with the stereo.

DS Ian Kerr and DCI Jacobson of Crowby CID can discern no obvious motive. Harvey didn't do serious drugs, have a criminal record, and wasn't gay. Not even Harvey's closest friends, John Kent and his beautiful wife, Annie, seem to be able to throw any light on the situation.

Despite Jacobson's dependence on booze and fags, and the fact that Kerr's marriage is disintegrating faster than his boss's liver, the two men are experienced policemen. But to solve the case they have to untangle the dark threads of a mystery which threatens to unravel in seemingly every direction...

Mind Games

Hilary Norman

'heart-stopping suspense' Mary Higgins Clark

On the face of it, the double homicide of Arnold and Marie Robbins looks like just another brutal Miami Beach murder – except Cathy Robbins, Marie's teenage daughter, is lying between the bodies, blood-drenched, traumatised but otherwise unharmed.

Is the teenager a silent witness to the slaying, or does Detective Sam Becket have to contemplate the horrific possibility that Cathy may be a killer? As more victims are murdered, each with an intimate link to the teenager, Becket no longer has any alternative but to arrest her.

Only child psychologist Grace Lucca believes Cathy incapable of the crime. But Sam fears that she may be risking more than her reputation in her belief in Cathy's innocence. She could be risking her life...

Praise for MIND GAMES:

'A nerve-shredding tale of murder, revenge and calculated cruelty and a plot which twists and turns to the end' *Jewish Chronicle*

'compulsive and gripping ... with a high body count and lots of intrigue' *The Bookseller*

'An absorbing, cleverly constructed thriller' *Books Magazine*

Deadly Games

Hilary Norman

Jake Woods gave up his law enforcement career a decade ago to settle down to life as a criminal justice professor and family man. Now widowed and bringing up two daughters, Jake is shocked by the inexplicable disappearance of the teenage son of good friends. In his efforts to help, he uncovers a link to a similar case in New York City, where Lydia Johanssen is currently going through every mother's hell after her sixteen-year-old son Robbie vanished on an evening out with friends. Soon the official missing persons database throws up more related cases, teenagers with three things in common: good looks, athleticism – and the fact that each of them disappeared after receiving an anonymous gift of *Limbo*, a violent, bestselling computer game.

Lydia has her own suspicions, but no one on the official FBI task force seems to be listening to her. Horrified by her plight, Jake can't help but get involved, but the deeper they get sucked in the greater and more terrifying the danger to their families and themselves. For this is no ordinary kidnapper. This is an individual for whom the margins between reality and fantasy have blurred beyond all recognition...

Praise for Hilary Norman:

'heart-stopping suspense' Mary Higgins Clark

'genuinely scary ... touches of sheer horror ... a real page turner' *Daily Telegraph*

'an accomplished novelist' *New York Times Book Review*

'an enthralling read' Gerald Kaufman, *The Scotsman*

'a goose-pimply, page-turning read right to the end' *Company*